..., Archaeological Space Adventure

Craig Martelle, Brad R. Torgersen

Craig Martelle, Inc

Website & Newsletter: https://craigmartelle.com

Facebook: https://www.facebook.com/AuthorCraigMartelle/

Brad Torgersen Social

Website & Newsletter:

Facebook:

Zenophobia Book 1—Heretic

Zenophobia Book 2—Messenger

Zenophobia Book 3—Extremist

This book is a work of fiction.

All of the characters, organizations, and events portrayed in this novel are either products of the author's imagination or are used fictitiously. Sometimes both.

Zenophobia Book 1 - *Heretic* (and what happens within / characters / situations / worlds) are Copyright (c) 2021 by Craig Martelle and Brad R. Torgersen

All rights reserved. No part of this publication may be reproduced, stored in a retrieval system, or transmitted in any form or by any means, electronic, mechanical, recording, or otherwise without the prior written permission of Craig Martelle

Version 1.0

Cover by

Editing by Lynne Stiegler

Cover by Ryan Schwarz, The Cover Designer

Published by Craig Martelle, Inc

PO Box 10235, Fairbanks, AK 99710

United States of America

Contents

1. CHAPTER ONE — 1
2. CHAPTER TWO — 13
3. CHAPTER THREE — 36
4. CHAPTER FOUR — 50
5. CHAPTER FIVE — 66
6. CHAPTER SIX — 83
7. CHAPTER SEVEN — 104
8. CHAPTER EIGHT — 118
9. CHAPTER NINE — 137
10. CHAPTER TEN — 152
11. CHAPTER ELEVEN — 170
12. CHAPTER TWELVE — 190
13. CHAPTER THIRTEEN — 203

14. CHAPTER FOURTEEN	227
15. CHAPTER FIFTEEN	241
16. CHAPTER SIXTEEN	255
17. CHAPTER SEVENTEEN	267
18. CHAPTER EIGHTEEN	280
19. CHAPTER NINETEEN	299
20. CHAPTER TWENTY	311
21. CHAPTER TWENTY-ONE	325
22. CHAPTER TWENTY-TWO	343
DEDICATION	354
Author Notes - Craig Martelle	355

CHAPTER ONE

"Fire," Sankar growled, and the twin ion cannons unleashed their fury into the void. The molecule-sized projectiles stitched across the Ursoid fighter, slicing it as finely as a surgical blade cuts flesh.

The ship lost power an instant before it started to tumble, and the stress of momentum split the small craft along the new seam. It broke in half, both sections following a single ballistic trajectory until the atomic powerplant lost containment and splashed a mini-supernova across the *Four-Claw*'s viewscreen.

"I'm bringing us around. There's one more out here. And where's that sow?" Sankar said.

The heavily muscled and oversized humanoids known as Ursoids called their mother ships by that name.

"Eyeballs, people!" Sankar commanded, scanning.

The humanoids known as Tigroids patrolled the space surrounding their home planet of Oterosan in the *Four-Claw*, a long-range interceptor with a crew of six. It retained the maneuverability and footprint of a smaller craft but had the punch of a heavier vessel. The Tigroids and Ursoids had been conducting an underground war with each other for as long as anyone could remember, despite the marginally open relations between the two planets.

Sankar's whiskers twitched. Instinctively, he yanked the ship hard to port and barrel-rolled. Pulse beams slashed through the space where he had just been. He arced through a bone-crushing loop to come in behind the Ursoid enemy.

The Ursoid fighter spun and twisted toward deep space, maneuvering away from Sankar's weapons envelope. He coaxed more speed from his quad-wing fighter. Sensing a maneuver from the ship in front of him, he slid sideways and fired his ion cannons. The enemy turned into the stream of fire, and disintegrated into space dust.

Sankar banked the *Four-Claw* through an expanding circular search pattern. "All scanners active, find me that sow!"

The mothership didn't have to be a large craft. Only two fighters had been delivered. They could have been dropped hours earlier and hung idle in space until an alluring target presented itself, like the Oterans' latest and greatest interceptor.

It took an hour to finish the spherical search to confirm that the sow was long gone.

"Call it a day," Sankar told the crew.

"Grace be to Traythor!" the five crewmembers shouted in unison.

"To Traythor for leading us to victory and to the Furd gods keeping us safe," Sankar said reverently, as the ship's commander—though his heart wasn't in it.

"Charting optimal course to Oterosan," Junak the co-pilot stated. Having a thin coat of light-colored fur, he looked far more human than tiger-like. His glasses didn't fight that impression. He had never yearned for combat but being best friends with the rising star of the Oteran Space Fleet had put him on the front lines of an undeclared war.

Oterosan protected its shipping lanes from "pirates" and "raiders" that looked too much like Ursoids, Goroids, and Wolfoids, while at the same time keeping the shipping lanes open for trade with their own planets.

Sankar pointed the nose of the *Four-Claw* on the course Junak had designated, before rising and stretching. He was larger than your average Tigroid, but leaner. He fit within the piloting school's constraints, not encumbered by bulk. Not by Oteran standards at least.

The rest of the crew had started the *de rigueur* victory celebration, toasting with a slightly fermented milk drink called testle. "Here you go, boss," Junak said, handing over a squeeze bottle. Sankar sucked it slowly. It tingled as it crossed his tongue. He enjoyed the beverage just like everyone else.

"Traythor gives you strength, wisdom, and courage," Sankar said, knowing his lines as the *Four-Claw's* leader. "We fight to keep Oterosan safe. We fight for each other." He raised his bottle in a toast.

The crew did likewise, and then the cabin was quiet. This was not their first sortie, nor would it be their last. After a year of conducting intercepts, he had little to say. The unofficial war with the bear-men of Medvegrad.

The *Four-Claw* continued to the landing field, where they would be relieved by the next watch. An older Dominator-class vessel lifted off and accelerated away. Not the equal of the *Four-Claw,* no. But still a formidable craft.

Sankar's crew powered down the ship, following their checklist, step by step. With six of them, they were able to complete post-flight in under ten minutes.

"Time for the pub, Commander? Testle is good, but we need something with a little more punch. Nothing like blasting a couple bears to make a tiger thirsty!" the first engineer quipped.

"You go ahead. We have a few hours of extra duty remaining for that last prank Junak pulled," Sankar said, waving his crew away.

"Right. Under. The. Bus," Junak said beneath his breath, then stepped away from his friend to glare appropriately at him.

"I wouldn't be your friend, otherwise," Sankar quipped. "Besides, we barely made it out of this one, but that's not because of the ship. It's because we never saw them. We have the best weapons, but our scanners are nothing more than gutter trash. We need an upgrade. We need what the Ursoids have."

"Akoni is not going to tell you," Junak said, then shook his head, his whiskers twitching.

"He may in time," Sankar replied. "Sooner than you think."

"Bet on it? A hundred duckets say no way. Not now, not ever, but we'll cap the timeframe at two months from now. Or you could just pay me now to save yourself grief."

Sankar held out his hand. "Slap on it."

Junak obliged. Sankar draped his arm over the shorter Oteran's shoulder. "Thanks for being my friend. I have something coming that I can't tell you about. I hope when you are able to look at it dispassionately, it will make you proud."

Junak pushed him away. "What's this?"

"Things are changing, Junak," Sankar said, but did not elaborate. They walked away from the spaceport and caught a common shuttle to take them downtown. From the central station, they walked to the nearby military zeno-detention facility and flashed their credentials.

"You two again?" the guard asked.

"You just come on shift, Torkus?" Sankar asked.

"I have. How can you tell? Maybe I don't look as dead as I will tomorrow: drooping whiskers, sagging eyes, matted fur..." He looked into the distance.

"Sounds like your tigresses will have you by your tail!" Sankar quipped, but down inside he felt nervous. He needed Torkus on shift. It was part of the plan. A plan which was not precisely approved by Sankar's bosses.

After they walked through the first gate, Sankar turned to Junak. "We don't have much time."

"Really?" Junak asked. "I'll follow your lead, but we have all night. If we finish early, the crew will expect to see us, even with your parents having something going. You *are* the *Four-Claw's* commander, after all."

"I am, but there may be times when you shouldn't go where I lead."

"What's that supposed to mean?" Junak said, raising an eyebrow behind his Tigroid-large spectacles.

"Save it," Sankar said, and kept walking.

They passed through two more barriers, waving at the guards on their way. Once inside, they went into the common area. Oteran guards from the ground forces watched from within guard towers.

The docile prisoners milled about an open area. Oversized humanoids as comfortable walking on four legs as two, the Ursoids had bristly hair and heavy builds. Next in size were the Goroids from Cornelior, humanoids with long arms, short legs, and broad chests with an abundance of thick hair. The Wolfoids—of the planet Angelos—were the smallest species, with triangular, pointed ears and black noses on an extended snout.

The two Oterans strolled in, smiling and nodding at the prisoners. "Make friends, not enemies," Sankar said.

"But they *are* enemies, and prisoners," Junak replied, following the commander to a massive Ursoid, who was the weight of three Oterans combined. He moved on all fours through the yard while the other races walked upright.

"Akoni, my friend, how are you faring this fine evening?"

The Ursoid reared up on his back legs and stood casually, looming over the Tigroids. "I'm not telling you anything."

"You can pay me now," Junak whispered. "The bear isn't telling you anything."

Sankar ignored him and spoke to Akoni in a hushed tone. "I want nothing from you besides your word that you'll be here a few hours from now."

"Where else would I be? Are all Oterans this dense? How could we possibly be losing our fights with you?" His voice rumbled from deep within his chest.

"Do you want to get out of here?" Sankar asked.

"Dense as the matter within a black hole. If you haven't figured it out yet, no one likes it here, and we would all be happier somewhere else. Anywhere else. What are you trying to imply, Sankar? Stop playing coy. Out with it."

"If you were to leave here, would it be worth your while to upgrade the scanners on my ship?"

"Go hump yourself," the Medvegradian bear-man said.

"It might be in your best interest, but there will be no strings," Sankar said, and patted the heavily muscled shoulder. "You are an engineer, aren't you?"

"Of course. Do you think an Ursoid landing team would have a runt like me?"

Junak snorted. Runt? Akoni was gargantuan.

"It's not funny," Akoni said. "You're small for your species, too."

"Hey!" Junak said, and his whiskers laid back against his face.

"See! How do you like it?" the bear-man countered. "I'll be in the yard. If you can get me out of here with no strings, I'm for it. I can't imagine what's in it for you, Sankar, but there has to be something. Once I'm out of here, I'll owe you nothing."

"Maybe I just want to do the right thing?" Sankar said, then left the Ursoid to contemplate the opportunity.

Sankar led Junak until Sankar had located the next zeno-prisoner of interest.

"Bayane, how are you this fine evening?"

The Wolfoid chuckled, "You smell funny."

"I'm a cat. You're a dog. We always smell funny to each other. Is that how you engineer, with your nose?"

"Hey! I'm a damn good engineer, unlike Gonzo here. He just looks at living stuff."

"*Gwarzo*," the Goroid corrected in a voice almost as deep as Akoni's. "Bioengineer, if you please."

"How did a bioengineer get captured?" Sankar asked.

"I was bored and signed on with a freighter crew that was creatively smuggling. They bailed out when confronted by an Oteran patrol. Left me high and dry, and in the Tigroids' eye."

Bayane laughed at the Goroid. "Such is the lot of all!"

Akoni had wandered over to listen.

Junak looked around him, nervously. But Sankar seemed satisfied with his audience.

"Why are we at war, even when there is no war declared?" Sankar asked them.

Bayane and Gwarzo intently watched the Oteran.

"Maybe there's something better out there," Sankar suggested, "starting with you good people in here. What have you done wrong? Other than serve your own? As if that can be wrong, on any world."

"They're prisoners," Junak reminded. "*Pirates and raiders.*"

"No, my friend," Sankar said, "I think perhaps they are much more. Why don't you join the crew of the *Four-Claw* at the bar and get yourself a drink. I'll be along shortly to celebrate with you. We fought well today, But I look forward to a time when there will be no need to fight."

"You are scaring me, Sankar, but I will go. Don't be too long, and don't fall under the spell of these zeno-criminals. They will just as likely kill you as look at you. *They are not like us.*"

"I think they are more like us than anyone will admit," Sankar said, and held up his hand for Junak to slap in the usual Tigroid gesture of greeting or departure. Junak obliged with a gentle tap, but his whiskers drooped from worry. Sankar watched his friend walk away, shoulders sagging.

Sankar turned to his audience, "Well, now. Where were we?"

Akoni was the first to reply. "We're at the part where we are intrigued by your words, and although your vision is cloudy, if it leads to our departure from here, then I'm all for it. For the record, I've looked at you plenty and have yet to kill you."

"That's comforting." Sankar chuckled at his sarcasm. "Have you ever thought you were here for a higher purpose? With your skills, two engineers and a bioengineer from the four races, we'll have access and the ability to get the answers we need. For permanent peace. That's right. But first, we have to get out of here. The wheels are already in motion. Here is what's going to happen..."

CHAPTER TWO

High Priest Zeon smoothed his robes for the third time. His wife Actiosa pawed his arms. "Stop it. You look fine."

"I'm nervous," he said. He took Actiosa by the shoulders to rub his furry face against hers before flicking her ear.

"It's hard." She said, and looked down to keep the tears from coming. "He's late. Maybe tonight is not the night."

"Tonight *is* the night. There is no other choice. Events have been put in motion that cannot be undone."

Actiosa sniffled but nodded. "I understand."

The door opened and closed. Actiosa held a hand over her heart and whispered a prayer to the Furd gods in relief.

Sankar walked into his parents' home without knocking, having not officially moved out since he remained un-mated.

"Is it ready?" he asked.

"It is, my son," Zeon droned as if lecturing from the pulpit. "You have a half-hour to change and be on your way. Are you packed?"

"What is there to take?" He nuzzled his mother. "I've never been an outcast before."

She lost the fight with her emotions and started to sob.

"Actiosa, please!" Zeon cautioned. "We knew this day would come—these twenty-some years. Now that it's here, we have to keep our wits about us. Keep our hunting instincts sharp. Get a grip on yourself. As for Sankar, at exactly eight tonight, I will say the words. At that moment, he will need to lift off and not come back until he has proof."

"I know." Actiosa said through her pain.

"I believe, Father," Sankar said bravely. "I believe that all the races came from one place, that we should be working together and not against each other. I believe that everything the temple teaches is wrong."

"Everything *I* teach, you mean," The old tiger said—without irony. "Because this battle cannot be fought from within. It needs another way. You are chosen to lead this new war."

"Not chosen," Sankar said. "I volunteered. I kept your secret while I grew up, and I believe in this enough to do it no matter the cost."

"My son, the Heretic," Zeon said, the word bitter on his pink tongue. Heretic was more than a term of derision. It was a word that came from on high and usually carried a death sentence. Zeon pulled his boy into a fierce hug while Actiosa fought to get herself under control. They all had roles to play if they wished to survive the night.

"I better go," Sankar said, lifting his chin and stretching to his full height. "Peace upon you both." He butted his forehead against each of theirs in turn. Sankar hurried to his bedroom to collect his pack, which had been previously prepared. In it, he had concealed tools to pick locks and do the intricate work required to break into a ship's computer system. He had a button drive filled with his memories—pictures, videos, stories, and sounds. He had few clothes, almost none. There was still so much he'd have to find along his way.

Sankar changed into a business casual outfit, all black with a unique belt only worn by temple security. He put his badge in his breast pocket and his military identification on the dresser. He wouldn't give them more reasons to hate him.

And hate him, they would. The entire planet of Oterosan. Unless he returned with proof, and even with that, they probably wouldn't listen.

Sankar allowed himself a moment to contemplate the pending upheaval in his life. The time had come for change. The question was, had he learned what he needed to know to manage it?

"You said you'd be back," Torkus said. "I didn't necessarily believe you. This place is unpleasant to visit, what with all the scum inside the wire. But your efforts with a few of them may be yielding progress, eh?"

"You are correct," Sankar said, then looked around conspiratorially before sliding a piece of paper across the counter and leaning close to continue in a low voice. "We are ready to move to phase two of this operation. I will be taking the three named prisoners with me to an alternate facility. There can't have an official record."

"Mum's the word," Torkus confirmed. He waved a second guard over to staff the front desk while Torkus personally escorted Sankar.

"Your work here is exemplary,' Sankar said. "These zeno-prisoners don't even try to escape."

"Spare the claw and lose control," Torkus said. "We've had plenty of upstarts who don't think they belong here. They've been made to understand. But not the three you've been working with. They're . . . different."

At each of the two security barriers, the guard talked to his peers—to smooth the way for the return trip. In the open yard, Akoni, Bayane, and Gwarzo waited. Sankar made a simple gesture, and they joined him near the entrance.

"You're being transferred," Sankar said. "Come with me. Any attempt to escape could result in your immediate death."

Torkus waved, and the gate opened. Sankar strode forward. Bayane hurried after him while the other two lumbered to catch up. Torkus followed. The next two gates opened as they approached. Sankar tipped his chin in recognition, keeping his expression somber while he passed through the main entrance to the outside, where he turned to address the three in his charge.

"There is a vehicle around the corner. Climb in and be quiet, please."

"But..." Akoni rumbled. Sankar held a finger to his lips before hurrying them down the street and around the corner. A nondescript van waited with the back doors open, and they climbed in. Once settled, they strained the vehicle's suspension.

Sankar puffed a breath through his whiskers, then steeled his resolve. The plan was in motion, and there was no turning back. He climbed in the front of the van, put it in gear, and drove away. Although sluggish, the van wouldn't have to climb or descend any hills between the prison and the spaceport.

Sankar drove to the far entrance. He arrived at ten minutes to eight, five minutes later than he'd planned, and waved his military badge at the guard, expecting to be let through.

"It's after hours," the guard said. "And you're not on the list for the flight line, sir."

"Here to prep the *Four-Claw* for a late mission," Sankar said officiously.

The Oteran guard considered—his whiskers twitching—then his eyes got large.

"Hey! You're the pilot who splashed two bears earlier today. Word gets around. Nice shooting, sir!"

The guard then activated the gate, and it rolled aside.

Sankar accelerated quickly to the speed limit and held steady. No matter how much of a hurry he was in, the last thing he needed was to get pulled over by the port police. He arrived at the ship two minutes before the hour, and arranged the van to block the tower's view of the ship's access hatch. Sankar then popped the back doors.

"Hurry up. We have to go!" he announced.

"You shot down two of our ships earlier today?" Akoni said dourly, his thick hands out, ready to grab Sankar by the throat.

"I did," Sankar admitted. "The two raiders had been dropped into a low orbit, and they attacked me first. Yes, I splashed them. But it wasn't personal. And now, if you'll get on the ship, we can be on our way."

Bayane didn't hesitate. He bolted through the hatch.

Gwarzo squeezed through, his huge torso making it difficult.

Akoni considered, then nodded once, and walked on all fours to the hatch. He twisted sideways, and with a gentle shove from behind, popped through. Sankar came in last and sealed the hatch.

"Strap yourselves in!" Sankar commanded, then squeezed around Akoni and vaulted over Bayane to land on the pilot's seat. He dropped down and frantically threw switches to power up the ship. "Come on!" he shouted, trying to encourage the ship to respond more quickly.

"Hey!" Akoni shouted, suddenly pointing to an unexpected passenger.

Junak had crawled out of one of the ship's tiny bunks.

"I was supposed to come get you," Sankar said. "Not the other way around."

"Yah, so," Junak said, and held up his paw-hands in surrender.

"Later," Sankar said, shaking his head. "We have to go!"

Sankar returned to his controls and hammered them. His watch said it was eight. He was out of time.

The Temple of Spheenix stood above all the other buildings. Worship required dominance, and the temple was the perfect symbol to put people in their place—not just now, but forever.

Inside, at the hour of keening, High Priest Zeon waited for quiet. Every pew was filled, the parishioners sensed the hour was close, and their excitement was palpable. More Tigroids stood in the back. Zeon raised his arms, his hands palms-down. Ushers appeared in the aisles and shushed the worshippers.

"Honor the Furd gods and Traythor, their prophet!" Zeon projected his voice into an amplifier that sent his words echoing through the temple. The congregation stood. "In the beginning, when primitive Tigroids prowled the wood, the Furd gods looked upon them with kindness and grace, before choosing their Prophet. Traythor was born, and from him, the wisdom of the Furd gods has been shared with all who followed. Pray with me."

As one, the worshippers bowed their heads. In a side alcove from the main altar, Actiosa bowed hers. Zeon caught the movement out of the corner of his eye and quickly looked away to avoid getting caught in his wife's grief. The stage was set. The only thing that remained was for the actors to say their lines. The words had to be spoken.

"The hour of keening is here. Unity of purpose. Atonement for those who have gone astray. And prayers. Always prayers for those who eschew the favor of the Furd gods. May Traythor guide us in his wisdom, show us the hallowed path where we may find enlightenment and peace forevermore. Amen."

A rumbled *amen* rolled through the temple as the worshippers sat.

Zeon waited an uncomfortably long time before speaking slowly. "We have one name today. One who has gone astray. I fear he has already run from his reckoning. Enlightenment will not be his until he has been found and brought back into the fold. *I* have failed you, and the Temple of Spheenix. This name stabs a dark spear through my heart. I have prayed and continue to pray, but I can only see the shadows of failure."

The congregation had no patience for delays.

"Give us the name!" a male Oteran voice shouted. Others soon joined.

Looking down, Zeon caught sight of the time: two minutes past eight. It would have to be good enough.

"We have a new Heretic, and his name is Sankar! And I am ashamed!"

The hall erupted. Zeon raised his arms for order. The first row rushed the altar.

"Such a terrible burden," said an older female Oteran. "Let me pray with you."

Actiosa eventually joined her husband on the raised dais, and together they waded into the crowd to receive the kindest of words and sympathies from the parishioners. Pink tongues licked at the fur of their faces. Zeon and Actiosa's smell broadcast their grief, and the dashing of their pride. Their momentum slowed until they had nowhere to go, quagmired in the morass of their people.

In the back of his mind, Zeon fervently hoped that Sankar was long gone.

Alarms sounded throughout the spaceport.

"Time to go," Sankar shouted. "Power is nominal. Wings deployed. Engaging antigravity engine."

The *Four-Claw* lifted into the air more slowly than it should have, but it carried more weight than usual and hadn't fully charged.

"You two are going on a diet," Sankar snarled at Akoni and Gwarzo, as the ship picked up speed at an agonizingly slow rate. Sankar then watched for a Dominator-class interceptor. He had no idea where the current patrol was located, but they could be on him at any moment.

"They'll shoot us down. Our lives are now measured in seconds," Akoni growled.

When the power reached one hundred percent, Sankar juiced the throttle, which threw Junak into the rear wall. Bayane howled with joy—freedom now seeming sure. Gwarzo gritted his teeth against the gee forces.

"You don't have inertial limiters?" Akoni complained, examining the display board.

The ship accelerated into the upper atmosphere before it throttled back to save fuel. "The latest limiters," Sankar corrected. "We're pulling ten gees, but only feel five felt. Standby. Two missiles inbound from the surface."

Bayane started to unbuckle.

"Stay there!" Sankar snapped, but didn't look behind him to see if he'd complied. He juked left, and a missile shot past. He rolled behind it, fired the ion cannons, and the missile exploded. Sankar pulled the ship to the right and accelerated again.

He turned the nose back toward the surface, sending the second missile in a wide exoatmospheric arc. Sankar cut power, banked hard, accelerated through fifteen gees—perhaps seven felt—and brought the cannons to bear. He sent a stream of particles into the path of the trailing missile and turned away the instant it started coming apart. The missile sent its explosive force forward in an expanding cone that Sankar was desperate to escape. He leaned into the maneuver.

The ship bumped enough to let them know it was not unscathed.

Junak stood, holding his shoulder. Akoni faced him, lips bared as he showed his fangs and growled.

"You owe me an explanation," Junak said over Sankar's shoulder.

Sankar set the autopilot to take them to deep space after checking the scanners to make sure they were free and clear of Oterosan. The *Four-Claw* was the fastest ship in the fleet. No other interceptor could catch it.

There was no sign of the Dominators on patrol. Sankar rubbed his chin, wondering where they might have gone. He double-checked, and once satisfied that they weren't being followed, he turned to the ship's company.

"I owe you *all* an explanation. Tonight is the hour of keening on my world, an annual ceremony. My father is the high priest in the Temple of Spheenix. At eight, he declared me a Heretic, which means I will be hunted until my people catch me, and then I will repent and live my days in a penal colony, or if I am insufficiently penitent, I will have my limbs ripped off and be left to die."

"Sounds barbaric," Gwarzo said. "I would expect no better from you cats."

Sankar threw his paw-hands up placatingly. "It had to be done."

"Why??" Junak demanded.

Sankar stared at his co-pilot. "We're in this together. I am on a search for the truth. I don't believe what the Temple tells us. I believe we evolved from the same genetic source. That the gorillas, the bears, the wolves, the tigers, and who knows what else is out there, have a common ancestor. I'm going to find evidence of it, and then I'm presenting it to all of the planetary governments—Oterosan, Medvegrad, Angelos, and Cornelior. I need all of you to help me."

The bunch stayed silent.

"Why didn't you say so? Why the coy games?" Bayane asked mockingly, giving Sankar the two-finger wave, an insult across all the cultures. He bared his fangs as he continued. "You total nutbag! I'd say stop and let me off this express jet to Psycholand, but that could be problematic at this point in time. When we have atmosphere again, can I go?"

"If I haven't convinced you by the time we've reached Medvegrad," Sankar said, "then we'll drop you off there."

"Why the Ursoid home planet first?" Akoni asked.

"I have a couple leads. Medvegrad seems the most promising, based on an initial archaeological dig over a hundred years ago. I am in possession of additional information suggesting there is more at the site than what the Ursoids found.

"I don't want to be let off on the bear planet," Bayane whimpered. "Take me to Angelos!"

"Eventually," Sankar promised. "We have to check all the planets to find what our governments have been keeping from us."

"Better to try Pangea," Junak said. "That's neutral ground. And we all know the stories about that place."

"If it comes to it," Sankar said. "But first, Medvegrad."

"They aren't going to let you sashay down there and open a new dig." Akoni said, and sat up.

"We're not going to sashay anywhere." Sankar smirked at the Ursoid. "I've spent my life learning what's illegal to know, and if said aloud could get me killed. I don't believe in the Furd gods or that the Oterans are better than any of you—no matter what my father or my mother are forced to say in public. Now that I've freed you from the Oteran zeno-prison, and can speak openly, I'm asking if you'll each join me in a search for the truth. I have to warn you that I think it'll make us the enemy of all the worlds. But I am also convinced that learning the truth of our existence is the only way Hinteran space can truly become free."

"What if your beautiful interceptor needs maintenance?" Akoni asked, then seemed to realize why he was aboard.

Sankar waggled his Tigroid eyebrows, and his whiskers angled forward—amused.

"I'm not bad with a spanner and circuit board myself," Bayane said, coughing. "A ship like this would take several maintainers to keep in flying condition."

"You're willing to join the crew?" Sankar asked.

"Why not?" Bayane said, reconsidering his prior outburst. "In the Wolfoid culture, getting captured alive is barely above defecting to the enemy. If I returned home, it would be without honor. I'd be digging for scraps for the rest of my days. And I admit, I too am curious about the old stories. They don't just exist on Oterosan, you know."

"Why me?" Gwarzo asked. "What is my role in this expedition?"

"Genetics," Sankar said. "We need to find you a lab where you can check the samples and verify that the similarities can be traced to a single ancestor."

"That's a tall order." The Cornelian looked from face to face. "A real lab takes a lot of money. Do you have any money?"

Sankar smiled at the passengers. "I might have access to a rather substantial fund. Money is not the problem. Our biggest issue is that I'm a Heretic, now. I will be arrested on sight wherever Oterans can be found. Perhaps even on Pangea. That's why I can't do this without you."

"I still don't think I grasp the nuance of your sentencing," Bayane admitted.

"Oterans are a spiritual people," Sankar said. "Our faith keeps us from fighting among ourselves. Our Furd gods are kind in most things, but where we came from is not one of them. We are born of the forests and the wild Tigroids by the grace of the Furd gods; only the Chosen One—Traythor—was brought forth. But it doesn't hold up to scientific scrutiny. So, we question quietly. But never openly. Our faith keeps us united against a common enemy—the other races. It may have worked millennia ago, but now we have trade, embassies, and more, but we still fight. I say there's no reason for it. Hinteran space is therefore our cage. Trapping all of us."

"And you've never told me any of this," Junak interjected. "Didn't you trust me?"

Sankar looked hurt. "Quite the opposite, friend. I respect you. The words I am saying could have gotten you killed, or worse. The best way to keep a secret is to tell no one."

"You've now told us," Gwarzo rumbled.

"Because we're all criminals together," Sankar said. "I'm on the run and you're along for the ride, also on the run."

"But you have shed Medvegradian blood," Akoni said dourly. "This cannot be easily forgotten."

"I have killed for my nation, same as the rest of you," Sankar said. "But now I am asking you all to put the past to rest. Again, Hinteran space cannot go forward until we know the truth. And it'll take all of us to survive it. Akoni, with your engineering skills, what can you do to extend our scanners?"

Akoni shrugged. "Need hardware and circuit boards. I know where to get them, but you're not going to like it."

"Medvegrad is already our destination," Sankar said.

"In the heart of the capital city," Akoni said.

"That does present a problem," Sankar admitted.

"I know my way around Oteran and Medvegradian technology," Bayane said. "I've worked with both, often enough."

"You need to learn how this ship operates, too," Sankar said. "And we're going to teach you. If we're to survive, it'll take all of us."

"I think I should be the leader of this fruit-and-nut roll," Akoni said.

"Let me guess," Gwarzo said, "we'll be dumped into a ring for single combat, and the survivor takes command?"

"Sounds like a barbaric Medvegradian custom," Bayane said.

"You may know our tech, but not our kind, wolf-boy," Akoni said. "No. We change command by delivering our vision to our troops and how we're going to accomplish that vision. Then we vote."

"You do *what?*" Sankar raised his eyebrows, and his whiskers jutted forward at the humor of the proposal. "We're not taking a vote. *I'm* the commander of this vessel. I fly the boat. I give the orders."

"Well, now, we're going to have to think about that. What's to keep us from taking it from you?" Gwarzo asked while cracking his knuckles.

"Can any of you fly this ship?" Junak interjected.

Gwarzo looked at Akoni and Bayane.

"I don't fit," Akoni nodded at the pilot's seat and controls, which were made for the hands of a Tigroid.

Gwarzo screwed his face up while looking at the controls. "Not built for Goroids, either."

They looked at Bayane. He held his hands up. "Not me. I don't fly. I'm a tech guy."

Junak shook his head. "What a crew we've got for this job," he lamented.

"Fine. I'll join you," Akoni's low and rumbling statement brought silence to the *Four-Claw*.

Sankar looked to the big ape next.

"Gwarzo? We need you every bit as much as these others."

"My people will welcome me home. I have a family," the Cornelian said. "But they probably think I'm dead. It may be best to let them remain believing this."

"How long have you been a prisoner?" Sankar wondered.

"Three years." He slouched against the wall, frowning and looking at the deck.

"Only two for me," Bayane added.

"A year is all," Akoni admitted. "I'm happy to be out of zeno-prison. Though, I don't yet trust this isn't an elaborate ruse to learn how to upgrade your Oteran scanners."

"Can't you make it so no one can reverse-engineer the system? I only want the improvements to give us a better chance at staying alive. That's pretty selfish on my part, but it's the truth. I think the dig on Medvegrad will address your concerns."

"About that," Bayane started. "Are we going to have to *actually* dig?"

"Maybe," Sankar admitted, then checked the screens to make sure they were still clear. Once that was confirmed, he turned back, crossed his arms, and watched the menagerie that was the new crew of the *Four-Claw*.

"You didn't ask me," Junak said softly.

"You said, 'Where you go, I follow.' I tried to steer you clear, but you saw fit to hide within the ship and ambush us after we secured the outer door." Sankar kept his voice even, but it sounded harsh to his own ears.

"And if I ultimately decide to say no?" Junak asked.

"I would honor it," Sankar said. "Though I hope I can convince you, just like I hope to convince these other people."

"Assuming you are worthy officer," Gwarzo said. "For someone so recently declared anathema on his own world, how do we trust you?"

Now it was Junak who spoke up. "Sankar *is* a very good commander, and a better friend."

Sankar added, "I don't feel any animosity toward anyone here. I don't care if you like flavored testle or not. I don't care if you're big or small, hairy or not. I don't care about any of that. Once I was declared a Heretic, my sole purpose became to find the truth."

"I suppose it's better then zeno-jail," Gwarzo finally admitted. "Count me in."

"Me too," said the rest, even Junak.

Sankar held his paw-hand up. "Deal," he said. All of them pressed paw-hands together, then broke.

Akoni experimentally tried to squeeze himself into one of the *Four-Claw's* auxiliary seats.

"We need a bigger damn ship," Akoni said, looking left and right at the confined space. The five were on top of each other.

Sankar worked his way past to touch foreheads with Junak. Without a word, he apologized to his friend by emitting the right scent, as did Junak in return. Bayane held his nose, but Gwarzo and Akoni remained oblivious.

"Junak, find us the best course to Medvegard's outer heliosphere. Once there, we'll have to plan our ingress to the home planet based on what we find."

"Set course for the gold moon of the hydrogen ice planet, Medved Seven," Akoni directed. "We need a bigger ship, and that's the Ursoid scrapyard. We'll find a tin can that'll be able to haul this ship *inside* of it."

"Launch the *Four-Claw* if we need firepower after flying through the scanner screens with no one the wiser," Sankar intuited, and nodded. "I like it."

"What do you think we use as sows?" Akoni said. "Our fighters can sit idle for weeks on end before activating. Don't tell me you've never heard of our ability to hibernate."

"I'll be damned," Sankar stated. "I hadn't put two and two together, because freighters are cleared through Customs before they are allowed to enter the atmosphere."

"And the ships queue up for the one day a week you make Customs checks. And your scanners are weak."

Sankar shook his head. "You make it sound so simple, but the Oterans haven't figured it out. What would prompt them to attack?"

Akoni waved his hands to take in the entire ship. "I expect we knew this ship was here and are testing it. I also believe there is a communications relay buoy where you won't find it that has already transferred the details of your engagements."

"The Ursoids won't have to worry about this ship anymore as it is no longer on duty with the Oteran Fleet."

Bayane chuckled. "We have not been trying to kill our sisters, the Tigroids."

"Since when?" Sankar countered.

"What year is it?" Bayane asked.

"You lying dogface. We've always been in conflict with Wolfoids, Ursoids, and Goroids. You are the 'oid brothers of conflict. By the Furd gods, Traythor, please help us see the way to salvation!"

Bayane chuckled and turned back to the console at his seat. "Salvation, huh? Which buttons should I avoid pressing to keep from exploding the ship?"

"Gather 'round, people. Let's talk about the *Four-Claw* and what she's capable of..."

CHAPTER THREE

"You could not have delivered us to a better spot, Master Astrogator. I'd salute you if I wasn't afraid of hitting somebody." Instead of saluting, Akoni nodded at Junak, who beamed at the compliment.

Many Oteran days had passed as they made the transit from Oterosan's system, to the Medvegradian system.

Junak gave off a smell of satisfaction only Sankar could understand. Astrogation wasn't as simple as pointing the nose at the desired star. By using gravity wells and spatial anomalies, trips could be made at a vastly reduced cost in travel time by appearing to travel far in excess of light speed. Small black holes dotted the known galaxy. Many were mapped. Intersystem wells could pull a ship into and through the gravity canyons. The antigravity engines augmented the apparent downhill slides to cover extreme distances by using high-gravity, high-speed sprints.

As soon as the ship hit the Medvegrad system's outer limits, Sankar killed the engines. He sat in the pilot's seat, watching the screens while the ship continued on a ballistic trajectory into the star's heliosphere. He would restart the engines to decelerate when they neared the seventh planet.

"Scopes are clear," Sankar announced for the benefit of his crew.

"Doesn't mean jack with your systems. Reduce the search distance by half and refine your beams," Akoni ordered.

Bayane tapped the buttons at his workstation. "Refinements in place. Still nothing."

"Thank you," Akoni said from where he was standing in the middle of the open deck, hovering over everyone else. Junak hunched away from the Ursoid's bulk. With Gwarzo occupying the seat next to Bayane, the space that had been comfortable for six Oterans was nearly filthy with zenos.

"Diet!" Sankar shouted as Gwarzo hulked on him.

"Akoni and I don't fit in that space you call a latrine," Gwarzo retorted." We better get where we're going soon, or we're going to have a problem."

"Hear, hear!" the Ursoid agreed.

"Your wish is my command." Sankar looked over his shoulders and smacked his lips but changed nothing he was doing. He leaned back in his chair and watched the immensity of space on his viewscreen.

A shipyard for junked ships. It was better than taking the *Four-Claw* directly to the Ursoid capital city. Thinking better of antagonizing the two biggest members of his crew, he powered up the engines.

"What will we find at the junkyard?" Sankar asked.

"Overweight and out-of-shape retired Ursoids running it, and a bunch of scavengers buying bits and pieces from the salvageable vessels. We should be able to roll in, find the most intact of the freighters, and then get to work."

"What kind of work?" Sankar winced while he waited for the answer he didn't want to hear.

"We'll have to fix whatever ship we buy. You said money wasn't a problem. I hope you were serious. We'll be able to find something that will work. With good money, we'll get the staff to look the other way. With *lots* of money, we'll get the spare parts we need to bring our new ship online."

"And maybe buy some food with Heretic's purse," Bayane said slyly.

"You can call me Commander, or Sankar," Sankar said, his hackles going up a bit.

The Angelo snorted, "Not likely."

"In any functional crew we each deserve respect according to our station," Sankar pointed out. "My callsign with the Oteran Fleet was Crosshair. You can call me that if you want."

Again, the Wolfoid snorted.

Akoni said, "Mine called me Runt."

Junak laughed, but held his hands up before the Ursoid got mad. "It's funny because you're one of the largest creatures I've ever met. I'll be happy to call you Runt as long as you know it means exactly the opposite to me."

"Well, dog, are you going to join the adults?" Akoni rumbled.

"Fine. You can call me Cat Hater."

"We're not calling you *Cat Hater*," Sankar said, sighing. Days in the confined cabin of the *Four-Claw* were having a deleterious effect on their sensibilities. He checked the course and speed. "Thirty minutes to orbit. We'll need to hide while you, Akoni, call them. Do you know the frequency and scramble codes?"

Akoni shook his head. "It's a junkyard. They don't have scramble codes. I know the freq. We'll be fine as long as the rest of you keep your ugly faces off the screen."

"What do you say, Gene?" Bayane poked Gwarzo's shoulder.

"Gene?" Gwarzo said, ape eyebrow raised.

"As in, gene sequencing."

He shrugged. "You could just call me Gwarzo."

"Do the others of your race have no humor too, or is it just you?" Bayane asked.

"I'm a bioengineer. Do you think I chose that profession because I'm a people person?"

"You *do* have a sense of humor." Sankar chuckled from the pilot's chair. "Now, Akoni, I'll maneuver us into orbit while you get us cleared to land. I'll have to try and fly it while crouching on the floor." Sankar curled and twisted to get between the seat and the flight console. He made himself appear half his usual size. Junak did the same, at the co-pilot's seat.

"That isn't normal," Akoni said.

"It is for us. That's why our beds look the way they do." Junak pointed at the small bunks to each side of the cabin.

"You'll be in for a treat on an Ursoid freighter. Space is not at a premium."

"Will this ship have any weapons or defensive systems?" Sankar mumbled from his position beneath the console, working the controls by reaching his hands over his head.

"Freighter. Not only will it *not* have any weapons or active defenses, there will be no way to install any. The power system isn't designed for that. And before you ask, I'm not upgrading it so we can wade into a firefight with a garbage scow. Your death wish is not my death wish. Ain't no one found the truth being dead."

"So, what are you trying to say?" Bayane asked before barking a laugh.

"You better be a good engineer, or we're chucking you out an airlock," Akoni grumbled.

"Keep it down. I'm trying to do this thing here." Sankar peeked over the edge of the console. Akoni loomed over the chair, tapping the communication controls.

"Get down back there. It's time to contact the junkyard." He checked over his shoulder to make sure the others were out of the way. Despite their jibes, they understood the deadly serious business of infiltrating another system was underway. A misstep now could get them all killed.

Akoni cleared his throat, then spoke into the broadcast mic. "Shipyard Medved Seven, Beos Region, this is Catamar One Three requesting clearance to land."

After a few moments of silence, the receiver brightened with an inbound message. "Is that you, Akoni, you twerp?" a disembodied voice replied before a broad face filled the holo in front of the forward canopy.

"Nice to see you too, brother," Akoni said. "I need some parts for my ship and think I can find them down there. Plus, maybe we can take one of those hulks off your hands. Have bajingos, will travel."

"I heard you were captured by those Oteran assholes."

"Not really. But it was embarrassing, so I cross-decked to a civilian freighter. Can we keep this just between us?"

"Anything for the cub who gave me his food so I could grow big and strong. Transmitting landing instructions now. I'll meet you on the pad in just a few. Med Seven out."

The screen went dark. Sankar corkscrewed himself out from under the console. "Your brother..."

"I figured you'd be against it if you knew." Akoni shrugged.

"No secrets!" Sankar's hair stood on end, and his whiskers flattened against his face.

"You kept your secret from him." Akoni pointed to Junak.

"That was to save his life," Sankar countered.

"As was this secret. My brother moved through the business world at the speed of light. His size helped him make better deals. Being head of the ship reclamation facility is a lucrative position that will lead to an executive billet on Medvegrad. Recently, he realized that if I had fought him in the womb for an equal share of the nutrients, we would have both been average."

"So you're *really* are a runt?" Junak wondered aloud.

Akoni shook his head and gave Junak the cross-species two-finger salute.

Sankar opened the transmission packet and guided the *Four-Claw* into the designated landing pattern. "Thanks for sharing, Akoni. It's your show down there. Tell us how we play this."

"Since you're the money man, I'll introduce you, but we'll keep the others under wraps. Once we have a ship that's salvageable, he'll see all of us working on it. He'll trust me, and this deal could do good things for him if it helps move some stock that he needs moved."

Sankar put the *Four-Claw* into manual flight mode to descend toward the moon and through the force field protecting the junkyard. He brought it into the designated landing pad between multiple massive warehouses, a short walk from the control facility. Derelict ships, parts, and pieces were scattered to the edge of all they could see. The others leaned forward to get a better look.

"A playground for adults," Bayane said in awe.

"Now you sound more like an engineer!" Akoni slapped the Wolfoid on the back. Bayane coughed and bounced off the wall. Sankar settled the ship softly, not a single bump. They realized they had landed when the pilot powered down the engines.

Sankar stood and faced Akoni. He held up his hand. "Thank you."

Akoni put his massive hand against the Oteran's. "I want to know the truth, too. A life back on Medvegrad would have me asking my brother for support. There is no future for runts like me."

"But there is with us. Imagine if we can change the fundamental understanding of the nature of our existence—for future generations who won't be declared Heretics, or for those who want to learn instead of fight."

"It's part of *our* nature, Oteran," Gwarzo interjected. "Make sure you acquire a ship where I can set up a fully functioning genetics laboratory. I hope you have lots of money like you promised, cat."

A massive Ursoid approached the *Four-Claw*. He stopped and studied the ship.

"That's my brother Koni," Akoni announced. The other crew members did a double-take. Sankar accepted the statement at face value.

"You better go, then."

"Once you push me out of this ship, I'm not getting back in, but for what it's worth, you have my word that I am a part of this crew."

"I trust you," Sankar gripped part of Akoni's massive arm. "We're dead in space without trust. Do you want me to join you outside?"

"Yeah. He's already suspicious since he's probably never seen anything like this ship."

"Very few have," Sankar said, and squeezed past the Ursoid and opened the hatch. He jumped out and waited. Akoni wedged himself as far through the opening as he could. With a push from those behind, he popped out. They secured the hatch behind him.

"You are looking wondrous," Akoni offered and ran forward. The larger Ursoid lunged at the last moment and the two collided, slamming their massive chests together. Akoni bounced back despite his momentum.

"What is this?" Koni demanded with his hands pushed into his sides and his legs braced wide. He held his head high to look down on his brother and the Oteran.

"This is the time for truth, not when we're on an open channel."

Koni crossed his arms and glared at the two before him.

"I was a prisoner of war, but Sankar broke me out. He's on a mission to find the nature of our existence—"

"You mean, *his* existence," Koni interrupted.

"No, I mean *all* of our existences. His point is, are we so different from the apes and dogs? Why have we never found aliens besides these other races? To think that life only formed on these planets and that life is so similar for animals that inhabit all the worlds. To think we're all unique, well, it stumps you when you think about it in detail. I've always wondered. I think we all have. But didn't worry about it because no one has been able to prove anything. Until now."

Koni threw his head back and howled with laughter. "And you think it's going to be you and a misfit cat who deign to destroy all we hold dear?"

"I do because of garbage like what you just said. Is it beyond the pale that I have friends?"

Koni grabbed his smaller brother and lifted him with one hand until only his toes were touching the landing pad.

"It's beyond the pale that you would be so stupid as to want to change how things are."

Akoni laughed and snorted until his brother set him down. "Things are great for *you*. I had no future here. Bayane had no future on Angelos, and I'm not sure about Gwarzo the Goroid. We need a ship to carry our little scooter on long-haul missions to all the planetary systems of Hinteran. I know you've got something in these warehouses that we can use. You've always cherry-picked the new arrivals."

"I ought to tear your head off. You come in here with your nonsense, demanding I help you..."

"I won't let you hurt Akoni," Sankar said, forcing his way between the two.

Koni roared over the head of the interloper, spittle flying from his mouth, and seized the Oteran's shoulder in a grossly oversized hand. Sankar extended the claws on his right hand and stabbed them deep into the Ursoid's wrist. Koni threw his head back and screamed, involuntarily letting go. His muscles spasmed from the injury.

Sankar ducked, turned, kicked the lumbering hulk between the legs, and dove out of the way to avoid Koni landing on him. As the big brother doubled over, Akoni swung a vicious uppercut, snapping his head back. The great creature's knees buckled, and he fell.

Koni's hands flew to his face to staunch the bleeding. He started to laugh as blood squished between his fingers and dripped on the pad.

"Well done!" the huge bear-man said.

Sankar stayed in battle stance, confused.

"No matter the fool's quest you're on, I like my little brother standing up for himself. I judge a bear by the quality of his friends, and you've got teeth, Tigroid."

"Thank you," Sankar mumbled, still confused. Akoni winked at him before helping his brother to his feet. The bigger Ursoid let go of his face and gripped the puncture wounds.

"I have to admit that I've never met an Oteran before. Let me see those claws." He crooked a finger covered in blood without letting go of his wrist.

Sankar stayed out of reach as he extended the claws from his knuckles. He retracted them where they settled safely under the skin on the backs of his hands. He extended them once more.

Koni watched with fascination. "Why don't we have those if we came from the same place?"

Akoni laughed and pointed. "If we had those, we wouldn't be alive to evolve. Can you imagine the fights?"

"Probably best, little brother." Koni gestured for the two to follow.

Akoni clapped the pilot on the back. "I think I'll call you 'Guts' because you have more of them than brains, getting in the middle of a bear family throwdown like that. But," he leaned close, "thank you. It made all the difference."

CHAPTER THREE

"You people are weird," Sankar said.

CHAPTER FOUR

"Bring your other friends, too. Friends of my brother are friends of mine," Koni called over his shoulder.

Sankar turned to wave at the cockpit of the *Four-Claw* since he knew the others were watching. He motioned for them to join him.

The hatch popped, and the three tumbled out of the ship as if they couldn't decide who should disembark first. Sankar shook his head and hurried to catch up with Akoni.

Inside the control facility, Koni led them around to the back so they remained out of sight of the yard's other workers.

"I gotta hit the can," Akoni said.

Gwarzo treated the words as a call to action. "Me, too!"

Koni looked at the Goroid. "You're almost as big as Runt." He jerked a thumb over his shoulder. "That tin can's facilities a little small for you?"

"It's small for them too, but they have double-jointed backs or something. Maybe I'll dissect one of them to find out."

Koni roared with laughter. "Who would have thought a Goroid had a sense of humor?"

"He doesn't have one. I better lock my door when I sleep," Sankar replied.

The large Ursoid laughed even harder, doubling over and slapping his thigh. "And I thought this day was going to be crap like every other day out here. But no! Akoni returns and brings better standup than what we have on the vid channel." He wiped the tears from his face before continuing. "I have something in Warehouse Three that might work for you."

"Now you're talking," Sankar replied, sitting at the breakroom table while he waited for Akoni and Gwarzo to take care of business.

The Ursoid returned from the latine with a big smile on his face. "You probably don't want to go in there for a while."

"Nice! Why didn't you let me go first?" Gwarzo complained.

"It's my brother's house. Dibs."

"You're already done. How can you call dibs?" Gwarzo brushed past the Ursoid and strode down a hallway large enough to accommodate the two of them side by side. Junak walked around to stretch his legs, looking like a little kid. He was so lean, comparatively, that he wasn't sure Koni had acknowledged his existence. Sankar gestured for Junak to join him. Side by side, they might look big enough that no one would sit on them.

"Dibs," Akoni called after him.

"Where'd you run across these rodents?" Koni asked, straddling a stool to rest his bulk. Akoni took a seat at the end where he could rest one leg on the tabletop. Someone's lunch was sitting there. He nudged it aside with his foot.

Bayane leaned halfway across and pointed at the sandwich. "Are you going to eat that?"

"Nah." Koni shook his head.

Bayane grabbed it and took a huge bite.

"Because it's not mine. Cromin might be a little miffed, though, when he returns to find his lunch missing."

Bayane took another bite to square off the sandwich, leaving half of what he had started with. He slid it back into the middle of the table while still chewing.

The bear smell in the control building was nearly overwhelming, but when it was added to the stench drifting down the hallway, Sankar felt like he was going to puke. Junak had his shirt pulled over his face.

"We were in the military zeno-prison," Akoni said. "Even though we didn't have prisoner of war status, since we're not officially at war. Not according to the politicians. But the troops know. We fight every day."

"What is that ship?" Koni fixed Sankar with a narrow-eyed gaze.

"It's the *Four-Claw*," Sankar said. "The latest and greatest long-range interceptor in the Oteran Fleet. I stole it to help liberate your brother, and the Wolfoid, and the Goroid. By the Furd gods, what is that *smell?*" Sankar couldn't stand it. "Can we continue this conversation outside?"

"Pussycat can't handle a little man-stench?" Koni roared.

"No, I can't. There is death and decay in there somewhere." Sankar covered his face as Gwarzo appeared.

"We're going outside because of you," Koni told the Goroid.

Gwarzo pointed at Akoni. "No open flames for the next fifteen minutes, for all our sakes."

Akoni threw his hands out. "Why are you looking at me?" He dropped his leg off the table and stood.

Koni led them outside.

"Warehouse Three?" Sankar asked. Koni pointed and headed toward the building on the far side of the *Four-Claw*.

He looked at the interceptor as they walked, detouring to examine it close up.

"Sexy." He waited for Sankar to catch up. "What makes it special?"

"Do you know about our Dominator-class fighters?"

"I do," Koni admitted.

"Maneuverability is twice as good with the *Four-Claw*, and speed is forty percent greater. The difference is the placement of the antigrav engine. It is the hull of the ship."

"The engine is the hull?"

"High risk, high reward." Sankar highlighted an area underneath where the grav plates were more obvious. Koni had to get on all fours before lying face-up on the pad to see. Once he was satisfied with his inspection, he heaved himself upright quicker than Sankar would have guessed.

"Interesting. What would it take for you to leave this with me for a couple weeks?"

Sankar shook his head. "I think the *Four-Claw* will be key to our survival. We may rub the wrong people the wrong way. I'll need my ship to keep our other ship safe."

"I had to ask. I don't work for the intelligence directorate, but if I was able to offer this prize to them, I think I'd earn myself the right favors from the right people. But it's best that no one knows this was ever here. You'll need to move it inside sooner rather than later." He gestured with his head, and they continued to the massive warehouse that doubled as a hangar.

They went through a narrow side door, but only Koni had to squeeze through. The others entered with ease. He worked his way between shelving units stacked with parts, all dust-free because of the forcefield-protected environment. Once clear of the shelves, they saw what Koni was leading them to. Sankar tried to look behind the boxy vessel with pieces hanging off it.

Akoni strolled forward. "The good news is that it will be cheap." He glared at his brother. "What the firepits of scat is this?"

"It's the only functioning ship I have right now. The next best isn't even close. This is the only one. It's an interplanetary transport with an upgraded drive, but the scanner suite was so bad that the owner was done paying to keep it flying since it was so ugly no captain would take it out."

Sankar twitched his nose as he contemplated his potential new ride. "The *Four-Claw* will fit in that cargo bay at the very least."

"If you won't say it, I will," Junak declared. "That is the ugliest ship I've ever seen."

"You must not get around much." Koni waved him away. "And you have no choice. It's this or nothing."

Akoni pulled Sankar aside and whispered, "He doesn't have to do this. Maybe bring the *Four-Claw* into the warehouse while we start the inventory and a repair plan."

"I'm not paying a whole lot for this," Sankar whispered back.

"I'll get a decent price, but we're going to need a lot of parts, and those will probably come at a premium."

"No doubt." Sankar held his hand up for Akoni to tap it. The others had already climbed into the cargo bay. "Open the door, and I'll bring the *Four-Claw* inside." Sankar left through the front door with Akoni headed to the controls. In less than ten minutes, the *Four-Claw* was secured behind the closed door, looking small and insignificant next to the flying crate.

"We could paint it," Akoni suggested.

"The more I think about it, the less concerned I am with how it looks unless that makes it stand out more. Tell me these things are common."

"These things are common." Akoni shrugged and entered the cargo ship through the cockpit hatch, which also turned out to be an airlock. "Lots of cargo transfers happen in space. So much easier to move freight when it's weightless."

Sankar followed the Ursoid into the ship, and its spaciousness struck him. Oversized doorways and room to turn around. Corridors wide enough to play ball games in. The cockpit looked more like a lounge, but it wasn't meant for high-speed maneuvers. Sankar climbed into the pilot's chair. His feet dangled not far from the floor.

"How do I look?" Sankar asked.

"Downright captainly, Commander Lieutenant, sir."

Sankar hopped down. "I don't know about you, Runt, but I'm starting to feel at home already."

"Well, Guts, she ain't pretty, but she's got it where it counts." Akoni pounded a fist on the dingey metal doorframe.

"Are you saying that because you want to believe it, or you want *me* to believe it?"

"A new coat of paint, definitely, and she'll be ready to fly," Akoni said, thereby nicely dodging the question.

Sankar stared at an empty panel in the pilot's console. "That looks like it was something important."

"Like I said. The ship will be cheap, but the parts to make it fly? Those will be expensive."

Sankar and Akoni started to laugh. "That's funny because it's true. Probably more than that, it's a truism that will follow us the rest of our days."

"May they be long, like a really large number of remaining days. Let me get a pad, and I'll start building a parts and tasks list. It won't be complete, but it'll give us a way ahead over the next week."

"What do you think it'll take to get it space-ready?"

"I've been on board as long as you and have seen exactly the same things you've seen. I could ask you the same question and expect you'll have the same answer I'd give." The Ursoid shrugged for emphasis.

"Shall we, then?" Akoni led the way through the interior of the ship, nodding as they meandered through the ship. The rest of the crew didn't appear to be happy.

"Look at all this room!" Sankar shouted. Bayane kept his hand over his nose. Junak kept his shirt over his noze. Gwarzo bounced from one place to another.

"We'll have to knock out a bulkhead, but I think I could make it work," the Goroid said, leaning into the first space off the cargo bay.

"Our first happy customer!" Koni declared. "Let's sign the paperwork and complete the transfer of funds for this gem. You could not have chosen more wisely, considering what a bear swarm you are." He motioned for peace. "Don't be offended. On Medvegrad, a bear swarm isn't a bad thing."

"Sounds like a bunch of scavengers whose efforts are mutually beneficial," Sankar replied.

"Or that, yes. Papers and documents. Then we'll take a look at the parts list, which will, of course, be a separate deal."

Koni took them to the freighter's lounge, a separate space on the deck above the cargo hold. He pulled a bear-sized datapad out of his pocket, tossed it on the table, tapped three or four things, and pushed it toward Sankar.

A standard contract with the vessel identifier.

"The *Bilkinmore*?" Sankar said, skeptically.

Koni shrugged one shoulder. "You can name it whatever you want. Only the registration number matters."

"I vote for *Bilkinmore*." Gwarzo raised his hand to reinforce his verbal commitment to the ship's name.

"I don't," Junak said through his shirt. Bayane only nodded. Sankar didn't ask if the Wolfoid was supporting the original name or Junak.

"We'll talk about the name later. What catches my eye is the derelict clause, as in, we'll never be able to validate the registration as a vessel that can fly."

"Are you actually going to check in wherever you're going?"

Sankar looked at Akoni. The Ursoid shook his head almost imperceptibly.

"This price assumes it is a functional vessel. Here's what I'll do. I'll double your price..."

Koni scowled and stepped back.

"What are you doing? You'll see the bottom of Traythor's heel at this rate." Junak inadvertently took a deep breath and started to cough. He pulled his shirt back over his face.

"I'm not going to get planted in the ground," Sankar replied. "Double the price, but that comes with all the spare parts to make this bird *fully* functional."

Koni considered the offer. He took the pad back, studied it, and sat down, then removed an old-school calculator from his pocket and started mashing buttons. He erased them all and went through it again, then adjusted the contract and put in a new number.

Sankar raised an eyebrow. He tapped in a different number.

Akoni watched the back-and-forth. "What is this, a Pangean Souk?"

"Shush!" Koni said, watching Sankar.

The Tigroid read through the entire two pages while everyone waited. He tapped a single letter into the contract and pressed his thumb against it, then slid it back to Koni.

It had read *Fully functional spacecraft as determined by Koni*. Sankar had put an "A" in front of it. Akoni would be the final arbiter of the quality vessel at double the original price. Sankar's funds had been skimmed from the Temple of Spheenix over the course of his whole life. He had twice that in his account. He hadn't expected to spend it all so quickly.

Koni grumbled for a short while before he jammed his thumb on the screen. He spat into his hand and held it out.

"Do I have to?" Sankar asked Akoni. The Ursoid nodded.

Sankar took a deep breath and slammed his palm against Koni's. The resultant splat made Junak gag.

"Take it easy, Tiny! You don't need to try and rip my hand off." Koni looked from face to face, then he and Akoni roared with laughter. "Send me the parts list. I have to get back to work."

"And tools," Akoni added.

"You can rent them."

"Without them, the ship will never be flight worthy. And food, because that's fuel for those who are going to fix this ship. Without food, not flightworthy. At least we're not asking for dancing girls."

"There will be Wolfoid girls in heat?" Bayane perked up.

Junak leaned close and whispered through his shirt, "They'll be Ursoid girls in heat."

"Oh." He contemplated that reality before making his decision. "Never mind."

"Any other extortion, Runt?" Koni wondered, tucking the pad into his pocket.

"No extortion to begin with. It's all about the contract. I guess we better get to work. Food now would be good. What about the parts in this warehouse?"

"Take what you need but maintain a running inventory. I need to keep my advanced inventory system up to date."

"Looked like piles of junk," Gwarzo mumbled.

"We have a system!" Koni swelled to his full height and girth.

"Relax, you big goony bastard. No one wants to fight you over the museum pieces filling the shelves."

Akoni stood and hugged his brother. "We'll take it from here, Twig."

He grunted and strolling away, tapping the pocket with the datapad. He started to whistle a gruff and rude tune.

Sankar stood up. The tabletop was level with his lower rib cage.

"We have a ship. We have a way ahead. We even have a name. Soon enough, we'll be flying this crate out of here. You *can* fix it, can't you?"

"With the right tools and parts, sure," Akoni said. "And we'll get to see if

Bayane's walk is as good as his talk, where tech is concerned. How *long* it'll take is the real question."

"I think since it is in your brother's best interest for us to be out of here as soon as possible, we'll get the red-carpet treatment," Sankar insisted.

"Gray carpet," Bayane clarified.

"What?" the others asked in unison.

The Wolfoid pointed to his eyes. "If we come from the same source, how come we can't see colors?"

"I'd like those claws, too. They would even the playing field with Twig." Akoni flexed his fists, imagining.

"What would he be like if he had them?" Sankar poked Akoni in the chest. "And why do you call him 'Twig?'"

"Koni was always taller than the others our age, but he didn't fill out until later. Twig, and I was Runt. Our parents were not proud."

"Gwarzo, start figuring out your lab space and equipment needs. We'll get access to a purchasing portal and see what we can acquire on the open market for a ship-to-ship transfer in space. It's nice having an airlock."

"I'll pick a space to start working on," Bayane said.

"Make sure I see what you're doing first."

"How about you sniff my ass?" the Wolfoid shot back at Akoni.

"Say what?" Akoni lumbered toward Bayane with his arms out.

"Stop!" Sankar shouted, and leapt to the top of the table with feline grace, landing crouched, claws extended. "I will not have you fighting each other. Bayane, you and Akoni work together until you're both comfortable knowing what's what. Maybe you'll each learn something? We'll get on what *we* can do, meanwhile. Into the warehouse on our first raid, and make sure you keep track of everything you take. Gwarzo, that'll be on you to inventory items we bring into the ship."

"I'm not sure Koni has a system," Akoni grumbled.

"We'll give him a list nonetheless. And here's a crazy thought. I bet a bunch of the missing equipment is out there and will bolt right back into place. How about that for a theory?"

"Damn. You're probably right," Akoni allowed. "I'll order us some food. We need to eat."

"And until we know the ship is up and running, don't use the latrines in here!" Sankar jumped off the table and landed lightly on the deck. He looked around the compartment before striding out. Junak hurried after him, face still under his shirt.

The others followed them down the steps and into the cargo bay, out the back ramp, and into the warehouse. Only a third of the overheads were lit. Sankar looked for the panel to turn on all the lights. He had no interest in saving power. They had a ship to fix. It required a lot of work, and there were only five of them to do it. They needed all the light they could muster.

The five scattered into the racks, each looking for what they thought the ship would require, but only Bayane and Akoni knew what bits and pieces they needed.

CHAPTER FIVE

"Yo!" Akoni called. First to join him was Junak.

"You've found something?" the co-pilot and astrogator asked. The Ursoid pointed at a collection of carts and pallet jacks.

"I think I've found my brother's system. They remove stuff they think has value, and it sits in these carts until they get around to putting it away. And judging by the others in the area," he waved toward at the rear area of the warehouse, "they never get around to putting them away."

Sankar and Gwarzo reached them. "Why do you think this is the right stuff?"

"Simple logic. These carts were most recently pushed in here because they aren't blocked in, and they say *Bilkinmore* on the side."

Junak felt stupid until he looked at it. He couldn't read the Ursoid common language.

Sankar didn't wait. He got behind the first cart in line and leaned into the handle. "Tell us which ones to take and let's go. Time's wasting."

It took every bit of his strength for Sankar to get the cart moving.

"Junak," he grunted, and the slighter Tigroid joined him. Together, they managed. Akoni and Gwarzo pushed the other two carts toward the ship.

"This is all," the Ursoid called over his treasures. "It also tells me that we won't find anything useful in the racks. The best and newest gear will still be in the carts."

"He has a system..." Sankar mumbled while leaning into the cart. Akoni snorted and laughed. The carts rolled easily once they got going. Humidity was low, and without dust, there was nothing to rust them. It was the perfect junkyard. Once on hand, the bits, pieces, parts, and props would remain as they'd been the day they were delivered.

Sankar and Junak were unable to get the cart up the ramp. Akoni jogged around the Goroid to give them a hand.

"Oof!" The Ursoid had to lean into it. "How did you guys pick the heaviest cart? And what in the name of Ursulis Major is in here?"

They manhandled it into the cargo bay. Akoni removed the top layer of parts. "Oh, my!" He reached in but couldn't move whatever he was touching. "Gene, give me a hand with this. You little people need to give us some space." He waved the others away.

Bayane appeared, carrying a box under his arm and a tree-shaped green trinket hanging from a string. He waved it past the Tigroids. "It smells of the mountain forests on Angelos."

Sankar and Junak sniffed and smiled. "A scent that I can rally around." Sankar's whiskers thrust forward.

"There's a whole box of them." He stabbed a thumb over his shoulder toward the two struggling with the contents of the cart. "To make life aboard this tub palatable."

Junak nodded vigorously. Sankar crossed his arms while Bayane headed into the ship, hanging the scented trinkets at various points in the corridor on his way to the cockpit and the second deck.

"Just a little more," Akoni muttered. He reached underneath an oversized part and gripped a square of deck plating, and it jerked upward. The Ursoid's head snapped back from the impact.

"Monkey balls! Sorry about that." Gwarzo guided the plate to the side and easily set it down.

Akoni staggered to the wall to hold himself upright. "What happened?" Sankar asked, hurrying across the cargo bay.

"An active antigrav plate that was upside down. Some worker probably did it as a joke," Akoni's eyes focused as he recovered from the violent blow to his head. He shook off Sankar's helping hand. "We Ursoids are a little tougher than the smaller Hinteran species."

Gwarzo checked the bear's head. "You have a lot of scars under this thick hair of yours. Did you use your head as a battering ram when you were younger?"

Akoni shook his head. "It sucked being the runt in my family. I did not, no, but someone else did." He nodded in the general direction of the control center.

"You're a big man for forgiving him," Sankar said.

"No sense trying to fight him. Don't we have work to do?"

Sankar and Junak moved the second cart into the cargo bay, and Gwarzo moved the third. Akoni removed the items, grouping those that were part of a single system and needed to be installed in sequence. Even Ursoid derelicts had been built with a modular plug-and-play system. Half the parts required minimal effort to be returned to operational status.

"Take these into the engine crawlspace." Akoni pointed at a pile of sockets and boards. "You should see where they belong, but I'll install them since they will fit in incorrect slots."

Sankar and Junak picked up what they could and headed up the stairs to the second deck. A ship with actual stairs, but it was a freighter.

Gwarzo started moving the heavier modules to the cockpit. Bayane reappeared, wearing one of the small trees like a necklace.

"Wolfoids are weak," Akoni said, taking a deep breath of the cargo bay's air.

"We have sensitive noses. Someday you'll be thankful that we can smell trouble before you step in it!"

"I work on spaceships. I won't be stepping in anything unless you and the cats aren't house-trained." Akoni looked over his shoulder at the Goroid. "And don't you dare start throwing your feculence around."

"Could you be any more offensive?" Bayane stood more upright than usual and held his short muzzle in the air. Akoni stared at him until he snorted. "If you're getting us food, you'll be my friend forever, even if you do smell horrible. You know, like a bear."

"We have work to do. Start on the cockpit." Akoni nudged a heavy electronic device with his toe that looked to be the same shape as the empty space in the pilot's control panel.

"Ah, the inertial inverter. I wondered where you'd gotten to. Come to Papa." Bayane picked up the module, grunting with the effort, and staggered toward the front of the craft.

"I don't smell, do I?" Akoni asked.

Gwarzo stared at him in disbelief. "You're asking me?" He shook his head. "I'll be in my future lab. Do we have access to purchase boards yet?"

Akoni threw up his hands. "I've been with you the whole time. How would I have been able to manage that?"

"Bite a guy's head off for asking a question. Maybe Sankar was right about you." Gwarzo carried a module as he left the cargo bay.

"What am I saying about you?"

"I don't know. Maybe you should tell me."

"I haven't said anything that you haven't already heard. And for the record, an Ursoid's idea of a crawlspace is a bit different than ours."

He and Junak gathered the second load and climbed upstairs.

Akoni took the largest remaining device. "I think I know where you go. Come with me, little friend."

Sankar and Junak stopped and looked back. "Is he talking to the equipment?" Junak asked.

"I'm not sure if answering that question will make me think better or worse of him. Maybe it's what engineers do. I've heard you talking to the astronavigation panel."

"Of course. It takes love to plot the best course that doesn't result in ripping the ship apart within a gravity eddy."

Sankar nodded. "Then, yes. He was talking to the equipment, and if it takes love to get this crate into space, then we'll give it all the love it can handle."

"Now you're being weird," Junak replied. "I don't think I can love this garbage scow."

"Feel the love, my friend!" Sankar continued climbing.

"I think I should thank you for saving me from my gambling debts. Things were going to come to a head soon. I am afraid that I was under internal investigation."

"Just in time, then. I'm glad you're with me. I don't think I could handle these other races on my own. When I'm looking to a Wolfoid for understanding and sympathy, I know the galaxy has been turned on its head."

"I was thinking the same thing." Junak looked at the deck. "What happens when they come after us?"

"We fight them. With every fiber of our beings, we fight them. We need small arms because we may encounter them on the ground, in the cities, at spaceports. We'll be the Swarm, a thing they don't want to see."

"There are only five of us."

"Then we'll have to shoot faster and straighter than anyone who tries to stop us."

"I don't know how to shoot a blaster well," Junak admitted.

"We'll have to train," Sankar said. "We need to be better at *everything*."

"If we're to survive, you mean." They reached the crawlspace, which was large enough for the Tigroids to enter by bowing their heads. They picked a spot between the engines to drop off the parts.

"If we're to survive, we need to be better. We'll train together so we can fight as one. And no matter what Akoni says, we'll need at least defensive systems on this tub. I have no doubt it'll come under fire at some point. We can't get blown away by a single missile that we know is coming."

"Aren't you a sunray of good cheer?" Junak left the crawlspace.

"I'm a realist. If you want a positive spin, I can do that. How about, 'at least bill collectors aren't scratching their claws on your front door.'"

"I didn't have a front door because the collectors already got that."

"Okay, Dark Cloud. I'll think of something. Until then, take ownership of your astronavigation station and bring it up to speed."

Junak nodded and hurried forward. Sankar took the opportunity to explore the second deck. Crew quarters lined the passage leading to the crawlspace. He checked each one. Some were in better shape than others. All were filthy. They'd need cleaning supplies. He added those to his list.

He selected one of the spaces, and with a greasy rag, wrote a name on the door. "Guts."

Sankar looked at it before tossing the rag into a box he designated for trash. He suspected they'd have boxes filled with boxes of trash before they were done. He ran his hand down the wall as he strolled, and a smile crept onto his face. A ship to carry them on their mission.

Akoni leaned in a darkened doorway, watching the Tigroid.

"Truth, Sankar. The mission to find the origin of the races. Is that real?"

"It's why I threw everything away." Sankar leaned against the wall opposite the Ursoid.

"I'll get those engines up and running for you, Captain. We'll have power, and that will make bringing everything else online a sight easier."

"We couldn't have come this far without you, Akoni."

"I know." He stepped forward, and with a movement as quick as a cat's, he ruffled the Tigroid's ears. "You little people are growing on me." He whistled as he walked away.

"Little people? I'm *captain* of a crew of misfits." He started to laugh.

He stood straighter. Could he sell that on the galactic stage? Would it keep the races away so the crew could work in peace? He added digging tools to his list. Medvegrad wouldn't be the only world where they sought answers underground. "*The Paleo Explorer*," he said as it came to him. "No one would question such a ship at an archaeological site."

Sankar strolled from the galley to the quarters to a second recreation room. He wanted to see them to visualize the ship and figure out what it would take to make it a home.

Two recreation rooms. They needed a workout and a sparring room. A firing range? What did larger combat vessels have? Training spaces for marines? Sankar had been fast-tracked through the fighter pilots' course at the war academy. He didn't exactly have whiskers for ground combat, though he'd taken pilots' survival training like everyone else—and excelled at it.

He continued down the steps that came out behind the cockpit, not far from the airlock.

There were a few cabins on the main level between the cargo bay and the cockpit. Sankar opened each door and walked through. Gwarzo worked within one of them.

"Can you make it work?"

"Got a grease pencil? Chalk will do if you don't."

Sankar pulled his pockets out to show he was carrying nothing.

"We'll need to upgrade the power to this space. The equipment for the lab will be power-hungry. You understand that we may not be able to buy what I need for a truly cutting-edge lab. You need me to have the best, don't you?"

"I do. We'll be doing work at the forefront of all research."

"You're going to save a lot of money," Gwarzo said, crossing his long arms across his chest.

"I don't follow." Sankar was confused.

"What I need won't be for sale because there is only one of them. We're going to have to steal it from the Cornelian University."

Sankar rubbed his temples. It resolved part of his money concerns while raising an entirely new set of challenges. "I was afraid you were going to say that. I don't mind stealing little bits and pieces in support of our mission, but this is a big piece of gear, isn't it?"

"Pieces. Big pieces, including an entire computer suite. We may have to make two trips." Gwarzo smiled half-heartedly.

"We'll figure it out," Sankar replied in a tired voice. "We'll keep climbing one mountain after the next until there aren't any left. Only then will we have our answer."

"It's okay if you call me Gene," Gwarzo said. "It's growing on me, but I'm not a fan of Crosshair."

"Runt wants to call me Guts for getting in between two bears getting ready to fight."

"Stupid is more like it, but Guts is easy."

"It's a little victory for today. I fear this is our home now, as crappy and dirty as it is. If we want to sleep, we'll need to move stuff in."

"I saw bedding in the warehouse racks. I think they used it as packing."

"We have blankets in the *Four-Claw*. Maybe there's hope to get some sleep."

"Don't you take catnaps?" Gene asked, raising one eyebrow.

"We do," Sankar said with a soft chuckle. "It's part of the Tigroid culture, but I haven't had one in a while. I've been up for nearly two days now."

"Go sleep on the *Four-Claw* in that box you call a bunk. We'll take care of things here. I don't think it'll take as long as you think."

"Let me find the others. I don't want to be that guy, the one who's just like a blister."

The Goroid shook his head. "I don't get it."

"Shows up after all the work's done, just like a blister."

"Ah. Must be Tigroid humor. You need sleep, so next time, you'll make more sense." Gene turned back to work on a small panel. He didn't explain what he was doing, and Sankar didn't ask.

Sankar left to go to the cockpit, where he found both Bayane and Junak. The flight consoles had already been restored.

"Just waiting for power to check them," Bayane offered.

Junak worked with a small screwdriver to adjust a monitor at the nav station. "Where'd you get that?"

He pointed at Bayane, who pointed at the toolkit on the captain's seat. It was from the *Four-Claw*. "The bears' idea of a small screwdriver is a little bit different from ours."

"We're going to look like a daycare facility, trying to fly this thing. We'll need to get stepstools. I don't like that my feet don't touch the floor. How do I pilot the ship when I'm not firmly in my seat?"

"It's not very ergonomic," Bayane replied. "Maybe you can do the hard piloting standing up. I think I can rig something."

"And for high gees?"

Bayane stopped working and stood up. "You're not pulling any erratic maneuvers in this hulk. You'll tear it apart. It has an inertial limiting system because this is a long-haul carrier. It has to survive the eddies and currents of the gravity wells, along with the stress of crossing the event horizons on the Black Hole Express. This is a freighter. Save your high gees for the *Four-Claw*. If you can't pilot it standing up, then you're doing something wrong."

"Defensive systems. We need mimics to draw off incoming missiles, then." Sankar stood in front of the pilot's seat to gauge how he could make it work.

"That's something we might be able to do. It won't require extra power. What it *will* require is the hardware. We may have to break into a military facility and steal them."

"While we're breaking in, we can steal the small arms we need so we can break in," Sankar stated, being somewhat self-sarcastic.

"You never said it was going to be easy," Junak noted.

A big hand slapped Sankar on the back. "Food's here," Gene announced.

Sankar jumped. "Where did you come from?"

Junak leaned close. "When a Tigroid and an Ursoid love each other very much..."

Gwarzo rolled his eyes. "Don't you have somewhere else to be?" The Goroid shooed him away. Bayane stretched and bolted.

"Was there a lot?" Junak wondered.

"I'm not sure," Gene replied. The three looked at each other before coming to the same conclusion. They ran for the hatch and down the corridor to find Akoni standing in front of a cart of food, using a chair to hold off the Wolfoid.

"You're lucky I got here first!" Akoni dodged back and forth, surprisingly light on his feet considering his size.

"Do all Wolfoids eat like you?" Sankar asked.

"You haven't seen me eat since you've been systematically starving all of us since we left prison. Ah, prison. Three hots and a cot. It didn't get much better than that."

"Did you land on your head or something?" Junak asked, walking around Akoni to get to the cart. "Looks like sandwiches and snacks, but it's Ursoidsized portions. Let him through." Junak handed over enough food to choke a hungry goat. Bayane looked at it as if he were getting shorted. "Take it!"

"You people are mean when you don't get enough food. At least I'm not raining on anyone else's parade. I know a callsign for you: Grumpy. And goes for you, too." He stabbed his sandwich at Sankar before biting it in half, filling his mouth. He chewed and swallowed too quickly. He gagged half of it back up and started chewing again.

Akoni stared at him. "Can you make him eat somewhere else?"

Sankar jumped a few steps up the stair to the second deck and faced the crew. "We start workouts first thing in the morning, kittens and cubs, because we are going to have to fight as a team, and fight we will. You saw how we were treated leaving Oterosan. You see how we have to work undercover here, and Koni is family! Heretics and pariahs. The unclean. The chosen few. We are *Bilkinmore*, all five of us. They'll never know what hit them, like they've been sent through a buzzsaw. We'll need something to use as weapons until we get real weapons, and then we'll keep acquiring better. No one will stand in our way."

Akoni nodded, grabbed a sandwich, and started eating while he walked. "I'll have the engines up in just a few, boss."

Gwarzo took some food and squatted on the deck next to the cart to eat. Junak took a sandwich and a chip bag to eat while leaning against the wall. He ate half of it since that was all he could hold and kept the bag for later. "Do you want this?" he asked Bayane.

"I do. Thanks for asking." He slowed down, eating Junak's half-sandwich before polishing off his chips and turning to a snack bar. Junak hadn't seen the bars. He returned to the cart, took one, and stuffed it in a pocket.

Bayane belched. "Sorry." He didn't sound sorry. "I'm ready to go." He staggered halfway down the passage, stopped, curled up on the floor, and went to sleep.

"Your motivational speech had a significant impact on our Wofloid," Gwarzo observed. "But I'm with you. I get what you're trying to accomplish, and I applaud you. I better start teaching myself how to use the gene-sequencing equipment."

Sankar's face fell. "You don't already know how to use it?"

"The right answer is, not yet, but I will. Every company's machinery is different. I trained on a specific set of instruments. Now I will re-train on another set."

CHAPTER SIX

The first three days aboard *Bilkinmore* passed in the blink of an eye. Sankar had not yet managed a single physical fitness and training session, per his original directive, but today was different. The *Four-Claw* was secured in the rear area of the cargo bay, and the fresh paint was drying. They intended to take the new ship for a test flight.

"Get up, you lazy scumbags!" Sankar pounded a metal pipe on the doors as he strolled down the corridor.

He went to tap on Gwarzo's door, but it was flung open mid-swing. The Goroid grabbed the pipe, ripped it out of Sankar's hand, and slammed the door in his face.

Sankar looked at his hand and then the door. "Give me my pipe back!"

"I'll give it back, all right. I'll shove it right up your ass."

Akoni stepped out of his room. "I'll thank you to never do that again." He walked down the corridor, bumping into the Tigroid even though there was plenty of room. He wedged Sankar against Gwarzo's door before sliding past. The ship's upper latrine was the next door down.

"Combat drills!" the captain yelled into the empty corridor. When no one materialized, he went down the stairs into the cargo bay by himself. He set up a target dummy, picked up the largest staff, and started hammering away. He beat it into submission, his tongue out of his mouth as he panted.

Akoni finally appeared, followed closely by Junak, then Bayane. They each picked up a staff, which were little more than carbon fiber pipes.

"What do we do with these?"

"You fight," Sankar replied. "A staff is an elegant weapon. It can redirect an inbound blow or block an attack. It can strike an enemy and paralyze him. Give us space. Runt, square off."

The others backed away. Gwarzo appeared at the top of the stairs and sat down to watch.

"I suppose you want me to attack you."

"Of course." Sankar bounced on his feet. The staff had been his weapon of choice at the war academy, though he did have reverence for the lethal *kabbar*—the traditional all-purpose military knife issued to Oteran war academy graduates.

Akoni took a step forward while swinging the staff over his head in large circles. He jumped toward Sankar and dropped, attempting a leg strike. Sankar jumped over the weapon and thrust his staff into Akoni's forehead. The Ursoid staggered, and Sankar followed up with a gentle tap to the side of his head.

"Felled like a mighty oak with two blows."

Akoni bowed his head in defeat.

"Until we have blasters of some sort, we'll have to make do with the weapons at hand. Maybe we'll look like monks. Do you have monks?"

"No." Akoni shook his head. "We'll look like a bunch of boneheads carrying sticks. People will shy away from us for that alone."

"If they leave us be, then we can go about our business. That is the best-case scenario."

"I'll take you on," Gwarzo called. He leapt down the stairs, skipping the entire flight, hit, and rolled. He took the staff from Akoni's hand as easily as he had earlier snagged the pipe from Sankar.

He spun and twisted with the staff until it was a blur. Sankar dodged and ducked, then ran aside to force the Goroid to change his approach. Gwarzo jumped over Sankar's head and thrust upward, hitting only empty air. He touched the wall and pushed off toward his opponent.

With a quick twist of his wrist, the staff changed direction, slipped past Sankar's block, and struck him across the midsection. Sankar bent over. Gene hit, rolled sideways, caught Sankar's legs, and jerked them upward. The Tigroid slammed face-first into the deck.

"That's how you fight with sticks," the ape said. "I'll have my breakfast now."

He strolled away, the undisputed champion of cargo bay combat.

"That looked painful," Junak said. "Who would have thought our bioengineer was such a stud with a staff?"

"He's a Goroid. They were born hanging onto sticks."

"And don't you forget it," Gwarzo yelled from down the corridor.

Bayane rubbed his stomach and started to inch away from the target dummy. "Pick up your staff and prepare to defend yourself."

"I'm an engineer," Bayane stated, pawing at a staff but not picking it up. Sankar rapped his knuckles. The Wolfoid pulled his hand away. "That hurt!"

Sankar pointed at the wall. "Out there, they are going to try and kill us. No pain, no gain, you little bitch."

"Hey!" Bayane snatched a staff and snarled.

Sankar stabbed at the Wolfoid, forcing him back on his heels. He responded by swinging wildly while off-balance. Sankar's jab in the crotch dropped him.

"I'm an engineer!" Bayane cried.

"Get up!" Sankar snarled.

"Maybe you should…" Junak stopped speaking at Sankar's wild-eyed look.

"We've been getting the ship ready, and now that we're there, we need to be ready for the next phase: going to Medvegrad and digging into our history."

"What's that have to do with getting beaten up with a stick?" Bayane rubbed his groin.

"People will try to stop us. People who benefit from hiding the truth."

"I'll dig. I'm good at it, and you guys can watch my back. Deal?"

Sankar closed his eyes and took a deep breath, trying to calm himself.

The impact to his chest drove the air from his lungs, and stars popped like fireworks in the dark of his mind. He staggered back and swung his staff to fight off the attack until he could recover his wits.

"That'll teach you to take your eye off your enemy," Bayane declared, working his way closer, spinning his staff before him.

With Tigroid quickness, Sankar smacked the Wolfoid's knuckles hard enough that he dropped his staff.

"I give!" he shouted before Sankar could follow up by clubbing him in the head.

Koni strolled up the ramp and into the ship. "I told you it would take no time to make the ship flightworthy! You test-fly it today, no?"

"We'll be ready for a flight check this afternoon," Sankar replied. He didn't thank their gregarious host because it was operational due to their hard work and not any effort on Koni's part.

"You play when you should be flying?" the Ursoid asked. He lost his smile and the projection of joy. "Why don't you test-fly it now, and once you leave, do not come back. There is nothing else here for you. I brought you a going-away gift." He pointed at a cart he'd left near the *Four-Claw*.

Sankar made eye contact with the Wolfoid, who accepted the task and checked it out. "Food and circuits," Bayane reported.

"For the scanners, big brother?"

Koni nodded. "It'll be better for this fine freighter if it can see farther than it is seen. These aren't off junked spacecraft, by the way. This is the latest tech."

Sankar bowed his head. "We thank you. We'll start preps for immediate departure. We'll head out to deep space and then to Cornelior, where we have an appointment. You've been a friend to us, and we won't forget that."

"Don't be confused. Akoni is my brother. It is for him alone you have this ship. It's probably best if you forget me and that you ever had anything to do with Medved Seven."

"Besides a bill of sale that says we purchased a spacecraft here," Sankar clarified.

"Are you sure that's what it says? I believe *Bilkinmore* was purchased directly from the previous owner at Orbital Platform One."

"You sly dog." Akoni meandered over and embraced his brother, grunting as he lifted and bounced him.

"Those are fighting words, Runt." Koni's voice boomed across the cargo bay. Akoni let go and twirled his hand in the air.

"We'll be on our way, big brother. Thank you for your help. I don't take it for granted."

Koni grunted and walked away. Akoni followed him to the end of the bay for a few private words before raising the ramp, then closing and sealing the cargo bay.

"We better hurry. He'll call the authorities if we take too long. His people are starting to ask questions."

Sankar nodded and handed his staff to Bayane. "Secure the gear and cargo. Junak, plot us a course to the outer limits of the heliosphere. Akoni, power us up and then take a look at upgrading the scanners. I expect we'll need them sooner rather than later. Gwarzo! Help Bayane secure the gear so he can join Akoni in helping to keep this bucket in the sky."

As the captain, Sankar jogged down the broad passage on his way to the cockpit. He stood in front of the captain's seat so he could reach the screens and controls. There was no documentation. He had to make up the pre-flight as he went.

The engines came to life and showed nominal power.

"Engines are green, beginning status check. Inertial systems." He looked over the panels until he found the right gauge. "Inertial limitation is nominal. Life support is online. It's yellow."

Sankar leaned against the chair and watched the status indicator stubbornly refuse to give him the green light. He punched the ship's intercom, a massive button on the arm of the captain's chair.

"Life support is yellow. Akoni and Bayane, we need to clear the issue."

The intercom flashed. "The issue is this harking thing is more a sieve than a bucket. We're leaking air. If we take this trash can to space right now, we all die. We could use a hand patching leaks, so get your hairy asses out here and grab a torch and a metal plate."

"Don't we have any fiber-fill?"

"That's for emergencies. It'll get you to a place where you'll have to make a real repair. How about we save it for an emergency? How many old ships have you flown? Never mind. I know the answer. It's zero. You don't need an engineer on a brand-new ship, and the pilot doesn't need to know anything about anything to fly one!"

"Are you finished?" Sankar asked softly. "You got your pound of flesh. We're on our way. Guts and Slim to the rescue."

"May your Furd gods save us. I'm going to burn incense and wave a mystical toker torch for good luck because you're turning me into a praying man."

"You're welcome," Sankar said before shutting off the intercom.

Junak shook his head.

"You're coming, too."

"I'm not done with the navigational calcs."

"We don't need those as much as we need to get off this rock. I felt Koni's sense of urgency and Akoni's too. They know something that they're trying to protect us from. Let's patch those holes and get airborne. We'll figure out where we want to go when we're out there."

"Cornelior or Medvegrad?"

"Probably Cornelior. For now. We'll both need to get used to flying by the seat of our pants."

Junak stepped away from his console. He had rigged a box to sit on and added a pillow from the bedding stacks in the warehouse. Sankar looked envious since he had opted for standing, not entertaining other options.

They hurried down the passage to the repair locker. The torch was there, but no metal panels to use as patches. Junak checked the cargo bay. It had been stripped.

"Request permission to leave the boat in search of repair parts," Junak shouted from the far end of the cargo bay with his hand hovering over the open button.

"I second that," Akoni added as he lumbered down the stairs and jogged toward the ramp.

"Go," Sankar replied. He slashed his hand downward in a gesture to hurry up. *Akoni is running. Urgency.*

Sankar could do nothing while he waited for direction from his engineer. He put the torches down and ran after his shipmates.

Junak and Akoni looked through the racks. Akoni grabbed an item and handed it over. Sankar ran for a cart and joined them. The Tigroids filled the cart with items Akoni chose. Sankar rushed it into *Bilkinmore*.

"Keep the cart and get another two," Akoni yelled, continuing to acquire parts and pieces.

Sankar delivered an empty cart and ran for a third. Fifteen minutes later, they trundled the two carts into the ship. Akoni's arms were filled as he waddled after them. They put the gear in front of the *Four-Claw* by the stairs to the second deck where it would be most easily accessible. Akoni handed them two plates each.

"Follow me."

With the torches and the plates, the Tigroids were hard-pressed to keep up. Akoni pointed at one of the crew quarters. "Bottom panel on the far-right side." He kept walking before pointing at his own room. "Top panel, far right."

Sankar stood before the empty room. "On it," he declared at Akoni's look.

Junak entered Akoni's quarters for only a moment before returning to the passage. Akoni was squatting to enter the crawlspace through the engine systems.

"I can't reach it," Junak said.

Akoni waved his hand over his shoulder. "You'll figure it out. I'll take care of a couple leaks in here. When you're finished, find Bayane. He's working on the patches behind the cockpit."

Junak watched the Ursoid crawl away. He joined Sankar, who had begun welding the panel into place. He fired his torch up and started on the other side.

"Can't reach the panel, and I'm going to need your help," Junak said over the hiss and crackle of melting metal.

Sankar nodded and continued drawing a bead around the outside of the plate, which was designed to melt into the base material. Junak finished his side, and they met at the middle top. They didn't have the right equipment to scan for densities to highlight weak points. Sankar looked it over and declared it sound.

"Are you sure?" Junak wondered.

"Nope. Space is the final arbiter of repair quality. At least it won't cave in. We'll find the pinholes the old-fashioned way and top off the repairs if anything else is needed."

They went to Akoni's room. The seam that needed to be repaired was obvious. It was nearly rusted through.

"How does scat like that happen?" Sankar asked. "Space isn't corrosive, and neither is this shipyard."

"Maybe it was abandoned on a planet before they brought it here. A rainy planet."

"I guess if they flew it here wearing self-contained suits, maintaining environmental integrity wouldn't have mattered. Climb on."

Junak jumped onto Sankar's shoulders and balanced himself against the wall, which was nothing more than a single plate of the hull.

While Junak worked, Sankar held his ankles and talked. "Our defense will have to be the advanced scanners. This single hull will collapse if someone looks angry at it."

"You're not lying. This ship looks like it was mass-produced, the last off the line on the day before vacation. And flown by people similarly detached." After a couple of tack welds, Junak was able to work with one hand against the wall. He traced a double bead around the outside of the plate to ensure it held. The damage it covered was extensive.

Sankar grunted and groaned as the repair dragged on.

Finally, Junak declared victory and jumped to the floor.

"Next time, we switch halfway through." Sankar rubbed out the boot prints in his shoulder hair before picking up his repair gear and heading into the corridor.

Akoni was exiting the crawlspace. "Don't tell me you just got done?"

"We had to do it our way because it was too high. Does this ship have a stepladder?"

"No. I can reach everything."

"Why didn't you take care of it?" Sankar shot back.

"Because I didn't want noobs like you sparking near the engines." Akoni stood and stretched. "Let's finish up downstairs and see if our work passes inspection."

They used the forward stairs to come out where Bayane was working inside an access panel. Only his feet stuck out as he welded while lying down. "There you are," he called while putting the finishing touches on his repair. "I think this is the last of it."

"You two gutter slugs took so long you only had to fix two spots." Akoni stabbed his finger at the Tigroids.

"Judge less and love more!" Junak shouted at the Ursoid, holding his arms out for a hug.

Bayane chuckled as he handed his equipment out of the hole and followed it.

Akoni couldn't come up with an appropriately witty retort. The Tigroids tapped hands at the verbal joust.

"Let's get this baby fired up." Sankar looked toward the aft end of the ship. "Seal the cargo bay."

Junak pointed at the cockpit, but Sankar pointed the other way.

"Fine." The astrogator handed his gear to the Wolfoid and ran off.

Back at the pilot's station, Sankar continued the pre-flight. "Woohoo! Life support is green. We're pulling air from the warehouse and liquifying to refill the emergency supply. Flight stabilization systems are at ninety-four percent. Akoni?"

"That's probably the gold standard for a flying box. Thumbs-up, sir." He held a massive thumb next to Sankar's head.

"Astrogation?" Sankar asked.

"Online, no course plotted," Junak emphasized before he climbed onto his ad hoc co-pilot's chair.

"Scanners are five by five." Sankar tapped the screen. The scanner pulses penetrated the warehouse as if it weren't there. The sky above Medved Seven was clear. "Communications?"

"Is that me?" Akoni asked.

"It's whoever is the race of the people we're trying to convince that we belong to." Sankar reached out and took the manual flight controls. "Take your seats, people. We're going airborne. Akoni, if you would do the honors?"

Akoni sat at the comm station. "Ooh. Comfy." He adjusted his bulk. "Medved Seven, Catamar One requesting clearance for immediate departure."

Koni's voice replied. "Opening the hangar door now. Cats and Dogs One, you are cleared on Route Four Seven One."

"Roger, out." Akoni signed off.

Junak stared at him. "Four Seven One?"

Akoni spun his chair around to meet the Tigroid's gaze. "You're the navigator; you figure it out."

"I don't have it figured it. There's nothing in the astro database showing such a flight profile."

"Antigrav system at three percent and climbing." Sankar lifted the ship off the deck and maneuvered out of the warehouse. "Anything on that course?"

"Nothing. We should request further instructions." Junak crossed his arms, refusing to deliver an unapproved course.

"That isn't going to happen," Akoni replied, crossing his arms.

"Going vertical." Sankar pulled back on the controls, expecting to be thrown back as the ship responded, delivering its power into his body, tingling his fingers as it responded to his every whim. Not the *Bilkinmore*. It sluggishly lifted higher. He jerked the controls to the right since it wasn't climbing fast enough. The flying box resisted his efforts to control it. It climbed of its own volition. It turned, maybe. Sankar screamed at the controls, and the ship lurched, dipped, and rose.

"Wahoo!" Gwarzo shouted from the rear of the cockpit, where he swung from a pipe in the overhead.

Bayane crouched on the floor. "Somebody tell me when it's over."

The ship climbed and picked up speed. "It's over," Akoni deadpanned. "We won't hit anything, at least not this time." He turned to Sankar. "I have to comment that your piloting leaves a lot to be desired. If you're the best the Oterans have, I'm amazed that we haven't conquered your world by now."

"Then you understand the greatest urgency in getting the scanners upgraded. Your brother understood they'd be key to our survival. Clearing the moon's atmosphere. We're in space. Give me a course to the far reaches of this system's heliosphere, as far from any living creatures as we can get."

"Roger." Junak started tapping his screens, finally getting to what he did best.

Akoni took Bayane with him as he left the flight deck.

Junak declared victory. "Sending you a flight path now."

The new course appeared on the flight screens. Sankar adjusted course and set the autopilot. It remained red. "Don't tell me." He tapped the screen and scrolled through the systems, looking for the autopilot.

He accessed the intercom. "Akoni, it doesn't appear to have the autopilot installed. Can you remedy that for us, please?"

"You think I have software hidden up my butt?" the Ursoid replied and started laughing.

"I think you have it somewhere. There has to be a backup system buried beneath the cobwebs. We can restore that and then tweak it. I can handle the flight instructions but need the core program first."

"Check it now."

Sankar tapped the screen, and the autopilot came online. The ship flowed onto Junak's course. Flowed like water running off a mountain as the ship jerked back and forth before settling into the course. "Did you hide it on purpose?" Sankar demanded.

"Of course not. Standard procedure is to disable the autopilot during the landing sequence, and when I say disable, I mean take it offline."

"I'm sure the reason for that procedure is written in blood." Sankar didn't envy the one who engaged the autopilot and crashed their ship.

"It wasn't our finest hour. On a *completely* different note, I'm almost done with the upgrades."

"Already?"

"Plug and play. Koni wasn't kidding with these circuit boards. He also gave me a technical manual with additional theory. I might be able to upgrade them further once I understand the math."

"Koni, looking out for his little brother and taking care of us in the process. Thanks, Runt. None of this would have been possible without you."

"Are we going to Cornelior?" Gwarzo asked.

"There is some genetic sequencing equipment that needs to be on this ship, so yes. We're going there, but we need to hit the dig on Medvegrad first. After that, we'll go to your home planet."

When Gwarzo left, Junak leaned close and asked, "Do you think we'll have a problem with Gene, assuming we get to Cornelior in one piece?"

"Have to trust all of these zenos sooner or later," Sankar said. "If Gwarzo betrays us, he betrays us. But you remember what he said: it might be best if everyone on his planet thinks he's dead. Plus, you're upset because you're not my number one. I'm sorry I've come across that way. We'll all have our roles to play when the time comes. I'll need you on the ship making sure we have top cover."

"You don't trust me aboard the *Four-Claw* anymore??"

"I trust you to shoot the bad guys while the rest of us are on the ground. We'll have a real bad day if you don't do your job. I need you, Junak. I need you every bit as much as anyone here. There are only five of us. That means we all have to contribute. You've seen us in action from the point we arrived at the *Four-Claw*. What do you think the chances are of anything we do going according to plan?"

Junak snorted and smiled before looking at the floor. "I see what you mean. I get why we're all wound a little tight, and maybe I *am* mad about not being your second. Too many unknowns for me to be comfortable. Here we are in the middle of nowhere, about three days' worth of food on hand. It's overwhelming."

"It is. Once we arrive at our hold point, we'll run through some ship drills. Then we'll make it an early day, see what kind of recreation there is on this tub."

"That's funny. You've been in all the spaces. The former crew must have been allergic to fun."

"If only we had a couple more days scrounging the junkyard, we would have been able to outfit the ship all the way." Sankar let the thought hang. Wishful thinking wasn't going to get them anywhere. He touched the autopilot, turned it off, and resumed manual control to practice flying the freighter. He chuckled. "This thing is such a barge."

Junak clapped him on the back. "But it's *our* barge."

CHAPTER SEVEN

"Scanners are great!" Sankar declared after running a series of tests. "If we could upgrade to a three-dimensional monitor, we'd be cutting edge all the way around."

"We can buy the display in the capital city," Akoni replied. "Maybe even have it delivered to the dig site."

"Bold move. But that would take them from great to magnificent." Ships orbited the home planet, the fourth from the star. It was a long way away, but there were the icons as clear as the sun on a cloudless day entering space and assuming intercept courses with one of the three space stations orbiting Medvegrad.

"Life support is still one hundred percent, and flight stabilization is now at ninety-five percent. A couple adjustments to the lateral grav plates increased their efficiency, but I won't get any more out of this flying box."

"As long as we're in a mostly frictionless environment, that's plenty." Sankar yawned and stretched. "I think we should go to minimal power and catch some shuteye."

"I've got something I want to try. Since the scanners actively project a signal, I think I can create a ghost image of the ship."

"As in, someone trying to kill us gets multiple targets to shoot at?"

"While reducing our signature from his scanners, making us the less likely candidate for delivery of a ship-killing missile, or in our case, a ship-killing spitball."

Sankar shrugged off the denigration of their freighter. He was growing to like it, with its cathedral-like ceilings and open space. "Whatever you need from us, let me know. When you are happy, I'm happy."

"You probably don't want to put that kind of pressure on yourself, but for the moment, yeah. I hate to admit it, but I'm happy being among you little people and doing my thing. I like figuring out the ship's systems and making things work."

"I can tell. Thanks, Runt."

"Anytime, Guts." Akoni hesitated. "For what it's worth, Bayane isn't bad at all. He knows things and can get into where I can't. He gets distracted easily, but when he has something to do and no time to do it, he gets it done."

"Dogs. Gotta love 'em," the Tigroid said on his way out the door, leaving Akoni on his own. He headed up the stairs to his quarters, and he was asleep before his head hit the pillow.

A clunk and a bang shocked Sankar awake. He jumped up, still in his clothes, and ran out the door. "What's going on?" he yelled on his way to the cockpit. He took the steps three at a time as he raced downward. He slid to a stop outside the cockpit and looked wide-eyed at the airlock as it cycled. Sankar took one step into the cockpit, and that was all he needed. The tail of the ship connected to their airlock sported Medvegrad colors. He jumped past the captain's chair.

Customs.

He punched the button on the console. "All hands, emergency! We're being boarded by Medvegradian Customs. Akoni, I need you down here."

Sankar stood on the flight deck by himself while he waited. Air hissed from the pressurized space of the airlock into the ship. The system wasn't equalized properly. He'd add it to the list of items that needed to be repaired.

An Ursoid in the official tan uniform of Medvegrad Security Services under which Customs operated appeared in the doorway, carrying a blaster on his hip and a notepad in his hand.

Sankar waved. "Hey there! Can we help you?"

"Have you stolen this ship?" he demanded, stepping into the doorway and blocking Sankar's escape.

"No. We bought it off some dude at Space Station One."

"Papers!"

Sankar glanced around the cockpit. "All digital." Peering through the small space between the Customs inspector and the doorframe, Sankar saw two more uniformed inspectors heading down the corridor toward the cargo bay.

Heavy steps coming down the stair announced Akoni's arrival.

"It's so nice to smell fresh Medvegradian air." Akoni's voice boomed into the cockpit.

The inspector turned. "Did you steal this ship?"

"What did the cat tell you?"

"What do you think he told me?" The inspector turned to face Akoni.

Running steps suggested the inspectors had found the *Four-Claw* and were less than amused by its presence on the freighter.

Sankar leapt, extending his hand snatching his *kabbar* from his belt as he flew through the air. He landed high on the inspector's back and viciously slashed the bear-man's throat from behind. Akoni stumbled backward at the violence of the Tigroid's attack. Blood shot out with each beat of the inspector's heart. Sankar dropped off the body, grabbing the blaster out of its holster when he touched down.

Ursoid blasters weren't designed for Tigroid hands. Sankar almost dropped the weapon but recovered and grasped it with both paw-hands. The Ursoid running up the passage came into Sankar's sights. He fired, hitting the second inspector in the upper chest. His feet flew out from under him, and he landed flat on his back.

The smell of the blaster's propellant filled the air.

Sankar jumped over the first and second Ursoid officials on his way to find the third. Akoni stood still, in shock over how quickly two of his kind had died.

Akoni stepped into the airlock and through. The hatch on the other side was secured and wouldn't open for him. He needed his tools if he were going to bypass the security protocols. He hurried back into the freighter, where he helped himself to the second fallen inspector's blaster. A shot rang out from down the passage, and a heavy slug zinged off the sidewall and into the frame behind him.

"Watch where you're shooting!" Akoni yelled before realizing it hadn't been Sankar who'd fired. That was the next shot since it wasn't as loud and the round headed away from him. As Akoni ran up the stairs, he spotted Gwarzo heading down into the cargo bay by swinging through the overhead. Bayane crouched at the top of the stairs and Junak looked through a crack in his door.

"Surrender!" Sankar shouted.

The remaining inspector replied by firing three times quickly. The slugs nipped at the metal of the corridor as they screeched and pinged into the forward wall.

Then, the heavy *thump* of a body hitting the cargo bay deck.

"Check on them!" Akoni shouted at Bayane. The Wolfoid hesitated for an instant before bounding down the stairs and into the cargo bay, where he found Sankar stalking forward, aiming the oversized blaster at a spot beyond the *Four-Claw*. Bayane hurried up behind him to find Gwarzo standing over the third Customs official.

"He's dead," the Goroid said. He picked up the blaster and nodded in appreciation of its heft.

"Where's Akoni?" Sankar asked and turned toward the cockpit.

"He went into his room?" Bayane replied.

Sankar redirected toward the stairs. From the passage, he heard the sounds of an Ursoid lumbering down the forward stairs. He ran that way, yelling for Gwarzo to join him. Akoni trundled past and into the airlock, and Sankar and Gwarzo followed.

"Airlock is secured. I needed my tools to bypass the lock."

"What's the chance they know about this little scuffle?"

"Unknown," Akoni replied while clipping a meter to the panel. He unbolted the slab of metal and peeked behind it, pulling it far enough away from the hull of the Customs ship to get behind it. He tipped the end of a screwdriver into it.

"Be ready, Gwarzo. We don't know what will greet us when this door opens."

"Did you have a plan, or are you a psychopath who enjoys killing?" the Goroid asked.

"There was no way they were going to leave us alone. It was us or them. I would have preferred they never stopped to check on us. What concerns me is how they hooked onto us without us ever seeing them. I'll need to review the scanner logs and see where we failed."

"Maybe we can focus on this right here first?" Gwarzo asked.

"Just trying to keep from having to go psychopath again. It's going to be a pain, cleaning up that blood. We'll hit the ship and go fast. I want to believe they don't know what happened over here. If that's the case, the quicker we can clear this ship, the better off we'll be."

"Finally, I can agree to something you say." Gwarzo checked his blaster. "Raining scat! There's only two shots left."

"Got it!" Akoni declared.

"It'll have to do," Sankar said, and prepared to jump through the door. It started to roll aside, and Akoni ducked out of the way. The Tigroid leapt an instant before the Goroid. They hit the deck beyond a quarter of a second apart. Sankar bolted to the right, and Gwarzo went left.

Two seconds later, Akoni entered the Customs ship, blaster at the ready. Torn between which way to go, the shot ringing out to his left made up his mind for him. He ran down the narrow corridor to the cockpit and flight deck.

Sankar reached the sparse engine room and found it empty. He retraced his steps, opening doorways as he passed—by punching the button next to the door and leaning around the opening with his blaster. Empty after empty.

After the shot from the cockpit, a door slid open between Sankar and Akoni. An Ursoid stuck his head out and roared a battle cry as he ran at Akoni's back.

Sankar fired. The impact of the heavy slug threw him into Akoni, who was trying to duck to the side and get turned around.

From the cockpit, Gwarzo shouted, "Clear!"

Sankar checked the last two spaces to find them empty.

Akoni's shoulders drooped. The blaster fell from his hand and clattered off the deck. He stood between two of his people, both dead. Though neither had died at his hand, he had done nothing to save them. Ursoids fought among themselves but rarely to the death. They fought to establish dominance. Not for murder.

"It's like they've been executed. They never had a chance, did they?" Akoni asked, tears welling in his big bear eyes as he looked to Sankar for an answer.

"They had the choice to leave us alone," Sankar reassured his comrade. "We were out here in the middle of nowhere, not bothering anyone. They shouldn't have boarded our ship."

Akoni nodded, but the tears flowed down his hairy face.

"We better get out of here," Sankar said. "Come on, big fella. Let's go back to *Bilkinmore*, where it's safe."

Sankar led the Ursoid to the airlock and through. Bayane and Junak waited on the other side.

"Help him into a seat in the cockpit," Sankar ordered. "Let's get these bodies onto their ship and rig it to blow. Can you do that, Gwarzo and Bayane?"

The Wolfoid nodded. "They'll be heavy, but we can manage."

Gwarzo took the legs of the dead inspector closest to the airlock. Sankar tried to lift him by the arms, but that didn't work. He joined Gwarzo, and together, they dragged the body into the Customs ship, dumping it unceremoniously in the corridor. The second body was heavier than the first, and by the time they got to the third, there was no way they were going to be able to haul it from the bay to the airlock.

"The carts," Sankar suggested. "Akoni knew they would come in handy."

Together, they manhandled the upper body of the Ursoid into one cart. He hung mostly out of it and the cart wouldn't budge, so they used a second one for his legs. They pushed and pulled the tandem carts to the airlock, where the door seals were too high for the wheels. Sankar hung his head.

Gwarzo jogged to the cargo bay and returned shortly with the antigrav plate. He slid it between the two carts and activated it. They balanced the body on it and guided it through the airlock and into the Customs ship.

"I'll rig the engines to overload and implode," Akoni said. "Give me a few minutes."

"Gwarzo," Sankar commanded, "We need to find ammunition and anything we might be able to use from this ship."

"Concur. Ammo and equipment. Cockpit looked to be state of the art." Gwarzo pointed for Sankar to look for himself. The Goroid entered the closest door, turned on the lights, and did a quick search.

Sankar hurried to the engineer's station behind the pilot's chair, where he found a pull-out cabinet. He opened the emergency repair panel and removed the tools to unhook the electronics. Unlike *Bilkinmore*, the Customs ship had new equipment and fresh tools, each in its designated place.

Sankar lugged the electronics for the display and the toolkit into the airlock, walked them through, and delivered them to the cockpit. He found Akoni sitting with his head between his knees while Junak stood, his hand on the Ursoid's shoulder.

He shook his head when his eyes met Sankar's.

"We need a course to Cornelior as soon as you can," Sankar said softly. Junak nodded.

Sankar and Gwarzo returned to the Customs ship for a second and third round of scavenging before Akoni cut them off.

"Time to go!" Sankar shouted. Gwarzo emerged with an armload of bedding and loped through the airlock. Sankar headed for the cockpit and brought the engines up to full power.

Akoni punched his activator and tossed it into the Customs ship before securing the airlock hatch and joining the others in the cockpit. "We're detached."

"Angling away. I need a course, Junak."

The co-pilot and astrogator had been at his station for less than ten seconds. "Deep space. I'll have a course once you get away from here."

Bilkinmore slowly accelerated away from the contact. The scanners swept the area, painting a clean picture. Nothing besides the Customs ship.

"They shouldn't have boarded us," Sankar said, and clenched his jaw—guiding the ship through the outer limits of the heliosphere, away from Medvegradian space.

"Come to course one three four, tack four seven one, tack eight," Junak called.

As the ship turned, a bright flash signaled the obliteration and demise of the Customs ship.

Sankar adjusted course. Gwarzo pulled Bayane into the corridor to help stow the added gear. "I'll put the weapons locker in the cargo bay. Looks like five blasters and about five hundred slugs."

Akoni seemed beside himself.

"I blew them up," Akoni mumbled, staring at his empty paw-hands.

"You do what you have to," Sankar replied, not taking his eyes off the screens while encouraging the sluggish brute of a ship to assume the course chosen by the astrogator.

"In Oteran space," Junak said, "they'd not have jurisdiction that far out."

"What about it?" Sankar asked Akoni.

"I didn't think of that," Akoni said. "It's possible those Customs boys were on a self-enrichment run. But I'm still not good with killing them. You Tigroids love murder, we're brawlers and brutes. I saw how you slashed the inspector's throat, Sankar. You have my respect. Perhaps, even, my fear."

"We have *each other's* backs on this ship," Sankar reminded. "I'm sorry, Akoni. I'm sorry that went in a bad direction at the speed of light. We have to set up a watch so we aren't surprised ever again. It'll be better for the authorities and better for us."

Akoni hung his head. "I'll install that display and rig up an alarm, but it'll be a local alarm. Someone will have to be in the cockpit at all times. This garbage scow's remote features are limited, shall we say."

"I'll rig a hammock and sleep in here." Sankar set the autopilot once the ship was on course and left the cockpit, leaving Akoni and Junak to their thoughts.

CHAPTER EIGHT

Sankar searched high and low but found nothing that would work as a hammock. He settled for one of the carts. He removed the wheels and wedged it into a corner between the systems engineer's position and the wall. He filled it with bedding and climbed in. It was small, but he found the box comfortable, better than the abundance of space in his quarters.

Akoni kept working, adjusting, syncing, moving, and resyncing. When he finally declared victory, it was well into the next morning. None of them had slept beyond the couple of hours last night before the government-sponsored pirates showed up.

"I'm going to catch a nap," Sankar said, curling up in his box. Within minutes he was sound asleep, his snores a soft purr vibrating the sides of the former cart.

Junak looked envious. "I'll be in my quarters. We shouldn't be near Cornelior space for another day, but we'll need to be up for transiting black hole Cornelior Three. That could be a rough ride."

"Which translates as the ship could break or be scattered in molecule-sized pieces across deep space, where no one would ever know what happened to us," Akoni suggested.

"Something like that. No. Exactly that. All things being equal, we might be okay, but a Heretic and his friends don't have a lot of options."

"Even when all of them are bad. I need to dig into the engineering panel. Something about the scanner schematics caught my eye. I can't sleep, so might as well do something."

Junak stood next to the Ursoid sitting in the captain's chair.

"For what it's worth, I'm sorry about your people," Junak said. "I just plot courses. I'm good at one thing, and that's being co-pilot. I'm not big like you, not strong like Gwarzo, not versatile like Bayane, and definitely not a blood-fighter like Sankar. But you can be sure that I'll do my best at anything I have to do. I wish I had your aptitude and skill, Akoni.

You are a marvel to watch while working on this equipment."

"Compliments from Tigroids," Akoni snorted. "What is the universe coming to?"

Then, after a long pause, "Thank you, Junak."

Junak smiled and left the cockpit on his way to his quarters. There was no schedule, maybe day on, stay on. None of them could count on downtime anytime soon.

Akoni leaned back in the captain's chair, which was almost the right size for him, and brought up his tech manual on the three-dimensional display. *Theory regarding scanner ghosts*...

Sankar raised his head above the walls of his bed. "What time is it?" he asked the empty cockpit. He jumped out of the cart, landing softly, feeling new energy in his legs. He checked the astrogation station. Ten hours had passed since he'd laid down. The scanner sweep showed clear space, but they were well between systems, riding an interstellar cavern for four more hours before they reached the Cornelior black hole to transit the rest of the way.

He strolled to the latrine and took care of business, then headed up the stairs to get something to eat. They needed to stock up on food. Sankar wanted a month's worth in case they needed to drop off the grid. That would have been best after the Customs debacle.

Instead, they were on their way to Cornelior to stop by an archaeological site listed in the records of the Temple of Spheenix. The records referenced sites on all the planets populated by the other races.

Gwarzo strolled into the cockpit while Sankar chewed on his two-day-old sandwich.

"How long to my home planet?"

"Looks like a little over four hours until we arrive in-system and maybe twelve until we're settled on Cornelian dirt."

"Roots, vines, bushes, and rough grass. Cornelior is a wet planet, almost a jungle. There's not a whole of dirt, not dry, anyway." Sankar showed the location of the ruins on the display. "Do you know this area?"

Gwarzo pressed his hands on his hips and looked sideways at Sankar. "I'm from the city of Vinidor. This is nowhere near a city. No. I don't know the area."

Sankar saw the humor in the reply. "City boy is going to rough it in the wilderness. Don't get lost. It would be embarrassing to have to be rescued by a Tigroid."

"I can climb a tree faster than you."

"I'll take that challenge. I fear I have nothing to bet with." Sankar turned out his empty pockets.

"Me neither. I was in your prison for a long time."

"Not *my* prison, but we'll settle for bragging rights." Sankar climbed into the captain's seat and watched the holodisplay. "I like this. It would be nice to have something like it in the *Four-Claw*."

"Akoni does good work," Gwarzo admitted. "And so do I when I get the chance." He looked over his shoulder before leaning close to Sankar. "But I don't think Bayane or even Junak are quite yet aware of the stakes, or the odds we face."

"They'll come around," Sankar said.

"When?" Gwarzo asked. "We'll be fighting with someone in twenty-four hours, and then we'll be fighting with someone else again, later. We'll fight our way out of the university. And so on, and so forth. All of us will have blood on our claws—or nails, if you're like me—sooner or later. Some of us need to get used to that idea."

"Hmph," Sankar said, not necessarily disagreeing.

"By the way," Gwarzo said, changing direction, "I like the grav plate idea. We'll need a few of those to move the sequencing equipment."

"We'll hit the university on our way off the planet because everyone and their brother will be after us for our disrespect of and brazen assault on higher education."

"They'll get over it. They'll need to shepherd their money to buy new equipment instead of paying bounty hunters."

"Bounty hunters. Isn't that choice?" Sankar shook his head.

"No sense in blowing smoke up your ass."

"Not even once?"

Gwarzo blinked rapidly. "It'll be a walk in a manicured park under clear skies with a Goroid choir singing Cornel's *Fourth Opera* in the background."

Sankar nodded. "Was that so hard?"

The Goroid hammered his long-fingered hand across Sankar's back. "I like you more and more with each passing hour."

Junak rolled down the stairs, passing Gwarzo on his way.

"Why was he so happy?" Junak asked, taking his seat on the box at astrogation. "We are on track for Cornelior Three."

"Gene is happy to be a member of the crew." Sankar made sure no one else was nearby. "I think he enjoyed the firefight more than a normal zeno should. Did anyone see him kill the Ursoids?"

"His eyes..." Junak shook his head.

"He didn't do anything I didn't do," Sankar reminded. "Besides, we're looking for our common roots, and Gwarzo is the key to that unless we find something else along the way. We need all the evidence. The temple documents hinted at the origin but never came out and said it. Maybe the other races have information that is more forthcoming."

"You mean honest? For my personal edification, how much digging are we going to have to do?" Junak wondered.

"It's not going to be pretty. Archaeology isn't for the impatient. We need to collect clean samples, find something to draw genetic material from. I suspect there will be a great deal of digging."

Junak grumbled without articulating his thoughts. He double-checked the flight path before leaning back and almost falling off his box.

"I was serious about the Customs officials not having jurisdiction that far out. They were nothing more than official pirates," Junak said while reorienting himself.

"Do you think there's a record of their course and our ship anywhere?" Sankar asked.

"I doubt it. If you're stealing, you don't want the boss to know where you're doing it."

Sankar nodded. "Do you know when the others racked out?"

Junak shook his head as he pulled up random bits of information and studied them. "I'll be in the back. I'm not sure what we have on this ship. I should probably know that."

Sankar waved indiscriminately.

In the cargo bay, Sankar found Gwarzo swinging through the overhead. The Goroid launched himself toward the wall and scampered down it to end up on the deck next to Sankar.

"Fitness training?"

"It's what my people do. We aren't exactly made for walking all day every day." He shook a bowed leg at the Tigroid.

Sankar couldn't let it go. "You're a bioengineer, but you seem rather efficient at killing Ursoids."

"I'm efficient at killing *all* the races." The Goroid's voice was cold, almost detached. "Are you shocked?"

"You were picked up on Oterosan as part of a crew that was smuggling?"

"Thank your Furd gods that your people didn't discover my real assignment. I didn't know those nutheads were smuggling."

"Your 'real' mission," Sankar pressed. He wanted the truth.

"To kill your commerce minister. He recommended tariffs on our wood products that were rather prohibitive. Cornelior couldn't have that."

"Are you really a bioengineer?"

"I am. A damn good one." He chuckled, the sound rumbling deep in his barrel-like chest. "But that's my hobby. I have other talents."

Sankar leaned close to look into Gwarzo's eyes. The Goroid leaned forward until their foreheads nearly touched.

"Do you see what you're looking for?" Gwarzo asked.

"I was trying to see if you were joking, but I don't think you are."

"Good. How come the candor?

"I didn't trust you before."

Sankar embraced the positive. "You trust me now." A statement, not a question.

"I do. You offed two of the big ones most efficiently, and you finished the one that may have caused me a little distress. I don't owe you, but I can respect you as a brother in arms. Tigroid arms, but arms nonetheless." He whipped a big hand around to clap Sankar on the shoulder. "It's your three to my two. I'll catch up soon enough, I figure. You aren't one to fly under the scanners."

"Unfortunately, no. We have things to do that will put us in the spotlight. Thanks, Gene. It's important to know where we all stand."

"That was my position, too. I had to make sure." He held up a long-fingered hand. Sankar slapped it appropriately. "Now that that's settled, you need better food on this tub. Have you no idea what Goroids eat?"

Sankar stammered but couldn't come up with words. He didn't know.

"We don't eat meat, you barbarians!" He launched himself into a backflip, hit the wall, and kicked off to reach the overhead. He swung from pipe to pipe toward the stairs, and with a final leap, landed on the top step. He strolled away as if what he had just done was nothing. No Tigroid would have ever been able to manage that level of upper body strength, but the aerobatics and gymnastics weren't such a stretch.

"I *will* learn to climb and swing like that," Sankar told the empty space in the cargo bay. He measured the jump to the wall and hesitated. "But not today." He returned to checking out the contents of the storage boxes along the wall.

"We're entering Cornelior's gravity well. Planetfall in one hour, twelve minutes," Junak reported.

Sankar took two huge bites to finish his sandwich and stood.

"More than an hour. What's the rush?" Akoni asked.

"Scanner sweep. I want to see what's out there. Come on, Gwarzo. You'll be the face of Catamar One for this."

"Is that our callsign? What about *Bilkinmore*? I was getting used to that."

"No, you weren't," Sankar countered.

Gwarzo shrugged. "Okay, maybe I wasn't. I guess 'Catamar' is as good as anything."

"There's no record of it because it doesn't exist. That's the part I like best." Sankar briefly gripped Akoni's shoulder before leaving the mess, where little food remained. Gwarzo reluctantly stood and ambled after him.

In the cockpit, Sankar stood in front of the holographic display and studied the information as it populated.

"Akoni?"

The Ursoid had not yet joined them, but Bayane was in the corridor.

"He's still a bit down about that Customs thing," Bayane offered and strolled onto the command deck. It looked more like a recreation room with loungers than an interstellar ship's flight control center.

Bilkinmore was built for utility, not speed.

Sankar pointed at the display.

"Let's see what we have." Bayane put his snout almost into the display as he examined the images within. "Ships are detailed by icon, nose pointing in the direction of travel. One, two, and three barrels indicate vessel size. These are freighters on approach to or away from the system's only planet. And this one here," he tapped a finger into the image, "is a smaller ship, probably a patrol vessel of some sort in orbit around the planet. Scanners can't penetrate the atmosphere from this far out, so that's what we have. The closer we get, the better the scanner readings."

"What if I want to know everything now?" Sankar asked, raising one hairy eyebrow.

"Prepare for disappointment."

Sankar wrestled with the flight controls to change the ship's course. He wanted to pick up a more intense gravity canyon to decrease the approach time. The ship lumbered into it and surged ahead once it reached the slipstream.

"Gwarzo, if you would be so kind?" Sankar stepped aside.

Gene reclined casually in the seat, propping one leg over the arm and leaning sideways. "Gwarzo Vinebender, at your service."

Junak sent the landing coordinates to the captain's station. "Those are just outside the restricted area within which we'll find the ruins."

"We're going to ignore restricted airspace?"

"No," Sankar interjected. "We'll land outside of it and hike in. I don't know how good their scanners are and don't want to push it."

"They aren't as good as the Medvegradian scanners. If you can see them, they might not be able to see you," Gene advised.

"On this, we take no chances."

"I'll tell them we're up for a vacation away from the hustle and bustle of city life. That'll fly on Cornelior. We're still partial to the wild while also liking our frothed frozen banana juice."

"Goroids are complex, clearly," Bayane chuckled and chittered. "Everything in the ship seems to be working like it's supposed to. I think we can land on the planet, and more importantly, I think we'll be able to take off again."

"I like your confidence," Sankar stated while giving the Wolfoid the side-eye.

"Out of the image, vile creatures!" Gwarzo waved his hand, and the others drifted to the sides.

"Cornelior Primary, this is Catamar One on final approach, requesting clearance to land in Angistan National Preserve for some jungle time to shake off this space dust, over."

"This is Primary. Stand by."

Gwarzo dropped a hand below what the viewscreen showed and gave the thumbs-up. He lounged in the captain's chair and looked everywhere but at the camera.

Primary reappeared.

"Catamar One is not in our database."

"I renamed it. I scoured the universe for exactly the right garbage scow to call home. I'm taking up interplanetary haulage. After a vacation, of course, because it took all I had to get this tug into the sky. It used to be called *Bilkinmore*. I bought it for salvage."

Sankar vigorously shook his head while drawing a line across his throat with a finger. The Goroid chuckled at the screen.

"Very well. Bring your flying junk pile to the preserve and enjoy yourself. Don't leave a grease stain, or there will be a five-thousand-bint fine for every drop that's discovered."

Gwarzo pounded his chest in a salute. "No problem, Primary. It stopped leaking a week ago when it ran out of lubricants. I should probably worry about that more than killing the weeds and bushes. Going down in glorious flames! Catamar One out." Gwarzo reached a finger to the panel and tapped the comm closed. He rolled his head sideways to look at Sankar. "Enough of the truth to satisfy even the strictest controller. They hate their jobs just like every race hates their jobs. I delivered them from boredom for a few moments."

The Goroid continued to lounge in the pilot's seat. Sankar stared at him before assuming his position in the space between the chair and the controls. He dragged the ship out of the gravity wave and into normal space to finish the approach to Cornelior.

Once in orbit, Sankar directed the *Bilkinmore's* descent through the atmosphere toward the jungle planet. The cities remained unrecognizable from space since they blended with the rest of the green landmasses throughout the planet's equatorial zone. Only the spaceports were clear of foliage, a testament to the modern society hidden beneath the jungle canopy. Water dominated the ice-free polar regions.

"Home. Hot and humid, just how we like it." Gwarzo sighed.

Junak rolled his eyes. "It's not how I like it."

"Nor I," Akoni said from the doorway. He squinted to focus on the landmass filling the viewscreen.

The Goroid laughed. "I have to admit that I don't like it either. I've grown accustomed to that dry and cool on Oterosan."

Sankar kept his eyes on the screen to continue following a narrow path toward the far side of the preserve as he spoke over his shoulder, "I was just going to mention that your skin has taken on a radiant satin-like glow."

He was unprepared for the blow that landed between his shoulder blades. "I like you, Guts!" Gene roared.

Akoni joined them in the extensive cockpit. Bayane and Junak turned toward the screen as all watched Sankar wrestle with the oversized controls to slow their descent. "Is there any way you can reconfigure these things to fit a Tigroid paw?"

"Sure. I can take the controls out of the *Four-Claw* and put them in here."

"Now, now. Let's not be hasty," Sankar retorted. "We'll need the *Four-Claw* to hold the minions of evil at bay."

"Do these minions have a name?" Akoni asked.

"Anyone who tries to stop us." Sankar's answer forestalled further questions. The crew focused on the planet below. "There's no way we'd survive walking through there."

At treetop level, the jungle looked unforgiving. Sankar posted the coordinates for the ruins on the display. At a constant speed, he left the preserve's airspace and headed into restricted airspace. "Junak, find us a landing spot as close as possible to the primary ruins."

Junak scanned the ground ahead until he found a gap in the trees. It was still a ten-minute hike from the coordinates on Sankar's display. He sent the location.

Sankar steered toward it, dropping the ship into the clearing and powering the systems down.

Gwarzo undraped himself from the pilot's chair. He bumped Sankar on his way off the command deck while the pilot finished the parking sequence.

"Are we going armed?" Junak asked as the others lined up at the airlock, with Gwarzo's finger paused over the button. He withdrew his hand and waited.

Sankar completed his landing checklist and joined the others. They looked at him for guidance. "I think we always have to be armed."

He didn't explain further. They had five blasters. Akoni popped the weapons locker in the corridor and started to hand them out.

"Can we lock the ship?" Sankar wondered.

Akoni shook his head.

"Someone needs to stay on board then. And we don't have comms. I didn't think to snag anything from the junkyard."

"I looked," Akoni started, "but there wasn't anything to take. You have a full account. We only need to get somewhere we can buy comms."

"There's the rub." Everyone looked at Junak. "You stay. Send up a flare if the natives start pounding on the doors."

"I resemble that remark." Gwarzo tapped the airlock button and the outer hatch popped. A wave of hot mist surged through the opening. "Ah! Smells like love is in the air."

Bayane grabbed the Goroid's arm. "I already hate your planet."

"Not quite mine, but if it were, there would have been a sign in orbit. *No dogs allowed.*" He stared at Bayane's hand until he removed it, then turned his gaze to Sankar. "*Or cats.*"

"You can suck my hairy nipples," Bayane shot back with a snort.

"Eight isn't normal," Gene said as he strolled out the door, breathing deeply with each step. The others grumbled on their way out. Junak pounded the button to close the door after them before returning to the cockpit to adjust the life support systems. He put his blaster on the counter and looked at it, unsure if he could fire it. He found the emergency flare access and wondered if it would work.

He headed upstairs to get something to eat, expecting a long wait.

CHAPTER NINE

Sankar carried the temple map in his head. He knew the landmarks would be different and steeled himself to figure it out. He had not shared the information with his team. In a warped way, he thought he was protecting them. The knowledge he carried could get them labeled as Heretics, too.

He realized he should have shared it. Each society was different while still the same: fiercely protective of the unique nature of their people.

Sankar stopped walking.

"What?" Akoni asked.

"I'm tearing down everything most people hold dear. Now's your chance if you want to bail out. No one will think poorly of you."

"Shut your tuna hole!" Bayane replied.

Gene nodded once and pointed at the Wolfoid. "What Grumpy said."

"Hey!"

"Listen." Akoni shuffled his feet, then dropped to all fours to be eye to eye with the others. "Maybe it's time to tear down the old ways and give people a new outlook. As you saw between me and my brother, I'm not a fan of the status quo."

"Me either." Gwarzo gestured with his head toward the ruins. "How about we tear down some walls?"

"Now you're speaking my language. I'm not an ichthyologist, so I'm okay with breaking stuff to get at the prize within."

"Ichthyologist is a fish doctor. I think you mean archaeologist," Bayane said.

"That, too." Sankar winked and strode ahead with renewed vigor. The crew followed Sankar. That was the last time he'd ask if they were in. There was no turning back after this.

They powered through the jungle, beating their own path until they stumbled across a rise. Sankar stooped to look before following the small ridge.

"This is the outer wall of the compound. We need to find the major structure centered within. The location we're looking for is east of there. It'll be the next building. It was called 'the archive' in the Spheenix document."

Sankar led the way into the interior of the ruins. "Looks the same to me," Bayane complained. He sniffed the air. "Smells like something died."

"That's the way Cornelior always smells. Even recycled spaceship air is better. Now you know why we became the first spacefaring race."

"Get out! The Tigroids—"

"Stop," Akoni commanded. "Everyone knows it was the dogs. They kicked themselves off their own planet for not being housebroken."

Gwarzo thrust a fist in the air and put a finger to his lips. Sankar pointed at his eyes and then into the jungle. The Goroid nodded and gestured upward. Sankar waved at Bayane to go left and for Akoni to stay where he was.

Sankar faded silently into the jungle. Gwarzo pulled himself into the canopy. Bayane cradled the oversized blaster in both hands before shooting into the jungle.

Akoni remained by himself, sniffing and listening. He watched intently, eyes darting back and forth as his senses failed him. He had no idea what had spooked the others.

Sankar slunk beneath the undergrowth toward the sounds of muffled footfalls. He slowed as he closed on his target, hoping to catch sight of it before it saw him. A commotion overhead signaled Gwarzo's arrival.

A diversion. Sankar lunged into the midst of three Goroids dressed in military-style clothing and heavily equipped. He froze. Two lost interest in the noises overhead. One reached for Sankar. He snap-fired with the Ursoid blaster.

The Goroid flew backward. Bayane fired from where he was in the brush, catching the second patrolman in the shoulder and spinning him around.

Gene dropped from the branches, landing on the shoulders of his broad-shouldered fellow Goroid. He twisted upside down to wrap his arms around the other's neck. The patrolman wasn't going to go without a fight. He caught Gene's arm and spun in an attempt to throw off his attacker.

Bayane fired again, hitting the patrolman in the back. The Goroid's eyes went wide, and he stared at Sankar in surprise. The Tigroid dove out of the way of the titanic struggle between Gene and the last of the patrol.

Sankar tried to get a clear shot, but the movements of the fight to the death were violently unpredictable. Bayane remained in the brush. Sankar stepped back farther and farther, giving the two more room as they intertwined themselves seeking advantage, one over the other.

Gwarzo freed himself and dropped to the ground to sweep the other's legs, but the patrolman jumped upward, caught a branch, and started to pull. Two blasters barked a deadly volley, ripping the Goroid free from the branch. He flipped into the underbrush and landed in a heap, lying still as his lifeblood dripped on the soft turf. Gene pulled at his arm, trying to get to his back.

"Damn, Gwarzo. Hold still," Sankar called and dropped his blaster to deal with the knife in Gwarzo's back.

"Never fight fair when you're fighting for your life," Gwarzo said.

"It's in the muscle. I'm going to pull it out on three." Sankar gripped the hilt. "One..." He jerked it free. Gene tensed, but too late. The deed was done.

"Have I said lately how much I hate Tigroids?" Gwarzo gasped through gritted teeth.

"We're going to need to sew this up." Sankar had no other choice.

"Take their gear. They won't need it anymore." Gwarzo pointed. Bayane and Sankar checked the combat harnesses, which held knives and non-lethal weapons, electric stunners.

Akoni lumbered up, saw the search of the bodies, didn't ask any questions, and proceeded to relieve the third corpse of its gear.

"What's the chance there are more of them?" Sankar asked.

"Three is a standard police patrol. They must have registered our intrusion," Gene replied, wincing and spasming from his injury.

"I'll take him back to the ship," Bayane said. "You and Akoni go dig a fine hole."

"How much time do we have?"

"Not a lot. They'll need to report in, so probably less than an hour."

Sankar handed the gear to Bayane, who carried two sets while Gwarzo took the third. Akoni slapped him on the shoulder. "Strong like a bear," he told his crewmate.

"Still hurts like hell." Bayane let Gene lean on him as they retraced their steps.

"You heard the zeno. We have less than an hour to find what centuries of fish doctors have not been able to find." Sankar dashed through into the jungle, eschewing stealth for speed. If anyone came for them, it would be because of the telltale blasts from the Ursoid slugthrowers.

Sankar slowed to orient himself and put his back to the border of the compound. He worked his way forward until he found the mound of the main structure, which was higher than the outer wall but not by much.

"This wasn't a big building?" Akoni wondered.

"It was, according to the records I saw, a solid three stories high, but it appears that it was made of wood."

"It is the most easily accessible building material."

Sankar followed the rough outline of the central building. He came to the corner and turned with it. Twenty steps in, he turned ninety degrees to walk due east. When he reached the next mound, he found it to be taller than head high, and it retained the shape of the original building.

"This one is made of stone." He reached into the vines and leaves to rap his knuckles against it. Two steps over, he found the entrance. "Walked to it like I knew what I was doing."

Across the entrance was a sign. *Contents of this building have been removed to the Cornelian University for cataloging, study, and presentation at the Museum of Antiquities.*

Akoni read it over Sankar's shoulder. "Looks like the real ichthyologists got here before us."

"Looks like we're going back to school," Sankar grumbled before tearing the sign down and heading inside to find a plain space with alcoves spaced throughout. Sankar checked each one, looking for a hidden catch to give access to an undiscovered chamber. He went outside and walked around the building to better estimate the size. The inside matched. "No secrets here."

"Back to the ship?"

"I think it's best we not get caught on the ground here." Sankar hurried out of the ruins and easily followed their earlier trail, which would be overgrown in a day or two. Akoni pounded after him. The Tigroid was not of the jungle, but he moved as if he were one with the trees and brush. He lithely slid through the spaces between the trunks and roots, barely moving the bushes as he passed. Akoni walked in a straight line, indifferent to the greenery.

The ship sat in the smallest of clearings. "Hey. That was some good flying to put that thing in here," Sankar said, looking around before leaving the cover of the jungle. The external hatch opened as they approached.

"Anything?" Bayane wondered.

"A sign that said anything we might want is in the museum. Where's Junak?"

"Playing nursemaid to an angry crybaby." Bayane pointed down the corridor.

Sankar wanted to check on them, but he needed to get the ship into the air. Akoni saw the competing desires on the Tigroid's face.

"I'll coddle our boy. You fly the crate. I'll send Junak, and Gene can deal with my stitching." He waggled his big fingers.

"Two zenos enter. One zeno leaves," Bayane joked. He joined Sankar on the flight deck, and they started running through an abbreviated pre-flight. Junak arrived moments later.

"Don't ask," he said. "Course?"

"Mountains to the north. We need them to lose our track. We'll reemerge with the traffic coming from space."

"Roger." Junak started tapping. It didn't take long. He transferred the course to the pilot's console.

"Taking us up." The antigrav drives lifted the ship vertically before transitioning to horizontal flight like a tray sliding across an oiled counter. Sankar kept *Bilkinmore* barely above the treetops as he accelerated away from the restricted area. "Scanners?"

He kept his eyes on the course and tree line. Images appeared on the holographic display in front of him.

"Screen is clear," Bayane replied. "Keep us low. I can't tell if anything is tracking us from orbit."

"We can't see through the atmosphere?" Sankar was growing less enamored of the Ursoid scanners.

"I'm sure they aren't adjusted right. We should be able to see birds flying on the other side of the planet."

Akoni announced his arrival. "Not so much, but you should see ships in orbit."

Bayane gave up the systems position and Akoni flopped down. "Nice shooting back there," the Ursoid said while accessing the software systems.

"Are you talking to me?" The Wolfoid puffed out his chest and raised his snout in the air.

Akoni continued. "It's amazing how lucky someone can get when shooting with their eyes closed."

"Hey!"

"You say that a lot. I'm beginning to think you are a mastiff grazer. Try it now." Bayane stood next to Sankar and tapped the keys. The display expanded to include both near and far space.

"Yep. There's one up there matching our course and speed. He's tracking us." Bayane pointed at an icon in a low orbit.

"Watch this." Akoni snapped his fingers before accessing the system. The display shimmered and disappeared.

Sankar pursed his lips. "That's not impressive."

"Wait for it."

When the screen came back to life, the point that was *Bilkinmore* split into five.

"Break left," Akoni requested.

Sankar pulled hard, and the ship responded sluggishly. One of the false signals continued on the previous course. The images accelerated at the same speed as the real ship. Then they started to change altitude, with four of them heading for orbit.

"That's pretty sexy." Akoni smiled and bobbed his head while urging the ship to greater speed. It didn't help, but Sankar was a fighter pilot flying a freighter. The *Bilkinmore* would never be fast enough for him.

Junak sent a new course to the pilot's console. "If he tucks us into that valley, what happens to the signals?"

"They continue if we don't get too low. We'll disappear from their screens." Akoni tapped his screen. "As soon as you dip us below the mountain, I'll make four of the other signals disappear and send that one into orbit and a gravity well to surge out of their reach."

He finished tapping and waited. The ship reached the cover of the hills, and Akoni executed his program.

"Hold here until our trail goes away." The screen shimmered and readjusted to the normal view. The ship that had been following them started to circle into a higher orbit. "Confused him, but they are only Goroids, after all."

Akoni rotated his chair toward the door, expecting to see Gwarzo, but he wasn't there.

"A good joke wasted. Then again, I can still use it on him."

"Next stop, the university. We need information. I doubt they're going to let us stroll in and help ourselves."

"Sounds like a midnight run," Bayane offered.

"Aren't Goroids nocturnal?" Sankar wondered.

Bayane shrugged, then shook his head. "I don't think so. I'll ask him."

The screen cleared, but they remained stationary. Yelling and something heavy hitting the bulkhead let them know Bayane had riled the injured Goroid.

Gene grumped onto the command deck. "Can't an injured teammate get a little shuteye?"

Akoni turned him around to check out his handiwork. The first half of the cut had a zipper of small and tight stitches. The second half had big x-shaped stitching anchored farther away from the wound. The cut was misaligned and would leave an ugly scar. "Ladies on my planet love scars. How about on Cornelior?"

"Is it that bad?" Gwarzo asked.

Sankar turned to look. "Point of order. Akoni never gets to stitch anyone up ever again."

"It's that bad," Gwarzo grumbled.

"It's not bleeding. Take it like am ape, you big baby," Akoni sat down and returned to the scanners.

"How can we get into the university and get your equipment?" Sankar asked.

Gwarzo chased Junak away from the astrogation station and brought up the standard flight maps for Cornelior. He magnified the area of the university. "It's in this building, in the basement, but there's a freight elevator. From my last trip there, I believe we can get what we need in two trips. We'll have to bring all the cabling too, so we only have to fashion one power converter and adaptor."

"Roger." Sankar studied the map. "When's the best time to make our visit?"

"Four in the morning," Gwarzo replied without hesitation. "That will give us two hours if we disable the alarms before anyone even thinks about coming in."

Akoni and Bayane looked at each other. "I suppose you think we'll disable the alarms without a problem."

"Isn't that what you do?" Sankar raised one eyebrow.

"That's what criminals do." He gestured around the ship. "We're flying in this crate because of engineers."

"Can you do it or not?" Sankar pressed.

"Of course. I don't want you to take us for granted, that's all."

"I don't. We'll take the Goroid stunners. I prefer non-lethal, and it's good to have that option. Akoni, you carry a blaster just in case. No one else can fire those damn things, not with any degree of grace. I guess we'll cool our heels right here. What is the local time?"

Junak accessed the navigation systems. "It's noon, local. We have almost a full day to kill."

Sankar guided the ship into a rocky area and gently set it down. "I'm going to grab some chow and shuteye."

"At least shuteye," Bayane corrected.

"Don't tell me." Sankar glared at the Wolfoid.

"We need to get some food, too, while we're out shopping," Akoni offered helpfully.

Sankar assumed his best *Furd-Gods-Don't-Care* expression and sauntered out of the cockpit. His stomach growled with the revelation that it was going to be a while before it was sated. Since he wasn't going upstairs, he returned, jumped into his cart-turned-bed, and curled up.

"How does he sleep in there?" Akoni pointed a big thumb at the Tigroid's bed.

"He sleeps well when there's no noise," Sankar replied.

The casual conversation dropped off as they left him to his nap. Gene retired to his workshop, into which he'd dragged a mattress. Junak turned to his charts and began an in-depth study of possible egress routes from the university. He watched the scanner picture of the ships in the skies above Cornelior.

Akoni excused himself to play with the engines; he wanted to see if he could eke out a little more power and speed. Bayane joined him to learn more about this ship and Ursoid engineering.

Once they were upstairs, the Ursoid shared a secret with the Wolfoid. "The ship doesn't have enough power to both fly and use the genetic sequencing equipment."

"Sankar will birth a bovine if he hears that."

"We won't tell him. It's probably best if we're not bouncing around while the gear is running, so we won't be flying and working at the same time."

"The chance of us not running from something is zero-point-zero."

"We'll tell him, then. He seems to fly better angry," Akoni noted.

Bayane had no comeback. He followed the Ursoid into the engine crawlspace.

CHAPTER TEN

At two in the morning, the crew assembled in 's lab to walk through the night's operation.

Sankar looked from face to face. Akoni's stomach growled its discontent at being empty for too long. "Gene. It's your show."

The Goroid nodded and pointed at the sketch of the university he had drawn on the blank metal wall. "We need to come in high as if landing at the spaceport, then adjust our flight profile. Airspace control will lose sight of us when we dip beyond the horizon, and then we'll come at the school from the far side, the southeast, to settle at the university's landing dock next to the research building.

"We'll need to access the roll-up door. Akoni and Bayane, work your magic to get us in without triggering any alarms."

Akoni raised his hand. "We'll need you to watch our backs since we'll be head-down in the backwards electronics of the Goroid homeworld."

"With genetic sequencing. I don't remember hearing anyone suggest we get the equipment from Medvegrad." Gwarzo waited for a counter to his counter.

Bayane spoke first. "I don't care who has what. I am okay sticking it to *the man*, but I'm not okay being arrested as a common criminal stealing from a university. Upending the entire belief system of our races is one thing, but ripping off college kids, even if they are grossly oversized Goroids, is something completely different."

"Don't get caught. Check," Sankar stated and rolled his finger for Gwarzo to continue.

"Once inside, we need to take the freight elevator to the basement. When we get off, the labs will be to the right. We'll need the one with the computers."

"What's in the other one?" Junak wondered.

"Live samples from which genetic material is taken." Gwarzo wouldn't look at anyone after his statement.

"It's going to turn my stomach, isn't it?" Junak pressed.

Gwarzo shook his head. "No, because you and Bayane won't be there. You'll be next door accessing the museum, looking for what they took from the Vineland One archive. Anything that might have genetic material, like a mummified finger or a brush with hair. I don't know what they took, and don't expect it to be on display. It's probably in a back room somewhere."

"*Somewhere...*" Bayane drew out the word.

Gwarzo waved off the response. "You have two hours to find it. Less, depending on how long it takes you to disable the security system."

Bayane scowled at the revelation.

"We'll disconnect the gear and use the pallet jacks that should be located near the freight elevator. They move pallets of feed and waste every day. The jacks will be there. We'll help ourselves."

"And no one will try to stop us?" Sankar asked.

"There won't be anyone to stop us," Gwarzo replied. "But if someone shows up to ask questions, we tell them we have delivered the newest equipment and are removing the old before the school day starts so as not to interrupt the important work they are doing. No one will be the wiser."

"Sounds like you have some experience ripping off universities."

Gwarzo crossed his arms and stared Sankar down, challenging him to comment. The Tigroid held up his hands in surrender. "Three for the gear and two for artifacts. But keep in mind that we have five willing test subjects right here."

"I'm sorry, you want to take samples from me?" Sankar had suspected they would all have to submit material for baseline testing.

"We may hold the key. Modern samples might be more telling than museum pieces."

"If it were that easy, then why wouldn't someone have already tested that hypothesis?"

"Who's to say they didn't? Remember, *you're* the Heretic. You may have special insight into why no one has given it serious study." Gwarzo dabbed a finger in Sankar's direction.

"Politics. Religion. And then there's us, the renegade brigade, tearing down the walls impeding progress."

"And beating the crap out of those who stand in our way," Akoni added.

"When does this plan fall apart?" Sankar asked.

"If we activate the alarm instead of bypassing it, we'll know right away, and we'll leave." Gwarzo shrugged.

"That's the contingency plan?"

Akoni raised his hand. "I think it's better than staying and fighting."

"That's the plan. Get in and get out as fast as possible. If things go bad, drop what you have and get back to the ship. I can always launch the *Four-Claw* and provide cover for the big nasty to get away."

The others looked around. "Anyone know how to fly?" Akoni asked. No one replied. "Looks like one pilot and two ships."

"Akoni, in the next ten minutes, I'm teaching you and Junak how to fly this trash can."

The two mumbled and grumbled, but the options were limited. Gwarzo returned his attention to the diagram on the wall, continuing to study it while he made small annotations. Bayane and Junak looked at each other. "We get to rob a museum. Oh, goody."

Junak slowly shook his head. "I try to think of worse fates but can't come up with anything. Maybe if we had to use a sewer pipe for entrance, it would be worse."

"Or rain. I smell bad when I get wet." Bayane checked himself and gave the thumbs-up.

"It isn't just when you get wet, my friend." Junak slapped him on the shoulder, looking one last time at the space where everything from the university raid would go.

The plasma torch had made short work of the wall between the two rooms of the ad hoc lab. It wasn't load-bearing, and being little more than sheet metal, it cut like a knife through tallow. The remnants from the wall were stored in neat square panels in the cargo bay, ready to slap over a leak in the hull as a temporary repair.

Sankar stopped Bayane. "Take two of the stunners. We'll take the other one, and Akoni will carry the Ursoid blaster. Gwarzo will go unarmed so he doesn't have to think about whether to hurt another Goroid or not." Sankar didn't tell the others that Gwarzo didn't need a weapon to be the deadliest member of the crew.

Akoni headed out to gear up. He wore the full harness of the Customs official, complete with badge and loaded blaster. He made sure the backup magazine was loaded and stored in the appropriate pouch, within easy reach in case he needed to reload.

He didn't want to get into a firefight, but he was ready, just in case. They didn't have a great record when it came to their operations going according to plan. He returned to the lab, where he found Gwarzo talking to himself.

"How's your back?"

Gwarzo raised his arm rotated it slowly. "Hurts like Cornelius himself is pouring lava on me."

"That painful, huh?" Akoni didn't show a great deal of sympathy because the Ursoid culture rewarded strength, but he was trying. "Sucks. Don't push it too hard. I'll do the heavy lifting for you."

"Wouldn't that confuse them if they found a blood trail down there?" Gwarzo joked and started to laugh.

"You are one strange character, Gene, but I'm glad you're here. You make the cats and dog seem normal." Akoni strolled out to meet Sankar and Junak in the cockpit so they could learn how to fly the ship.

When the ship lifted off, Gene joined them to find Sankar pulling at his hair and shouting.

"Meathead!" Akoni yelled back. "Not my fault you make it look easy." His overcorrections forced the ship to respond with exaggerated movements. It lumbered back and forth.

"Small movements, like you're rerouting a circuit board's power supply!" Sankar was thrown against the engineer's station before Akoni brought the ship back under control. "Now, set us down without breaking the ship."

Akoni caressed the controls, and the ship settled without an issue. "There you go."

"I only had to visualize what you wanted. The controls are sensitive. Not bad for my first time. We walk away in one piece. I am a pilot now." Akoni pounded his chest, Goroid style.

"Junak, you're up." Sankar pointed at the skinny Tigroid. None of them had eaten in a while, but Junak had come with no extra weight.

The Wolfoid had to stand to operate the controls. He caressed them but far too gently.

"Grab them like you mean it!" Sankar advised.

The ship scraped sideways along the rock before it gained altitude. He shot it straight upward. The crew bowed under the surprising amount of pressure from the old can. He overcorrected as Akoni had done, and the ship dropped like a stone. The crew nearly rose off the floor.

"No!" Sankar flinched, expecting an impact that would flatten them. The ship pulled up and hovered close to the rocks. He bent his knees with the gravity fluctuations.

"Sorry about that. I'm used to co-piloting the *Four-Claw*. Starting to get the feel of this mammoth thing." The ship lunged skyward before dropping again. Both movements were much tempered compared to their predecessors. He transitioned the ship into lateral flight, made a circle, and landed.

"Good enough. We don't want you two to think about it for too long." The ship had already gone through pre-flight and was warmed up. Sankar smoothly accelerated up and away. He locked onto the course that Junak had prepared earlier.

"ETA, five minutes," Junak announced.

"Get ready to disembark. Cargo ramp toward the loading ramp. We'll drop it when we're ready to load. We'll keep the doors closed while we're at work."

"At work..." Akoni repeated. "Who would have ever thought Tigroids had a sense of humor?"

Sankar raised a hand while keeping his eyes on the course. "We are a very funny race. You could learn something from us."

"And more humor! You're killing me, Sankar!" Akoni roared.

Sankar guided the ship in low, hugging the roofs on his final approach. He slowed and rotated the ship before landing. He kept it on minimal power and jumped over the seat on his way out. Bayane popped the side hatch, and they walked outside into complete darkness. The Goroid harnesses had flashlights. Gene grunted in pain with his first step toward the lab.

"I'll get them." Sankar dashed away. The others walked outside, stepping carefully and watching for movements in the shadows. Bayane and Akoni carried small packets of tools, ready to open the doors as soon as they could see.

No one had expected there to be no lights, and they hadn't planned for it. They'd brought hand towels to mop their hands should the sweat prove too much. The heat and humidity pressed in on them while they were outside the ship.

Sankar handed a flashlight to Junak, kept one for himself, and gave the other to Gene. He punched the outside access panel, and the door closed behind him. Now able to light the way, the two groups set out.

Junak and Bayane disappeared around the corner while Akoni got to work on the panel adjacent to the freight loading door. With two lights, he made short work of the electronic lock and alarm.

"Make sure you look for another panel before opening a door. Each one will have to be bypassed."

They hurried inside and eased the door to a point where it was barely open and not going to close. To be certain it remained open, Gwarzo kicked a sliver of pallet under it and wedged it in place. They took the freight elevator down, and as Gwarzo had suspected, pallet jacks and carts were stored nearby. They took two carts and a pallet jack with them to the gene-sequencing laboratory.

They knew when they were next to the animal storage area since the stench rolled from the room like a physical barrier through which only the strong could pass. Sankar pulled up abruptly when he saw what was inside. Wild animals of all sorts, but they also had cats and dogs that were half the size of their Tigroid and Wolfoid cousins. Livestock and wild mountain beasts lunged at the light shining into their cages.

"Come on!" Gwarzo growled. Akoni forced himself not to look, although he could feel as much as hear the deep-chested rumble of a creature similar to the Ursoids.

Akoni forced himself forward, focused on the panel where Gwarzo was shining his light, and got to work. Sankar caught up, but he clenched his jaw and glared at the Goroid. Gene held up his hand to block the line of sight.

"Don't hold me responsible for what my people have done."

"But you tested some of those animals."

"Of course. It's why they are there."

"We're freeing them," Sankar stated in no uncertain terms.

"Do what you want. There's jungle all around; they *could* make it."

"Then they're coming with us, and we'll turn them loose where they have the best chance." Sankar put his hands on his hips and tipped his head back as he stared down the Goroid.

"Lights." Akoni was still working on the access pad, but the two had lost their focus on illuminating it.

"Sure," Gene agreed. "We'll rip off the university and then take a joy ride into the wilderness to drop them off. How long do you think it's going to take to move those cages?"

Sankar's lip curled into a snarl, and his whiskers flattened against his face. He growled but left it at that. They both knew Gwarzo was right.

"I'm taking the cats and dogs," Sankar declared an instant before Akoni cheered and the door to the sequencing lab opened. "Your show, Gene. Tell us what to take."

The three hurried into the lab and turned on the lights. Being underground, there was no chance of bleed-through to the outside.

Gene pulled out the chalk he'd used to draw the diagram on the wall of the ship's lab. He started at one side of the room and checked the equipment, marking what he wanted. "And take all the cabling attached to these, too." Sankar and Akoni started unplugging and moving the bits and pieces to the center of the room. Most of it fit in the carts, but the primary scanning device was bigger and impressively heavy. It would take all of them working together to put it on the pallet jack.

Akoni and Sankar hurried with the loading and Gene followed them, marking the tables.

"You want the tables, too?" Sankar asked while he took a short break to wipe off the sweat rolling down his head.

"You've seen my lab. I'm not sitting on the floor." With a flourish, he marked two of the chairs.

Akoni and Sankar pushed the first two carts to the elevator. "Take them up, and I think the rest will fit in the last two. Then it's pallet jack city for the scanner and the computing mainframe," Sankar said. They loaded the two carts into the elevator, and Akoni punched the button from inside.

When the doors closed, Sankar grabbed two more carts, pushing one and pulling the other as he ran back to the lab. Gene was already breaking the tables down. They stacked them in the cart on their ends. Sankar wedged in the chairs to hold them steady. He had to tip the cart to get it through the doorway because of how tall the tables were, but he saw the reasoning in bringing them along. He rushed the cart to the elevator.

On his way back, he stopped and entered the area with the animals. Their cries pulled at his heart; he couldn't let it go. Sankar unwired the cages for a few of the smaller animals: a tiger a quarter of the size of the Tigroid and a smaller, fuzzier catlike creature. He pulled open a large dog cage, the animal smaller than a wolf but larger than an average canine.

The larger animals were too big to move, but there was another compelling need. The bovine could serve another purpose. Sankar's mouth started to water. "You're coming too. Your sacrifice will be greatly appreciated." He pulled aside a bag of feed that looked akin to the vegetation Goroids ate. "Probably not the best, but starvation isn't an option. We need you, Gene."

A clap from the doorway surprised Sankar. "That's nice," the Goroid said. "Get your ass back in the lab. We need to move this last piece and get out of here."

Sankar looked at the three cages he'd set aside and the bovine behind the bars of its stall. "I'll be back," he told them.

He hurried to the lab, where the final cart filled with cabling and the last bits and pieces was ready to roll to the elevator. Gene was looking at the last piece of equipment to see if he could take it apart.

Sankar took the cart and rushed down the hallway. Akoni arrived with another cart. They pushed one inside and blocked the door with the other. Akoni noticed the cages that had been staged for movement and stopped Sankar. "I will help you move them."

"Thanks, Akoni. That means a lot to me. On a completely different note, would you know how to slaughter a bovine for steaks and burgers?"

Akoni's head snapped toward the enclosure. "I like how you think, my friend. I'm starving."

"Me, too. Let's get that piece of gear and get out of here. Did you hear any alarms or anything while you were outside?"

"Nothing. I think the others have not triggered anything. It is a calm night. Hot as the sun's corona, but typical for Cornelior." When they reached the lab, they found an impatient Gene leaning on the scanner. The pallet jack was in place. All that remained was to lift it from the floor to the jack for movement to the ship.

"I'll take this side, and you little people can lift the other." They arranged themselves appropriately. "On three."

Akoni counted down, and on one, they strained to lift the behemoth off the ground. Akoni roared as he powered through three finger-lengths. Gwarzo refused to be outdone. The muscles in his arms bulged to fantastic sizes. Sankar put all he had into the lift. With one foot, Akoni slid the pallet jack under the equipment right up to the handle. They set the gear down.

"Time to go," Gene declared. He waited at the doorway for Akoni to use his bulk to push the pallet jack, angling to get it through even though the doorway was oversized. He continued down the hall while Gene ran ahead to remove the cart from the door. Sankar detoured into the area with the animals.

When the scanner and the last of the equipment were on board, Gene shut the door. It closed while Sankar struggled with the two cat cages. He set them at the elevator's door and went back for the wolflike creature.

Maybe Bayane would know what it was.

He slid the last cage down the hallway. The elevator had not returned. Sankar used the time to run back for the bovine. A rope lead hung on a hook aside the stall. Sankar attached it to the bovine's head—it seemed accustomed to the handling—and guided it out of the stall and into the corridor. Once there, it tried to bolt, although it had nowhere to run. It slammed Sankar into the wall. He cooed to it and yanked on the rope, trying to bring the terrified creature back under control. Maybe it knew it was going to be their dinner. Or maybe it was simply afraid after being awoken in the middle of the night.

The elevator arrived, empty of carts and help. Sankar used a foot to push the cages inside and dragged the bovine in last. It decided it didn't want to go. Sankar had had enough, so he used the stunner on it. It jerked and fell halfway through the elevator door. It twitched while he tried to slide it. He flipped the legs over and pushed.

Sankar punched the button for the ground floor. Breathing hard, he was happy to see Akoni waiting for him at the top.

"What did you do?" Akoni asked.

"Let's get these other cages into the ship. Maybe it'll wake up so we don't have to carry it."

Sankar tied the rope to a handrail outside the elevator to keep the bovine from running off and handed out the cages one by one. The cats snarled and slapped at the Ursoid.

"I see you're making friends." Sankar manhandled the wolf cage out the door, getting the same treatment from its occupant.

"These are wild animals," Akoni said as he lumbered along with two cages filled with outraged cats. "They may be a bit too angry to have on the ship."

"I know what you mean." The wolf slavered and snapped as if he could get through the bars by sheer determination.

They deposited the cages toward the front of the cargo bay. The genetic sequencing equipment was nowhere to be seen.

Akoni sensed the question. "We took it all straight into the lab."

Sankar nodded as he ran down the cargo ramp and back into the building to find the bovine straining at the lead. With Akoni's arrival, the creature started tossing its head and kicking. Sankar hammered the butt of the flashlight into its forehead. It staggered but remained standing. He untied the lead, and together, they guided it toward the ship.

"Where are Bayane and Junak?" Sankar asked. The bovine started running when they hit the bottom of the ramp. Akoni took it straight to the back of the bay. "I'm going to check on them." Sankar peeled off and ran to the museum.

CHAPTER ELEVEN

Junak shined his flashlight at the lock on a side entrance into the museum. "Do you know what you're doing?" he hissed. Bayane continued to fumble with the pad. The toolkit was of Ursoid design and didn't fit his hands properly. Bayane levered the oversized tools and finally broke the circuit without activating the alarm. The door lock released.

"We can go in," he announced.

Junak pulled the door open and shined his flashlight inside. Bayane followed him into a service hallway. He walked in one direction for a few seconds before turning around and retracing his steps. Junak looked at his companion. "You go that way, and I'll go this. Shout when you reach the end."

"One problem with that," Bayane said. "No light."

"We better hurry. That took way longer to get in..."

"Leave it!" Bayane growled.

Junak threw up his free hand and started jogging in one direction. When it dead-ended at locked offices, they tried the other direction with the same result. They settled for a side corridor that turned twice and ended at a windowed door that opened to the museum proper. The door was locked manually.

The astrogator said, "No sense trying to be subtle. They'll know we've been here."

Bayane launched himself at the door and kicked it in.

Junak continued, "We're looking for anything related to the dig at that site. What was it called again?"

"Vineland One. Let's grab a map." Bayane raced for the main entrance, hoping to find a handout with museum details. Junak followed, shining his light on the way ahead.

The main entrance was utilitarian, with nothing in the way of artwork or glamor. Calling it plain was overselling it.

"The Goroids need to add a little style to their lives," Junak remarked while rummaging through papers behind the high desk at the entrance. He found a Cornelian coin and tucked it into his pocket. Bayane looked at him. "If we're going to be thieves, might as well go all-in."

"We're on a mission for the truth if we're to believe your fellow cat. Put it back." Bayane hammered a fist into his palm.

"You're right. When they hang us for our crimes against the truth, they'll make special mention of this coin that I didn't take when it was sitting in the open, unloved."

Bayane waved him away. "I'm not finding anything that looks like a map."

"Behind us," Junak grumbled. The backdrop of the desk was a tall carved-wood map showing the museum's three levels. "Archive of Vineland One..."

They studied the oversized display but didn't find anything that suggested a display dedicated to the archive.

"This section to our left is the display for prehistoric settlements."

"Sounds like the timeframe we're looking for." Bayane waited for Junak to lead the way and trundled behind him. They both looked quickly as Junak illuminated the displays with a precise methodology of left to right, top to bottom. The fourth case showed promise.

"My Goroid is a little rusty," Junak said.

"Mine isn't too bad." The two looked at the picture on the display that showed a settlement in the shape of the one Sankar had taken them to.

"This is a disclaimer that the rest of the display isn't ready. And here's a number for the remainder of the collection's location. Assuming we're on floor one, this suggests the rest is on minus one. The basement?"

"The others were headed to the basement. Must be where Goroids hide their good stuff. Thanks, Bayane." Junak used his elbow to shatter the glass of the case. He took the scrap of parchment and a bowl. Bayane opened his toolkit, and Junak gently placed the items inside. He thought for a moment before ripping off the sign from where the items had been and tucking that into the bag with them.

"The steps." Junak pointed at a door with a faintly glowing sign above it.

"Now we're eating the meat!" Junak declared.

"Is that a cat saying?" Bayane walked to the side, keeping Junak's flashlight where he could see it.

"Tigroid. Dogs don't use that?"

"Wolfoid," Bayane corrected. "You know they have us pegged as the weak sisters."

"I know," Junak said. "Sankar saved me on Oterosan, from the fate of the runt—just like Akoni. I wouldn't be in the service if Sankar hadn't vouched for me. I'm a good astrogator, and I can fly the *Four-*

Claw well, but I'm not the martial spirit Sankar is."

"I'm average," Bayane said. "Newer generations are getting smaller and smaller, but the litters are getting bigger. I have nine brothers and sisters. The other races seem to be getting bigger, but I don't think your families are as large. Akoni's brother was ridiculous. I've never seen a sentient creature that size."

The door was locked, so Junak tried to kick it in, but he failed and limped away, the light bouncing around the museum. Bayane tore the locking hasp off with one vicious mule kick that burst the door inward. They hurried down the stairs, Junak gimping as fast as he could.

When they reached the bottom, they found a storage paradise. Bagged treasures were piled to the ceiling, with no labels on the shelves. One had to lift each item to see what was in the bag. "Gwarzo has a lot to apologize for," Junak complained.

"No kidding. I'm turning on the lights." Bayane left the sanctity of the flashlight beam to prowl the wall. Junak helped by showing him the way. Once the lights were on and increasing in brightness, the immensity of the task before them became apparent. "How much time do we have?"

Junak checked his watch. "Less than an hour."

"That's a firepit of scat!" Bayane chuckled to himself at his linguistic fluidity and started at one end, scanning the piles and randomly checking the labels on the bags.

Junak struggled with his search. He didn't read Goroid, and none of it made sense to him. He looked for things that might have genetic material on them, like brushes and grooming tools since the Goroids were heavily into that, even from the earliest age. The first tools they'd made were to harvest banana leaves, but the second were to comb their hair.

With that revelation, the search went faster. When Junak found one, he took the bag. When his hands were full of brushes, he jogged to Bayane for him to read the labels. The Wolfoid did his best but remained uncertain. "Get a bag and take them all."

"I like that plan." Junak headed for the side cabinets and rummaged through them until he found a cloth bag that smelled like something had died within. He broke chunks of dried mud off the outside before dumping his comb samples into it.

Bayane watched him. "You couldn't find anything else?"

"The samples are in bags and I'm dumping this thing in Gwarzo's lab, so no hair off my ears."

Bayane stopped midway to reaching for another sample when a red light started flashing and a siren chirped at regular intervals.

"What'd you do?" they called at the same time.

Without another word, they knew their next move. Junak ran for the stairs, his limp gone in the adrenaline rush of trying to escape. Bayane caught him and trailed him closely to the ground floor. The light swung wildly as Junak tried to keep it aimed at their way out.

They burst through the broken door leading to the side entrance and straight into another light.

"I'll shoot you!" Junak cried.

"It's me, dumbass!" Sankar shouted back.

"Nice family reunion. Now let's go." Bayane pushed past Junak, accelerated toward Sankar, and shined the light past the Wolfoid. They slid through the corner and raced for the outside door.

The outside door was unlocked, but the alarm had reset after Junak and Bayane passed through the first time. It had triggered when Sankar entered.

Bayane noticed that in the heartbeat it took to pass through the door. They ran like only cats and dogs could. Flashing lights in the distance signaled they would soon have company. They flew like the wind over the open ground around the main building and up the ramp into the back of *Bilkinmore*.

"Shut that." Sankar pointed at Bayane, then the cargo ramp. He and Junak headed for the cockpit. Akoni had already powered up the systems. The vessel thrummed with the energy surging through it. Sankar vaulted the captain's chair and landed in front of it. He stroked the controls, and the ship lumbered into the sky.

Akoni activated the scanners. "Ground targets fading into the distance. Two new targets, airborne, coming at us from the spaceport."

"Thirty-degree climb to space. No, wait. We can't depressurize the cargo bay without killing our cargo. Junak, set a course toward the mountains. Akoni, you have the controls. I'm taking the *Four-Claw* to deal with our new friends."

Sankar waited until Akoni stood next to him before transferring control. He bolted out of the cockpit and ran into Bayane. "Come on, need to open the cargo ramp."

"I just closed it!" But the Wolfoid followed him. Sankar jumped into the *Four-Claw*, breathing a sigh of relief at the familiarity of the interceptor's responsive controls. He prepared to unlock the magnetic clamps as soon as he saw the ramp drop. Bayane clung to the wall like his life depended on it—because it did. He tapped the controls, and the ramp started to descend.

Sankar touched the controls and lifted off. The ship came up faster than he'd intended. He corrected and leveled it within the large cargo bay. As soon as the ramp was open wide enough, Sankar punched the controls and rocketed out the back. He didn't look to see the ramp ascend. His eyes were on the screen.

The *Four-Claw*'s shortcoming was the amount of time it took to reach full power. Once he was outside the freighter, he cut the power and let the ship drop almost to the tree line to build up its energy before transitioning to horizontal flight and accelerating far enough to ensure that the Goroid interceptors were following the *Bilkinmore* and not the *Four-Claw*. The two ships climbed to get into position above the freighter.

Sankar rolled in well beneath them before pointing his nose skyward and coming at them from below. He triggered the ion cannons, sending hypervelocity particles in a wave across both ships. The first exploded. The second juked enough to save it from blowing up, but it lost power and control. The scanner showed the pilot ejecting and the ship spiraling into the jungle, then a brief fireball erupted in the distance. Sankar caught up to *Bilkinmore*. He didn't have to contact them to request the ramp open.

The freighter lumbered ahead on autopilot. Sankar brought the *Four-Claw* in fast, and once inside, jammed to a full stop before easing it back into position. He activated the magnetic clamps and powered the ship's systems down. He checked the time. He'd been outside the ship for a grand total of three minutes.

When he stepped through the hatch to the deck of the cargo bay, the ramp was closed. The heat inside was oppressive. The wolf in the cage howled, and Bayane joined him. He quieted immediately and started to whimper.

The Wolfoid opened the cage and turned the animal loose.

"What are you doing?"

"Taking care of my friend. Look at him!" The wolf growled at Sankar.

"Make sure he doesn't bite anyone." Sankar eased past and hurried to the cockpit. He relieved Akoni of his duties and took control. He turned the *Bilkinmore's* nose toward space and accelerated as fast as the old tub would go. "Immediate screen is clear, but it looks like we stirred up a hornet's nest. Junak, find me the nearest black hole and the shortest route to get there."

Sankar leaned forward, trying to will the *Bilkinmore* to greater speed. The freighter lumbered toward the upper atmosphere. Their run from the city had given them a good standoff distance, and the polar route into orbit took them away from the main equatorial patrol lanes.

"Move the animals. We may have to decompress the cargo bay."

Junak continued to furiously work at astrogation. Akoni was the only one available, but he didn't move. Sankar stared at him.

"Look what the little bastards did to my legs." Akoni stood to show scratches where they clawed him through the bars. His pants were ripped and sticking to the bloody flesh beneath.

"Take the controls." Sankar stepped aside without a second look at Akoni's legs. The Ursoid moved in. The Tigroid ran for the cargo bay, where both cats were voicing displeasure with their situation. The bovine mooed from where it was tied to the side wall. Sankar yelled in frustration. He unlocked the cage and caught the bigger cat first, then raced up the stairs to throw it in his room.

He put the second cat in Junak's quarters. Sankar ran into Bayane in the upper-level passage. "The dog?"

"Crassius the *wolf* is in my cabin, where he will get a good night's sleep."

Sankar returned to the cargo bay, unhooked the bovine, and dragged it down the corridor to the airlock. He jammed it inside and sealed the hatch.

In the cockpit, it was as if nothing had happened. Akoni lounged in the captain's seat while Junak was head-down in a display of the system's gravity waves, wells, swells, and micro-sized black holes.

The scanner screen showed increasing numbers of pursuing ships, their sole purpose to prevent the *Bilkinmore* from escaping.

"I think we need a scanner ghost to scatter our pursuers." Sankar looked at Akoni.

"I don't want to use that one too often because then they'll figure a way to defeat it. The pursuers are still a ways off. It'll be best if we beat them into a gravity swell, where we'll disappear from their screens."

Sankar nodded at the sound logic. He turned to Junak to stare at his back.

"I know you're looking at me," the astrogator said. "It's not helping."

"Sooner rather than later, my friend. And take care opening the door to your room. The smaller cat's in there."

"The what? Why? I don't like those little creatures. They are like ill-mannered children."

"I think you need to work on your acceptance of the future generations once you're done *getting us out of here!*"

"Yeah, yeah," Junak grumbled.

"I'm hungry." Akoni pointed at the door.

"No food." Sankar caught the Ursoid's intent. "I put him in the airlock."

"Perfect place to work. Once I'm done, we pop the outer hatch and send the trash into space."

"Is there enough room for you both?" Sankar didn't think there was.

Akoni patted the Ursoid pistol at his side. "You let me worry about that." He strode off the command deck, then the airlock's inner hatch opened. Following a brief scuffle, it closed again. Sankar glanced at the hatch to see if Akoni had changed his mind. Bayane was coming down the steps, but Akoni had not returned.

Junak cheered and sent the revised flight path to Sankar's station. The pilot adjusted the heading and smiled. "They won't catch us." Sankar gave his astrogator a quick thumbs-up before returning his attention to flying the tub.

"That's what took so long," Junak explained. "Close and slower or farther away and faster. Once we descend into the trough, we'll disappear and barely be faster than the pursuing craft, but it'll get us to a cross wave where we'll jump out and back in. They might see us for a few moments, or..."

The muffled report of the slugthrower joined the reverberations through the hull. Sankar jumped and rushed out of the cockpit. Bayane stood with his mouth open, staring in disbelief.

The inner hatch opened, and Akoni crawled out.

"Why did you fire a slugthrower inside a closed airlock?" Sankar tried to help him up, but Akoni preferred to lie on the floor.

"Next time, I will not do it that way. You sound funny."

"You're lucky you can hear at all."

"Good genes," Akoni replied, chuckling. "Today, we will eat like kings."

Behind him, the bovine was lying facing into the ship, the bullet hole in its head a testament to its recent demise.

"Bring me a cart," Akoni said and worked his way to all fours. He raised his head. "Who's driving the boat?"

Sankar returned to the pilot's station to find the ship had drifted off-course. He muscled it back on track before checking the trailing ships. The *Bilkinmore* was going to disappear before they closed to weapons range.

He ignored the sound of a knife being sharpened and Akoni's oohs and aahs while he worked. Bayane hovered and asked for various bits for the wolf.

Junak stood and stretched, blinking rapidly to relieve the screen glare.

"You better grab a little something for the cats in our quarters," Sankar said.

"You mean a chunk of liver or a kidney, don't you?"

"Entrails. I'm going for the good stuff. They can eat what we give them. They'll like it. They're cats." To Sankar, it made perfect sense.

"Yeah, yeah..." Junak moped away. The butchering was moving forward quickly. Akoni chewed something while he carved. He caught Junak watching him and winked.

"I don't want to know." Junak climbed the stairs, went into the mess, took a couple of serving bowls, and returned to the bloodbath.

"Can I get some kibble for my kittens?" he asked.

"Nothing but choice bits for the little demons." He sliced something out of sight and slopped it into each bowl. One contained twice the amount of the other, relative to the size of the two beasts.

Junak leaned into the cockpit. "Which cabin has the big one?"

"Mine."

Junak took the bowls upstairs and set the bigger one outside Sankar's door. He went to his room, blocking the door with his body as he slowly opened it. The cat was on his bed. He hurried in and dropped the bowl. The cat hesitated for a moment before jumping down and circling. Junak's nose wrinkled at the smell. He saw the reason.

"You dumped on my pillow?" he snarled. The cat froze and started hissing, its hackles raised. Junak removed the pillow, dumped the offending pile into the oversized toilet, and left the room.

He opened Sankar's door the same way, but this time he carried the pillow in addition to the bowl. Inside, he saw no sign of the small tiger. He put the bowl down and circled the room, keeping his back to the wall. A flash of orange and black shot out from under the bed and pounced on the bowl, eating the sloppy mess in huge bites. Junak swapped his pillow with Sankar's and eased out of the room.

Junak found the cat perched over the half-empty bowl, ears back as it ripped its meal apart. He tossed the clean pillow on the bed and took a seat on the floor by the bowl. The cat looked at him but kept eating. When it was finished, it sat and started grooming its face. Junak tentatively reached out and ran his fingers down its furry side.

After a moment, its hair stood on end, and it hissed and slapped at his arm with claws extended. Junak hissed back while extending the claws from the back of his hand. He jabbed his claws at the cat to make sure it knew who the dominant feline in the room was. It stopped hissing and sniffed the claws before licking one.

It returned to grooming itself. "Stay off my pillow or you'll feel my full wrath, right before I chuck you out the airlock." He petted the cat, and it purred in response. "Now you understand."

He lost track of time before deciding he had best return to the cockpit. He found Sankar easing the ship over the swell and into the tidal pull of the system's gravity waves. *Bilkinmore* increased speed until it settled into an easy pace. "One hour before we have to roll over to the second well and onto the black hole," Sankar announced. "How far is Akoni? I'm hungry."

"We're all hungry except for the animals in our charge. What happened to dropping them off in the wild?" Junak wondered.

"Bad guys chasing us. We had to change our plan." Sankar joined Junak at the back of the command deck and slapped him heartily on the arm. "We got what we came for, didn't we?"

Junak grimaced. "Kind of. That's a definite maybe. We have tentative confirmation that we may have acquired what we were looking for, but possibly not."

"Please stop talking." Sankar waved his hand. "Such equivocation. I'll ask Gene."

Sankar stopped at the airlock.

"You look far too happy."

"If we can get someone to start cooking, that would be great. No need to wait until I'm done." He sliced away happily, throwing slabs of meat into the cart.

Sankar continued to the lab, where he found all the equipment exactly as they'd left it. Gwarzo was propped on bedding, reading one of the manuals.

"Can I help you?" the Goroid asked.

Sankar looked around before shaking his head. "I just wanted to let you know that we're heading out of the system. Wave goodbye to Cornelior. After that spectacular departure, I don't know when we'll be back."

Gwarzo waved and returned to his reading.

Bayane pushed the cart down the corridor.

"Have you taken over cooking duties?"

"I'm the hungriest, and since the rest of you knotheads seem indifferent about it, yes, I have taken over as head chef."

"Where are you going?"

"To the freight elevator."

"We have a freight elevator?" Sankar scoured his memory but came up with nothing. He decided to follow Bayane into the cargo bay.

"You tried to park your ship on it, but there's room." Bayane put the cart in the middle of a square outlined on the floor. He lifted a flap covering a button and punched it. The square rose out of the floor, following a girder on the wall. A square in the ceiling retracted. Bayane waggled his fingers as he disappeared through the hole.

Sankar loped up the steps to see where the freight elevator deposited its cargo. The area was clear. The square was on the deck in the passage between Akoni's room and Junak's.

"I didn't have time to properly assess the ship's full capabilities."

"Of course. Open the door to the mess." Bayane pushed the cart down the corridor. Sankar complied and held the door. In the kitchen part of the space, Bayane put most of the meat in the refrigerator, keeping out enough for the four crewmen who weren't vegetarians. Gwarzo wouldn't be in the mess while they were grilling the steaks and roasts.

Bayane fired up the stove and put the available pans on the induction heating coils. "Take the cart back to Akoni. There's enough bovine to fill it a couple more times. We'll have to get creative with our storage."

Sankar took the cart and used the freight lift, happy they had such a thing. Of course they did since the ship's main living area was on the second deck.

He dropped off the cart and returned to the cockpit.

"When's dinner?" Junak asked.

"It's cooking now. It won't be long." Sankar checked the course, speed, and holographic scanner display, which was distorted by the gravity trough in which they rode. "Thirty-five minutes until we have to exit the wave."

CHAPTER TWELVE

"I'll help Bayane." Junak excused himself but stopped when he made it to the corridor. Akoni bobbed to a rhythm that played within his mind as he happily carved, throwing slice after slice into the cart. "Did you ever work as a butcher?"

Akoni swallowed before he replied, "No, but we Ursoids know how to prepare meat. Bovines are a staple on Medvegrad. Also, lowland porcines. So good!"

"What were you eating?"

Akoni ducked his head and went back to work.

Most Tigroids weren't opposed to raw meat, but Junak had never had a taste for it. He preferred his meat cooked like most of the newer generation. He headed upstairs to check on Bayane and found the Wolfoid dancing in front of the stove, where steaks sizzled in myriad pans. Bayane guided the meat around, sliding the pieces in their own fat. He tossed a series of small pieces into a rounded pan and snapped his fingers at Junak.

"Want a taste?"

"You are a master!" Junak took one of the plates and held it out. The chef dropped in a great spoonful of the bite-sized pieces, which were seared to a light brown.

Junak bit the first one gently, testing how hot it was before inhaling the rest. Bayane ate with one hand while tending the steaks with the other.

"More?" Junak asked.

"What about the others?" Bayane continued to eat the small strips he had cooked separately.

"I'll let them know. Is it ready?"

"We haven't eaten in three days. How ready do you think it needs to be?"

"Fair point." Junak held his plate out for more. Bayane obliged him by cutting a steak in half. Rare to medium-rare, almost perfect. "I'll eat in the cockpit to give Sankar a break. We'll need him soon to get to and through the black hole."

"Roger," the engineer-turned-chef replied.

Junak stabbed the steak with a fork and bit off a chunk instead of bothering to cut it. He hurried down the stairs and into the cockpit.

"Is that mine?"

"If you don't mind bite marks and a little drool on it." Junak held out the plate. "I'm spotting you so you can get something hot before you transition the ship from this well to the next."

Sankar jumped up, clapped Junak on the shoulder hard enough that he almost lost his plate, and rushed to the stairs.

"Soup's on!" he yelled at Akoni as he passed and took the stairs three steps at a time. "I can feel my ribs!"

"Good. You're supposed to feel a few ribs; otherwise, you're overweight." Bayane took the other half of the cut piece and held it out for Sankar.

Sankar almost dropped to his knees in relief and joy. He started eating it like Bayane, spearing the steak with a fork and biting off chunks while he was still standing.

Bayane turned down the heat and helped himself to the second biggest steak. He left the biggest for Akoni. He took a huge bite and strolled to the door, choking the meat down after not chewing enough. He cupped his hand and yelled toward the steps, "Akoni! Your steak is ready. Wipe your nasty ass off and get up here."

"This is how we call people for dinner?" Sankar asked through a full mouth.

"I'm going to eat my bodyweight in bovine, and then I'm going to sleep. Wait. I better take a steak to my good boy." He dug open the refrigerator with a hand held out to keep anything from falling. He removed a massive cut of meat and headed to his room.

Sankar ate fast but was still chewing when Bayane returned. He held one hand in the other, trying to look casual at the sink while rinsing off the wound.

He caught Sankar staring.

And judging.

"He bit me."

"Aren't you his sugar daddy?" Sankar took another bite.

"He is my good boy, and I'm keeping him."

"Is that good for him? Living on a ship isn't exactly optimal for a creature of his stature."

"We'll figure it out by the time we have to make the decision. We are kind of stuck, and I'm already attached. He reminds me of me when I was young."

Sankar had no words for the starry-eyed expression on the Wolfoid's face. He finished his portion and sat back to let it digest for a few moments before he took control of the ship for the next leg in their escape from Cornelian space.

Bayane returned to eating. Akoni showed up, covered in blood. He sat down at the table with a squish from his wet pants.

"The cleaning service has the day off, so you should probably not touch anything that we don't have to wipe up ourselves. I better put together a roster," Bayane said.

"Stick-in-the-mud!" Akoni declared.

Bayane tossed the massive steak on a plate, where it towered high and hung over the ends. He delivered it to the Ursoid.

"That's for doing the hard work getting this stuff ready, Runt. We need proper spices and groceries, a real food run. Guts has the money, and I'm willing to spend it."

Sankar helped himself to a drink before heading back to the cockpit. Akoni was already halfway finished eating his side of beef. "Thanks, man," the captain said, touching the Ursoid's massive shoulder as he passed.

In the cockpit, Junak had finished and was fiddling with the astro charts. "Five minutes to wave exit," he announced.

Sankar took his place at the pilot's station before running in place in a near-futile attempt to get his blood moving. "I could use a nap."

"No kidding." Junak yawned, pushed his plate aside, and rechecked his charts.

Sankar tested the scanners, but being within the gravity wave and at the bottom of the trough, they could only see what was directly above them. He jiggled the controls to make sure the ship would respond when he needed it to.

"Transition window in thirty seconds." Junak waved over his shoulder at twenty seconds and then at ten. At zero, he pumped his fist.

Sankar pulled on the controls, adjusting the antigrav to force a turn, then drive the ship up the wave and over the top. *Bilkinmore* lumbered out of the trough and into normal space.

Junak and Sankar saw it at the same time, and their jaws dropped. A massive warship stood between them and the next gravity wave. Sankar tried to dodge, but the freighter was too slow. He pulled back on the controls and brought the ship to a stop.

The comm buzzed. Junak ran from the command deck to get Gene.

Sankar waited. A laser lit the sky in front of the screen. Sankar tapped the control. "This is Catamar One."

"We suspect you are the ones who raided the university and then destroyed two pursuit units." A Goroid face with piercing eyes and a high-collared jacket filled the screen.

"I'm sure I don't know what you're talking about." Sankar wasn't sure about the sequence to create ghosts with the scanners. He studied the panel, but it didn't come to him. After arguing and shouting, Gwarzo appeared. He lost his resistance when he saw the ship before him.

"I've never seen one like that." He shook his head.

Sankar turned around. "Not Goroid military," he mouthed.

"No."

Junak ran up the stairs to get the others.

"Ah, you have one of our people on board. I didn't think a cat could pull this off by himself."

Bayane and Akoni hurried down the steps and joined Sankar and Gwarzo in the cockpit.

"My, what a menagerie you have. Is the bear covered in blood?"

"Pickle juice. We were doing some canning," Sankar said. "You should smell it in here. This old tub doesn't have the ventilation for that kind of thing."

"Funny. I expect you're carrying the ship you used to dispatch those two pursuit vessels inside your cargo bay."

No one answered.

"Don't bother trying to launch it. We will destroy you well before you get the outer doors open. But I don't want to do that. I have a business proposition."

Sankar tapped Mute and turned to the crew. "I don't see where we have much choice, even though I have no idea what he's going to offer."

"Find out how he got in front of us. How does he know what he knows, and who is he?"

Sankar reactivated the comm. "How do you know about what happened on Cornelior, and how did you get in front of us?"

"If we're going to be business associates, you should know who you are dealing with. My name is Maglor. I run a rather substantial multi-planetary private conglomerate. I live on this ship out here so I can get where I need to go when I need to go. Your escapades spun up the authorities, but your departure is what caught my attention. I have the need to recover certain items from a former associate who is currently on Medvegrad. I would like you to recover them."

Gwarzo nodded when he heard the name. He knew of him.

"I'm also surprised and pleased at your multi-racial crew. I personally don't care which race I deal with. I care about very little, actually. Loyalty. Adhering to a contract. Bottom line. Maybe a little dedication, but my ego doesn't need to be stroked to that degree. I want my items back."

"Or you'll destroy us if we don't agree to get them for you?"

"Don't be an idiot. I thought those who could pull off such a heist from the university would be a little smarter. We both know that to make that threat work, I would have to be constantly watching you. Fear is no way to motivate one's associates, don't you agree?"

"I agree that it is of little utility."

"Then let's cut to the chase. I will pay well to get my property back. And I will pay a bonus if it is accompanied by my former associate, too. Looking at your ship, I assume you are in need of certain support."

"We do the job for you, and then you let us go?"

"I have a number of jobs that need to be done. Success will give you more opportunities to be successful."

"We have our own mission that we're trying to accomplish." Sankar climbed into the captain's chair and leaned back. He was too small to cut an impressive figure in the chair, but Maglor didn't use that to belittle him.

"Pray tell, what could a mash-up of Tigroid, Wolfoid, Ursoid, and Goroid be doing together that would supersede an opportunity for action and adventure, followed by untold riches?"

"That is our business, but we are in need of returning to Medvegrad. Two birds with one stone. Half upfront, half when we complete the mission?"

"What are you doing?" Junak whispered. Gwarzo thumped him with a big hand.

"A quarter upfront."

"Barely enough to pay landing fees."

"Then it's even more incentive to succeed."

"We need supplies, consumables, food." Sankar crossed his arms.

Akoni raised a hand. "Power inverters, converters, transfer coils, and about two hundred kolams of extra cabling and fiber."

Bayane nudged him. "Maybe ten emergency packs of plastoseal."

"What is holding that ship together?" Maglor roared with laughter. "I've activated the light on my airlock. Please bring your ship in and link up. I'll meet you there. *You* don't come on board unless you clean up first." He pointed at Akoni. The screen went blank.

"It's a trap," Bayane suggested.

"We don't have much choice." Sankar clenched his jaw and whistled through his teeth. "Prepare to board Maglor's ship."

"Hang on." Akoni blocked the doorway. "Have you seen the airlock lately?"

Sankar closed his eyes and swore under his breath. "May the Furd gods have mercy on our souls. We aren't making it easy on them. Flush the airlock right now before we get too close."

"I'm not finished butchering yet. Bring me another cart and give me two minutes." Akoni returned to the airlock while Bayane bolted past him and down the corridor. The butcher twisted the bovine around, making broad cuts but still leaving much behind.

He chucked the quarters into the cart as soon as Bayane delivered it. Akoni stepped out of the airlock, stripped off his clothes, threw them on top of the carcass, closed the door, and hit the button. He hurried up the stairs before it depressurized and ejected the refuse.

"You know you wanted to see that," he shouted over his shoulder.

Sankar looked to the rest of the crew to confirm. "No! No one wanted to see that."

They left the outer door open to freeze the blood splatters, hoping they would crack off and be pulled into space. Sankar used the manual override to send air into the chamber to create a stronger wind.

Since Goroids were vegetarians, the blood could be a source of friction. Sankar wanted nothing to set off their host. He returned to the cockpit to guide the *Bilkinmore* to link up with Maglor's ship. As they closed, they found it was nearly the same size as the freighter, but weapons bristled outside the sleek armored hull. Sankar slowed and adjusted the course until the flying box's airlock married with the warship.

Sankar joined the others in the passage outside the airlock. "Who is this ape?"

Gwarzo said, "A businessman. He gets what he wants. So successful, that if he directs the government to do something, *they do it*. But he lives on his ship in secret because of his enemies."

"Not so secret, it seems," Sankar said, and watched the airlock seal and start equalizing the air pressure between the two ships. "What are the risks if we do his bidding?"

"We can talk about that, but the real risk is in not doing his bidding. We may be able to leverage his influence to have a safe haven. Until about ten minutes ago, we didn't have one of those. He keeps us off the radar, erases any mention of our existence, then we might be free to accomplish what you want. Find the source for intelligent life on our planets. Did we sprout from a single seed, or were there multiple seeds? Enquiring minds want to know."

Sankar nodded. "Thanks. That's good insight. I don't mind if someone has our back if all we have to do are little favors."

The airlock light showed green. Akoni pounded down the steps, still wet but wearing clean clothes. Gwarzo put his hand on Sankar's shoulder. "Look at his ship. These won't be *little* favors."

"We'll find out soon enough." He punched the button, opened the hatch, and led the others through.

CHAPTER THIRTEEN

Armed Goroid security guards met them on the other side of the airlock. The two hulking brutes didn't speak. One led the way, and the other followed them.

Sankar shrugged and stayed close to the guard in front of him. He could kill the Goroid with a *kabbar* slash across his throat—before he even knew he'd been attacked. Sankar glanced over his shoulder to find that Gwarzo had the same thought. Who then drifted back to get close to his guard, and spoke to him in the Conrelian trade tongue.

"What's this gig like?"

"It's fine. Good work. I get to meet interesting people."

" And kill them?" Gwarzo finished the thought before laughing with hearty head bobs. The guard joined his mirth. "We'll be in and out in a hurry. We have work to do for the old man. Just need a couple tidbits of info, and we'll be on our way."

"I know you won't be long," the guard replied. "Mr. Maglor keeps a tight schedule. He will have you for no more than fifteen minutes."

Gwarzo switched to the standard zeno, for his comrades' sake. "We got fifteen with the old man. I thought we'd get five. He must think highly of us."

They were led to a receiving room, where they were checked for weapons. The Goroids snapped at Akoni because he still smelled of blood. He shrugged. "My diet is different from yours, little ape," he told one of the guards. He liked being the largest in the room, a far cry from the world in which he was raised.

Sankar maintained his poise, with Junak and Bayane close by. Gwarzo took a position in the room where he could maintain eye contact with Sankar while also watching the guards. Akoni was in the middle of the room, lording his size over the Goroids, creating a distraction.

A new guard appeared. Fierce and scowling, his expression stopped all the antics in the room as he looked from one face to the next. The other guards faded into the background. He stopped and looked long and hard at Gwarzo, then tipped his head slightly before speaking. "I will conduct you to your meeting with Maglor. You will stand away from his desk in a line. You will answer questions directed at you. You will ask no questions of your own. You will agree to his terms, and then you will leave. Should you accomplish the task he sets before you, then the next time you meet will be under less stringent conditions."

"And if we don't accomplish the task?" Bayane pressed.

The Goroid took one small step forward. Bayane didn't back down. "I've seen your ship. You will neither be able to run, nor hide."

Without hesitation, Bayane snorted and replied, "I've ridden on our ship, and you know it, brother. We won't be messing around."

The new guard contemplated the Wolfoid's self-deprecating response. His mouth twisted into a smile. "I think you may surprise us." He headed through a set of double doors and down a short hallway. They passed doors on each side before continuing into the room at the far end.

A massive desk stood on a raised dais. Behind it sat Maglor, surrounded by screens from which he managed his empire. When the visitors arrived, the screens went dark. There were no chairs in the room. They stood in a line before the desk as instructed, with Sankar in the middle. Maglor was at eye level with Akoni but was able to look down on everyone else.

He took the greatest interest in Gwarzo. The senior guard walked around the desk and whispered in Maglor's ear. The businessman nodded, and the guard stepped back to assume a position to the rear of his boss.

"My former business associate is an Ursoid who lives on Medvegrad in Medved Central, the capital city. He has in his possession certain technology that we developed. It creates a personal forcefield around its user, and a larger version for space ships provides a screen against energy weapons. These would change the face of warfare if they were to be monopolized by one race's military."

"Which means we'll recover the technology, and you'll make it available to *all* sides," Sankar said.

The Goroid behind Maglor glowered.

"But you're a businessman," Sankar said. "I understand that. Can we get names, contacts, addresses, and anything to help us hunt this individual down and secure your property? Do you care about your associate's final disposition?"

Maglor leaned over his desk to glare at the Tigroid.

"I believe you were instructed not to speak or ask questions. Did you hear your instructions?"

"I heard that if we fail, we die. I have no intention of failing. You had the means to destroy our ship and us with it if you wanted. You could kill us right now. We have no leverage besides the promise of doing your bidding. Please forgive my impatience to make sure that we are successful. I have no desire to die." Sankar kept his hands behind his back as he spoke.

"Did you hear that, Wargo?" Maglor said, amused. "No leverage besides the promise of doing my bidding. How long have we been at this?"

The security guard took one step forward. "Nineteen Cornelian years."

"Nineteen! Has it been so long?" He waved impatiently at his own reverie. "No matter. For the first time, a suitor understands his position."

Sankar waited. He had made his point, but he wanted the information. Going in blind wouldn't help anyone.

"I'll transmit the information to your ship, everything I know, even though I fear much of it is dated. He has remained elusive." Maglor scratched his neck and studied the five zenos from four different races as they stood before him, trying not to fidget. "What do you call yourselves?"

"We are the Veracity Corporation," Sankar said.

"How quaint," Maglor said. "My people tell me that your ship smells appalling. And you appear to have wild beasts running free."

"You caught us in the middle of something," Sankar replied. "It's not our finest hour."

"The only thing we caught was you making it up as you go, but had I not been here when you conducted your raid, you would have gotten away. Maybe there is a little truth and a lot of luck on your side. Tell me, what are you *really* doing?"

Sankar swallowed hard. He expected the ship to be searched but that they would be subtle about it.

"We're looking for the nature of our existence. I believe that all the races come from a single source. That is what we are trying to prove. Even the contemplation of the pursuit has made me a Heretic on Oterosan."

The Goroid raised his ape eyebrows and held them there. "I would think so. What makes you go on such a fool's quest? There will be no reward for what you discover."

"What *will* we discover?"

Maglor shook his head before continuing in a soft voice, "You are on a search for truth. I am only interested in business. Find Breon. Obtain my hardware. And if the opportunity presents itself, it's okay if you finish Breon. Trust me when I tell you that you are not my first choice for this, but it is based on what I just saw you accomplish on Cornelior. My business does well because I seize opportunities when I see them before anyone else. I would hate to let a potential talent like Veracity Corp slip through my fingers."

"You're *hiring* us," Sankar said, looking at the floor, feeling the situation out. "So, if we're successful with this task, we'll get another job, and then another. I'm not necessarily opposed, as long as we can continue *our* search unimpeded."

"Also," Maglor said, "The ship in your cargo bay is of great interest to me. I need it."

"You can't fly it," Sankar replied flatly.

"Don't make me cut your hands off to activate the controls," Maglor said, smiling with an ape's grin. "I'm sure this Gwarzo has informed you of my reputation that I will do what I have to, to get what I want."

Sankar shrugged one shoulder. "The *Four-Claw* is non-negotiable."

Junak shuffled his feet. Gwarzo stood rock-still, and stared at Wargo. Akoni tried to see what was on Maglor's desk. Bayane looked forlorn.

"You bargain like a worthy Cornelian," Maglor said. "Yet your team is feral, like your pets, and you live in squalor."

Sankar smiled—sensing that the moment of crisis had passed—and held his paw-hands out. "Veracity is an evolving enterprise. Or work can get messy. If you have extra cleaning supplies, we would appreciate the tactical assist. Everything has been a blur since we departed Oteran space. I don't even know when that was—two weeks ago, maybe?"

Maglor shook his head. "We *are* providing, what did you call it, a tactical assist. Extra freezers. It appears you have your own meat, and I don't want to know about that. And most importantly, cleaning bots. They'll be automated because you look like a pack of slobs, but I expect nothing less than cutting-edge military minds. You defeated the university's security and planetary security with that flying trash can, and more than that, they never had a chance. Imagine what you'd be able to accomplish if you had real equipment. I will leave your *Four-Claw, for now*. When you return with my shield generators, we will discuss your ship over a nice glass of thick port."

"I look forward to that, Maglor." Sankar stepped forward with his hand raised to slap palms and seal the contract, but Wargo nearly vaulted the desk to stop him.

Maglor put his hands up. "I don't shake hands with anyone. Please respect my wishes. Wargo will see to your needs." Maglor faced away, and his screens reactivated. The doors behind them opened, and they were hurried out. Akoni ducked to exit, but not much.

Once in the outer chamber, a waitstaff appeared with trays of food, all of it Goroid, but there was nothing any of the crew couldn't eat. Bayane and Gene dug in as if they hadn't eaten. Gene probably hadn't because his only food was the animal biomass from the lab.

"You're going to get fat," Sankar told the Wolfoid.

"I look forward to that day. Judging by what you just committed us to, I doubt we'll be eating regularly."

"We weren't eating regularly before I committed us to anything. I figured it was best to stay alive between meals." Sankar turned away before Bayane could press the issue. This wasn't the place to carry on a philosophical conversation about doing an arms dealer's bidding.

"When can we go?" Sankar asked their escort.

Wargo remained stoic.

"I know you," Gwarzo told him.

"And I know you." It didn't sound friendly.

"Not all of us fight wars in the same way, but we all fight for the same reason," Gwarzo explained.

"You liked it more than the rest of us," Wargo replied, facing off against the smaller Goroid.

"Please don't question my honor, and I won't question yours," Gwarzo said, and pointed at the double doors behind which Maglor spun his interstellar deals.

They shook, gripping each other's forearms.

"You will be conducted back to your ship," Wargo said. "Your mission parameters have been transmitted. Good luck."

As they approached the airlock, the escort held them up to wait for a veritable army of workers leaving *Bilkinmore*.

Junak leaned close. "How do you feel about getting in bed with this guy now?"

"We are alive. Be thankful for that. Every day we live is another chance to do what we're out here to do. Doesn't look like our road is going to be a straight one, but being able to do this alone was becoming less likely. Take it in stride, Junak."

Sankar waited as impatiently as the others to board their ship. The stream of workers trickled until the guards finally let the crew by.

"Thanks," Sankar grumbled as he hurried past. The airlock was sparkling where they had disinfected it and scrubbed it clean. The pilot waited for the others to get in before closing the hatch and sealing the *Bilkinmore*.

Why would they clean our ship? Sankar wondered. His tired mind could come up with no reason besides Maglor expecting a long-term relationship and establishing a standard that didn't involve a ship that looked like a slaughterhouse.

"Junak, plot us a course out of here."

The Tigroids headed into the cockpit, where everything looked the same. A color caught Sankar's eye. A different blanket was in the cart he used for a bed. He pulled it to his face and sniffed it. Clean. Soft, unlike the industrial-strength Ursoid bedding. He tucked it back in. The fatigue of the past twelve hours was already catching up with him. The low after the adrenaline high.

It was like a switch had been flipped, and he had to force himself to keep moving.

He assumed his position behind the pilot's station and searched for the transmission from Maglor.

It was there, as promised. Sankar opened a file that was built like a military brief. Executive summary upfront, breakdown of terms, detailed research in the appendices. It lacked the most important details, and that was why Maglor needed a team with an Ursoid.

Akoni would have to stroll the streets of Medved Central in search of one of his fellows. The individual would probably be in hiding, but he also might be higher profile because he had technology that could make him wealthy beyond avarice.

Unless he was the one who'd designed it. *Associate*, Maglor had said. The details surrounding the establishment of their relationship were gray and sketchy. Sankar guessed at an answer based on what he read between the lines. Maglor had provided money to support the research, and after it panned out, Breon had reneged.

Making a bad deal didn't mean one could easily extricate oneself. Breon knew that; otherwise, Maglor would have found him already. Ergo, the Ursoid associate was in hiding.

The airlocks released, and Sankar vectored *Bilkinmore* away from Maglor's corporate headquarters, from which he ran his business outside of planetary jurisdictions. It was also a heavily armed warship because a boss like Maglor had capable enemies.

Little by little, Sankar felt himself getting more comfortable piloting the big, ugly ship.

Akoni strolled through, carrying a device from his toolkit. He put his finger to his lips. From time to time, he pulled bits and pieces from beneath the consoles. At one point, he laid down on the floor to crawl head-first under a panel. He reached as far as he could before using a screwdriver to stab something underneath.

When Akoni stood, he gave two thumbs-up. "Numerous listening bugs, and two tracking bugs, but that's just in here. We found eight more elsewhere on the ship. I haven't checked the *Four-Claw*, but there will be something in there, too. You're free to talk in the cockpit and the dining area, but expect that we're being tracked and recorded until I can verify the complete inside and outside."

Sankar chewed his furry cheek. "Take care with our words, yes, but there was never an option to not go to Medvegrad. Junak, update the course, and let's transit the black hole. Once on the other side, we need to rest and plan. I want a better look at this packet, and so do you."

"Breon?" Akoni asked. Sankar nodded. "I'll bring it up at my station."

Sankar muscled the freighter into the nearby gravity trough, sliding sideways into place until the ship picked up the wave and raced forward at a fantastic speed toward the micro-sized black hole.

"Time?" he asked out loud, even though he was talking to himself. He checked the navigation inset on the holographic display. "An hour and a half before I need to be back at the helm."

"Breon will not be easy to find," Akoni mumbled while slowly scrolling through the screens of information. Sankar looked over his shoulder.

"What's your plan?"

Akoni shrugged. "It is gelling within my mind. I'll let you know when I have it. I may need a pet because cute pets help start conversations."

"You mean, like Bayane's wolf?"

"I mean Bayane himself. I can get a collar, and a chain leash." Akoni winked, but Sankar suspected he wasn't kidding.

"Bayane's going to love that."

"Did you forget that I'm right here?" Bayane stood with his hand-paw giving them the two-finger salute.

"I think you should hear him out," Sankar suggested. "You want to be at the front of finding this technology. Imagine what else you'll find."

Bayane was torn. "But...a collar? Ghastly."

Sankar left him to contemplate his fate. Upstairs, he went into the spotless mess, where a cleaning robot waited in the corner. "You are going to make it easy for these guys to be slobs. They'll never clean up after themselves now."

The bot remained as it was, unpersuaded by Sankar's claim. It continued to wait to do what it was programmed to do, its sole purpose for existing.

Junak watched with mild amusement as his fellow Tigroid philosophized with a cleaning robot.

A new refrigerator stood to the side. Inside was a stock of plant-based foods. The ship's primary fridge was untouched, still filled with plastic-wrapped meat, but drips of blood had collected in the bottom and pooled within a brown-tinged border as it dried. Sankar looked at the cleaning bot but shook his head. Once the meat was gone, they'd clean it out, but not before. He didn't trust a Goroid cleaning bot to leave the choice bits. Sankar selected a slab of meat and gristle to take to the small tiger in his quarters.

He found his room untouched besides what looked like a tuft of Goroid hair near the door. "Where'd you go, little friend?" Sankar dropped the meat into the pan and waited. The cat popped out from under the bed. Sankar sat by the bowl and waited. Closer and closer the small tiger stalked until the call of food was too great. It pounced and started to eat.

Sankar tried to pet it, but it growled and snapped at him. "Hey! Cut the crap," he shouted. The tiger tucked its ears back and hissed. Sankar extended his claws and tapped the bowl. "Eat."

The cat returned to the bowl, eyes on Sankar, but it started eating, and this time, it let Sankar pet its soft orange and black fur.

"That's a good kitty. Maybe we'll keep you aboard if you're going to protect the ship from intruders. At least my room if nowhere else."

He checked to see if anything had been disturbed. That was when he found the pillow. "Did you...?" He sniffed it. "That's not you, but I know who's responsible for this."

Sankar took the pillow, snuck down the corridor and into Junak's room, chased the domestic cat under the bed, swapped out pillows, and returned to his room, where he locked his recovered belonging in the wardrobe.

"Eat well, my friend." The big cat continued to tear and gulp, even purring with the return of its new master.

Later, in the recreation room, fresh linens of the softest Goroid weave were stacked. Sankar ran his hand over them and then a second time since he'd never experienced the softwood fibers.

With his hands clasped behind his back, he paced, using the time and space to think.

He had become a mercenary because he was given no other choice. How could he use that to his benefit? He rested his hand on the linens. In the mess, they had food. The ship was clean. Spare parts and other bonus items had found their way to the cargo bay.

Sankar winced, thinking about the bloodbath the Goroid crew had encountered on *Bilkinmore*. "They caught us at a bad time. I should have told them to come back tomorrow after we had time to clean up. But would we have? I'm trapped on a ship with a bunch of slobs." He licked the back of his hand and ran it over his whiskers, smoothing them against his face and ending with a flourish. "Talented slobs, mind you, and we need to look better. We should buy some clothes."

His mind wandered because he was tired. He shook his head and left the rec room, taking the back steps to check the cargo bay. He found Akoni and Bayane there, digging through a crate that hadn't been there before.

He looked up the stairs and then down the passage toward the cockpit as if expecting clones of the crew where he had last seen them.

"Anything good?"

"Looks like a PDS," Akoni said, examining a rectangular metal box. He flipped it over before moving on to the next item.

"Point defense system," Bayane said. He dug out a small turret with an even smaller tuning-fork-like protrusion.

"That doesn't look like much."

"This is a high-energy pulse weapon. The only challenge is in upgrading the power system, but Maglor provided a stopgap generator and converter. That's over there." He waved a hand, but Sankar couldn't see anything in the indicated direction.

A throaty snore sounded from within the *Four-Claw*. Sankar peeked inside to find the wolf curled up in a bottom bunk.

"Why is your dog in my ship?"

Bayane threw his hands up. "I'm trying to do a job here, and Crassius' presence is comforting."

"He's sleeping in *my* ship, Bayane!"

"I can hear his calming snores. Rumble-snort. Rumble-snort. See? Soothing, isn't it?"

Akoni raised an eyebrow but didn't look up. He continued to remove equipment, cataloging it for installation.

"It will be a sorry day when you people don't mess with me. Did you sweep the *Four-Claw*?"

Bayane nodded. "It's clear of active transmissions, but we have the scanners tuned for random bursts if the trackers and bugs are dormant for a certain amount of time. I'm sure there are some that will activate later. All we can is pick them off when they pop up. But, Bayane has a super sniffer, and we checked everywhere they touched."

Bayane poked the side of his short snout. The wolf appeared in the interceptor's doorway, stretching before jumping out. It sniffed Sankar before running to the far end of the cargo bay to relieve itself. A cleaning robot slowly rolled after it. Bayane beamed like a proud father.

Sankar didn't have the energy to fight with Bayane about leaving his pet in his cabin.

"You better teach that thing to get along with the cats because at some point, they are going to get out and run free throughout the ship."

Junak shouted obscenities from the second level. As if making Sankar a prophet, the tiger raced down the stairs and bolted behind the *Four-Claw*. Crassius growled and stalked toward the ship.

Bayane inched toward the wolf.

"You wanted to release them together into the wild," Akoni said. With a snarl and snapping jaws, the two beasts launched at each other. With a feint, a slash, and a leap, the tiger ended on the wolf's back, dug in, and started chewing on an ear. The wolf tried to throw it off, but the cat wouldn't budge.

Crassius laid down and started to whimper. The tiger hopped off and strolled away, tail held high. Bayane looked crushed. He kneeled by the wolf to look at its ear. Chewed and a little bloody, but it didn't need any major repairs.

"Come on, Crassius. Let's get you cleaned up." The wolf walked in Bayane's shadow as he strode toward the steps.

Sankar held his hands out and shrugged. "I hope that's the end of it." The small tiger looked at him. He scratched its ears. "You did well. Thanks for not putting a bigger hurt on the dog. He knows his place now. What should we call you?"

The tiger purred like a smaller cat. He kneaded his claws on the deck plating with the vigor of Sankar's scratches.

"You shall be known forevermore as 'Deathblade.'"

Akoni rolled his eyes so hard he almost fell over.

"I better check on Gene," Sankar mumbled, scratching the cat's ears once more before disengaging from his domestic duties.

In the laboratory, Gene sat on the floor, still reading the manual from earlier. Nothing else had changed within the room.

"Gene? How long until you have this thing up and running?"

"Are you going to need me on Medvegrad?"

"Probably, but not in the hunting-the-guy-down part, only the direct-action work when we have our cubs aligned."

"Then it'll be about a week. It helps to have good food. I'll be able to work faster." He lifted the manual and renewed his reading before getting the last word. "For the record, I do know what I'm doing when it comes to bioengineering, but the Oterans kept me in prison so damn long that this is all-new equipment, which also means that it's better and faster. When we are running, we'll be operating at high-speed with the greatest fidelity."

Sankar returned to the cockpit to find Junak back in place at his station. "Twenty minutes," he reported.

"I have the ship. Twenty minutes to wave departure, then transiting the black hole to Medvegradian space. If you would be so kind, fix the stitches in Gene's back. That little wrestling match of his pulled Akoni's threads."

"But mine stayed?"

"Yes, and because of your fine work, you are designated as the crew's medic."

"Hang on..."

"Too late. You're it. As soon as we get through the hole, we'll be shutting down for a spell to rest. I'm beat. It won't take you too long. I'll let you know before we bump across the event horizon. Don't want you to stab Gene in the back and get yourself killed because of it."

"Thank you for that. I used to be an astrogator."

"And that'll teach you to mess with my pillow because your cat is undisciplined."

The tiger padded into the cockpit, stood on its back legs to look into the cart, and jumped in to make itself at home.

"Behold!" Sankar pointed with a knife-hand at the cart. "Deathblade."

Junak strolled off the command deck, shaking his head.

Sankar checked the scanners and the countdown clock. When they climbed out of the trough, they'd enter the black hole, and almost instantaneously, they'd exit at the fifth planet's distance from the system's star, but at ninety degrees to the planetary rotational plane.

He ran through his systems and upped the inertial limiters, but the freighter's design was bottom-heavy, so that was where the artificial gravity pulled, nearly eliminating inertia while limiting transverse stress. The ship's weak acceleration meant the antigravity plates wouldn't be stressed to the point that the limiters kicked in.

A black hole changed all that. To transit the black hole, the ship's hull had to be energized, and for the brief moment of transit, the antigrav plates cycled from pull to push and back to pull. If the transit was too slow, everything would be thrown into the ceiling and come crashing down moments later. But with reasonable speed, the only thing anyone felt was a slight bump.

Sankar activated the ship-wide communication system. "Listen up, people. We're leaving the wave and heading into the black hole. Don't be doing anything delicate for the next minute."

He pulled the controls, still unused to the ship's seeming reluctance to respond to commands. It climbed toward the crest and out. Sankar yanked down on the controls to avoid running into a heavy freighter that had just exited the black hole. *Bilkinmore* plunged into the sidewall of the wave.

The ship jerked left and right, dropped, then rose as it fought its way through the gravity walls.

The freighter cleared the space overhead and Sankar raised the nose, pulling it out of a swell. The ship rotated over the top and immediately plunged into and through the black hole...

Out the other side and into Medvegradian space.

Akoni shouted from somewhere. He wasn't delivering accolades.

Sankar turned the ship away from the planetary plane and accelerated. Thirty minutes later, he powered down the systems and turned the *Bilkinmore* into a great hole in space.

He looked to crawl into the cart, but the tiger was there. Sankar's addled mind wondered what to do, but inconveniencing the cat didn't come to him as an option. He reached in and gently lifted the cat to carry him upstairs to bed, where they could both sleep. Sankar had to dig into his cabinet for his pillow. That brief respite almost lost him his place in bed as the tiger spread out.

In the morning, they had a great deal of work to do, and Sankar had to be ready for it.

CHAPTER FOURTEEN

Sankar headed to the cockpit after blocking his door open to give Deathblade free run of the ship. After yesterday's struggle for domination, Sankar expected the animals to maintain an uneasy peace.

He walked by himself, but his circle consisted of everyone on that ship: four people and three animals. No one waited for him on Oterosan besides his parents, and only if he returned with overwhelming evidence. Even on the ship, Sankar stood apart.

In the cockpit, he found space clear around them for as far as their scanners reached. He strolled down the empty corridor, knocking on Gene's lab door before opening it. The Goroid was sound asleep, toppled sideways but where he had been the last time Sankar had seen him.

A dirty plate provided the only evidence that he had moved. Sankar took the plate and left the lab, which was nothing more than a room full of equipment waiting to be connected and powered up.

On the crew level of the ship, Sankar deposited the plate in the cleaning rack and found something to eat in the non-meat refrigerator. After finishing it, he knew he could never become a vegetarian. His body craved meat. He took out a thin steak and cut it up so it would cook more quickly. With additions from the new spice and seasoning rack, he was able to create an exotic-smelling breakfast.

When Junak and Bayane showed up, sniffing the air, he realized his mistake.

"Got any extra?" they asked in unison.

"Check the scans and make sure we're still in the clear. I'll do the cooking this morning."

"I like that!" Akoni's booming voice announced from the corridor.

"Just like a pack of weeds, you find a little fertile soil and dig in." Sankar returned to the refrigerator to pull out enough meat for the mess's morning crowd. "Get over here, knucklehead. I've seen you around a kitchen, and it amazes me that you're alive at all."

Junak pointed to Bayane. "He's talking to you. I'm the scan guy." He walked out to forestall any argument.

Bayane looked shocked.

"Junak's right. I am talking to you, dogface."

"What's with all the names? It has put me off the creative spirit."

Akoni blocked the doorway. "It hasn't put you off eating. Get over there."

"I'm on a ship full of bullies. Look out, you're blocking Crassius. He'd like steak niblets for breakfast, too."

Akoni stepped aside and the wolf walked in, head held high as it sniffed the air. Akoni went next door to the stack of linens, brought back a blanket, and threw it on the floor. Before Crassius could lie on it, Deathblade scampered in and plopped down.

The wolf looked at the Ursoid. Akoni snagged a second blanket and put it on the other side of the room. The two pets maintained their distance.

Junak returned with Gene. "It's clear as far as the electronic eye can see. And look who I found."

The Goroid wrinkled his nose at the smell of cooking meat, despite the spices. He helped himself to the plant-based refrigerator, snagging something extra for the wolf who hurried up to him when he held it low. Bayane narrowed his eyes, and his snout twitched as Gene fed the wolf and then scratched behind its ears.

"Have you had a chance to look at the info packet?" Sankar asked.

"I have. And I have a plan, but we need help. I'll contact Koni, and then we'll have to stop by the scrapyard."

Sankar grimaced but kept stirring to avoid facing the team. "He seemed emphatic that we were not to return, and here it is...what, ten days later? Look at us; we've returned."

"Believe me when I tell you that it wasn't my first choice or even my third, but it's got the highest probability for success. And it'll only cost us half the bovine."

"Just when we were starting to eat well," Bayane lamented.

Sankar sprinkled salt in the pan where the melted fat was collecting and swirled the meat chunks through the salty oil.

"We'll get more meat, but only if we can complete this mission."

"'Mission.'" Bayane said the word slowly. "It's like I'm back in the army."

Akoni laughed. "We've all been drafted, first by this lunatic," he jabbed his huge thumb toward the morning's chef, "and then by that Goroid psycho."

"He's a psychopath, make no mistake," Gene added. "But a good zeno to have on our side. We need to do this right, and we'll keep getting funds. We did get a quarter upfront, didn't we?"

Sankar looked into the pan, but the answer wasn't there. "I don't know."

"What is wrong with you people? We accept the job, we get paid. We do the job, and we get paid the rest."

"I don't even know where to look for the funds."

"Your account? The same one you used to pay Koni."

"I didn't give him the number." Sankar tossed the morsels one last time before shoveling them onto four plates. Bayane joined the others at the table. Sankar took his plate and sat down. "You can help yourselves. I'm not your manservant."

They raced for the counter. Akoni elbowed Bayane out of the way to keep him from taking the Ursoid's plate with the double portion. The three joined Sankar while Gene sat at the far end.

After a hearty round of compliments to the chef, they ate in silence.

"It's a small price to pay, Sankar," Akoni pressed. "If we can pull this off, we'll be able to buy our own bovine ranch."

Gene shook his head. "I need an assistant to get the genetic sequencing equipment online. There are too many moving parts for one person to manage." He looked purposefully at Junak.

"I heard the word 'volunteer' does not have to start with the letter 'I.' Although you think you want Junak, Bayane is the best choice because power is going to be a big issue, and you need an engineer for that. Bayane—tag, you're it. And Crassius seems to have embraced Gene. You guys can all hang out together."

"How am I it? I think Junak should volunteer."

"Have you taken a good look at the ship?" Akoni asked. "I need help!"

"Bayane stands ready. He can be everywhere all the time." Sankar took the last bite after his declaration.

"How did I become the ship's butt boy?"

"Because you eat like an Ursoid and can barely cook. We'll feed you, and you do everything else that needs done on the ship. We all have full plates."

"I'll help Gene when you don't need me in the cockpit," Junak said before putting his plate on the floor for the wolf to lick clean.

Bayane nodded at Junak.

"Make your call, Akoni, and let's pay big bro another visit. I'm not going to have to school him about fighting again, am I?"

"School him? I think you're serious." Akoni chuckled. "You wouldn't last ten seconds in a real fight with an Ursoid, my friend. Don't attempt it. You will not be better for it. But if you die, I get to stay home but have no purpose there. Here, you appreciate what I do. I like having you around, so don't start a fight with one of my people."

"I'll take that under advisement." Sankar winked at Akoni. They quickly cleaned up, each stuffing their own dishes in the cleaner. The other bailed out before Sankar could volunteer someone to clean the pan and the stirring spoon. He put it in the sink and added dish soap, kindly provided by Maglor. "I can't believe people saw our ship as it was. He gave us soap."

When Sankar looked around for sympathy, he found no one there, not even Deathblade.

"I'm putting together a cleaning schedule, and you're all going to be on it!" he shouted.

He headed for the cockpit by going through the cargo bay as part of his effort to be better aware of the ship. Sankar listened to it: the nuances of the environmental control system, the hydraulic pumps, the recycling system. He entered the *Four-Claw* and sat in the pilot's seat. It was like a comfortable blanket wrapped around him. He shot around when he heard a click on the deck behind him.

Deathblade looked up at him before leaping to the control panel and trying to perch on it, but it was canted, and the smooth surface gave him nothing to dig his claws into. He slid off, claws screeching, and landed lightly. He strolled off the ship as if he had meant to do all of it.

"You're kind of a jerk," Sankar told the cat. Deathblade didn't notice. Sankar sighed while looking at the blank screen before him. Upgraded scanners. He needed Akoni to work on them when they had the time. And if they could acquire the new screening technology to put on the *Four-Claw*, the little ship would become nearly invincible. Each planet only had one battlewagon, as per the Hinteran Peace Mandate of 2731. Those ships were ridiculous in size and armament, but to a ship like a screened *Four-Claw*, they would be vulnerable.

Sankar wasn't greedy. His mission was to find the truth, but it would be much easier if he commanded the most powerful warship in all Hinteran. He left the ship with a newfound desire to complete the task Maglor had laid at his feet.

In the cockpit, he found Akoni sitting in the pilot's seat. "Let me guess. He said he can't wait to see his little brother."

"I haven't called yet."

Sankar reached past the Ursoid, activated the comm system, and brought up the frequency log they'd used the last time he called the shipyard. He let his finger hover over the call button. "Call your brother."

Akoni nodded, and Sankar tapped the button.

"Shipyard Medved Seven, Beos Region, this is Catamar One Three requesting clearance to enter orbit."

Only the static of space replied. After a full minute, Akoni called again.

"You better have a good reason for this." Koni sounded the same as he had when they were last on Medved Seven.

"We need to talk in private about tech that'll bring tears to your eyes," Akoni replied.

"And bajingos. Time is money."

"You'll take what I have to offer you and no more. And you're going to like it. Clear us to land because we're coming in." Akoni closed the channel.

Sankar leaned against the engineering console with his arms crossed. "What are we giving him?"

"The technology for the screens once we have it, but just a copy. And it will probably be missing one or two key components, so it's not replicable. Koni is not an engineer, so he won't know. He'll be sold on it but won't be able to sell it, assuming that we are able to recover anything. He'll give me what I need on the promise alone."

"And us? For the *Four-Claw*, maybe?"

"We will secure a full copy of whatever we get," Akoni stated. "I need Koni's help to get access to the government databases. He knows people."

"To search for Breon?"

"Waste of time. We need to search for tidbits and breadcrumbs leading to the technology. Breon will be there, but that won't be his name. He'll have changed it. He's running for his life, but he still needs either money or the accolades, depending on his role. I bet he's a scientist. He'll want to keep doing that, which means he'll share his thoughts and breakthroughs with someone. If it's not him, then the other will try to cash in. That is who I'm looking for."

"Makes sense." Sankar shooed Akoni out of the command chair to clear the area in front of it where he stood to pilot the ship.

A message came through while he was bringing the flight systems online. It contained the approval and navigation instructions to bring the ship onto the same pad they'd used last time.

The intercom snapped and crackled, then hissed when Sankar tried to tell the group they were underway.

"I'll get on that," Akoni said, returning to his console and checking system statuses.

After a brief review, he jumped up and hurried away, shouting down the passage that the ship was on its way to Medved Seven.

"That's one way to do it." Sankar chuckled and accelerated the freighter at the speed of a marble forcing its way through cold grease.

Koni stood on the landing pad, arms crossed as he impatiently waited for the *Bilkinmore* to land. The ship lumbered in smoothly and touched down. The rear cargo ramp descended and Akoni strolled off by himself, then a small wolf ran past him on its way to the edge of the landing pad. A Wolfoid ran after him calling for, "Crassius!"

Akoni never looked at his teammate's antics. His focus was on his brother. He strode up to him with the confidence he had gained from being a valued member of Sankar's crew.

He didn't bother with a preamble. "I need access to the government databases for a detailed search for new technology."

"I told you not to come back here, and then you tell me you have something worth my while. I suspect you don't have what you promised, *Runt*."

"Knowing that it exists is a rare piece of information. Energy shields for spaceships. The technology is no longer simply theoretical, but the one with the design has gone into hiding. I need to find him and the information he has."

"And then what, Runt? Are you going to steal it? Is that what my family has become? I always thought you'd be a useless toad, but not a criminal. Your time in an Oteran prison turned you into a vile and disgusting creature."

Akoni smacked his lips and tossed his head back and forth before pulling the Ursoid pistol from his belt and charging into his bigger brother. He hit him under the chin and delivered a knee to Koni's ample belly that sent him staggering back. Akoni jumped on him and rode him to the ground, then shoved the pistol into his mouth.

Koni's eyes flashed wide with the realization that his brother had become dangerous.

"You are going to help me, or I have no use for you," Akoni growled. He pushed harder, driving the barrel deeper into Koni's mouth. "A soft pull on the trigger, and your torment ends. Or maybe that's your torment of me—your ridicule, your juvenile boasting. Are you going to link me through to the databases, or am I going to end you? If I blast a hole through the back of your thick skull, then I don't have to share anything with you. I believe that works better. What do you think?"

Sankar eased into Akoni's view to let him know he was there. The tiger appeared by Akoni's feet and inched forward to sniff Koni's face.

Akoni pulled the pistol out of his brother's mouth. "What will it be?"

"You have changed, brother," Koni coughed and swallowed. "Very well. What is it to me if you search an open database or three? I want the shields or screens or whatever you call them. And I want them functional, as in, you stay here until they are installed and working."

"You need me? Is that what I just heard?" Akoni stood and backed away. He held the pistol waist-high, aimed at his brother, and kept his finger on the trigger.

"Oh stop being so melodramatic," Koni gusted, rubbing his belly where his brother had assaulted him. "I *always* needed you, Akoni. Yes, I made your life hell a lot of the time. It's just what older brothers are supposed to do. It was never personal. And you've got nothing to prove to me! Not anymore, okay?"

Akoni blinked several times, then lowered his weapon.

"The one who funded the research and development of the technology is keen to get it in his hands," Akoni said. "That's who we work for, now. That's who we'll deliver the tech to. I'm going to tell him the cost of recovering the screens is to give copies to you. Fair enough?"

"Fair enough," Koni said.

Akoni nodded and looked at Bayane. "Can you bring half a cart of fresh meat into the control center?"

"I can do that."

Koni pointed at a side entrance. "Bring it through that door. We don't need to let anyone else know what we have. Not yet, anyway."

They knew what he meant. After helping himself to the choicest cuts, he'd share with the rest of his crew. Koni was all about Koni.

A rough-looking ship angled in to land on the pad on the opposite side of the operations building.

"We'd better get out of the open," Sankar said. Koni hurried away but stopped to look at Sankar and the small tiger.

"You probably don't want to bring that inside."

Sankar knew he was right. "I'll help Bayane. We'll be there soon."

Akoni walked side by side with his brother, a fragile peace between the two that promised to strengthen.

CHAPTER FIFTEEN

"How do you have this?" Akoni wondered.

"They thought it was easier for me to have direct access to find what broke, sooner, to fill needs before they had to ask. The security and merchant fleets break down more than anyone suspects. We have a ship right now scavenging parts for a broken Riggs-class freighter ferrying supplies to a military outpost. They have to get in and out quickly. We had everything set up for them before the rescue ship arrived."

"Efficiency at its finest." Akoni dug deeper, looking for elements of the technology based on the information Maglor had shared. The screens needed a list of sub-components, each unique and challenging to sell.

That was what made his search different from anyone else who was looking for Breon. It was easy for a name and an average face to disappear on Medvegrad. It wasn't so easy to peddle unique technology.

After half a day searching through the security and commercial databases, he switched to academic. "This is moronic," Akoni complained. Sankar tried to look over his shoulder, but he blocked the screen. Sankar didn't have enough motivation to stand after listening to Akoni talk to himself all day. Bayane had surrendered earlier and returned to the ship.

The smell of a grilled bovine reached them. Just wisps, not anything an Ursoid could pick up, but Sankar's Tigroid senses registered the scent loud and clear.

"Do you think Koni will be able to hook us up with personal comm devices?"

"Like, handheld wireless?" Akoni asked without taking his eyes off the screen.

"Exactly like that."

"Yes, but these are for Ursoid hands, not your tiny little cat paws."

"Didn't you people ever hear of miniaturization?" Sankar started pacing around the room.

"These are small enough. Do you want comms or not?" He leaned back, grinning.

"I'll take what I can get. It'll be better than nothing, which is what I have now. Maybe we'll take a side trip to Oterosan. Why are you so happy?"

He pointed at the screen.

Sankar looked at it briefly before giving up. "My Ursoid is a little rough. Maybe you can give me an executive summary?"

"The cycling power source and translational module that are the foundations of the shield technology. And look at the name of the designer." He stabbed a big finger at the screen. Sankar crossed his arms and waited. "Nober. An anagram."

"How has this guy not been found?" Sankar shook his head.

"Ours is not to question why." Akoni transferred the information to a memory stick he'd acquired from his brother.

"Did you scan that thing?"

Akoni laughed. "I see you understand. I removed two viruses and two separate input-tracking programs before I did anything, then scrubbed it further before reformatting a locked-down area that is password-protected. Koni will get nothing from this."

They passed through the kitchen on their way out. A massive fan pointed toward an open window loudly droned with its efforts.

"I can still smell it," Sankar said.

"But they can't." Koni chuckled as he flipped a massive hunk of meat in an aged and stained pan. "A little butter, salt, and the finest cut this planet has ever seen. My compliments to you and your rancher. When is the next shipment?"

"We're taking these." Akoni unplugged a four-pack charger and picked it up with its four comm units still inserted. "It all depends if we survive the trip to Medvegrad. We need to get going."

"Do not forget to stop here on your way out. You will need me again. I know it." He dipped his head to pass his snout over the pan. "You can have whatever parts you need if you can keep us in fresh bovine. You have my word on that, Akoni."

Akoni studied the beatific expression on his brother's face. "Akoni," he had said. He never used his younger brother's name. Was that grudging respect?

"We will not forget, but if they are chasing us, we'll need to escape any way we can. I give you my promise that we'll be back when we can make it."

"That will do, little brother. Good luck." Koni shut off the stove and slapped his lunch on the serving platter he was using as a plate. He sat down with a knife in one hand and a fork in the other.

"This would be a good picture of you."

Koni shook his head. "We can't let the crew know that I might have skimmed part of our take on the latest deal. They should expect it. This is me, after all. As soon as I finish, I'll inform them, while you'll be well on your way home."

Akoni waved and headed out. The sound of a knife raking across a plate and a long moan of gratification followed them down the hall.

"That was easy," Sankar said. They walked outside and made a direct line toward the *Bilkinmore*.

"Getting to Breon will not be. I'll need you to drop me off on the outskirts of Medved Central, and I'll work my way to him."

Sankar yanked Akoni's arm. "You know what that means? We can hit the archaeological site, too. We have comms. Call when you need us to pick you up."

Akoni started walking to the ship again. "I like how you never forget about your main mission. We're going to have some detours, but in the end..."

"Prepare the ship for immediate departure," Sankar announced. "We're going to Medvegrad."

"You found him?"

"We think so, and while Akoni is working his magic, we'll be digging holes in the dirt."

"Come on!" Bayane threw his hands up before calling for Crassius. The small wolf trotted up to him, and Bayane hugged him like a stuffed toy.

"What would you have us do?" Sankar asked.

"Something else..." Bayane mumbled into Crassius' fur.

"Digging to find the truth is what we're out here to do. Sometimes, it's in a museum, and other times, it's in the dirt. Get the ship ready to go. Time is wasting."

Junak was in the cockpit plotting their course. "Heading to Central, I assume?" The astrogator kept tapping his screen and adjusting flight paths as the software delivered the waypoints on a complex in-system transit. "We can be there on the ground in six hours."

"Running the checklist now." A red light flashed at him. Sankar didn't bother with the intercom. "Bayane! Shut the cargo bay door!"

He checked the next system as the engines came online. The light started to flash before going out.

"Thank you!" he shouted over his shoulder. Deathblade strolled in and leapt into the cart to curl up and sleep.

Akoni appeared. "Comm charger and units are in the rec room." He ran through his pre-flight checklist. "All systems are good. Take her out, Captain."

"Roger on clear. Systems are go, scanners are operational, and the sky is open. We are clear of the landing pad and rising at a mind-numbing acceleration of point two. Maybe Maglor can help us find a better ship? This thing is trash."

"This thing doesn't look like a threat," Akoni countered.

"And this thing rides the gravity waves better than the *Four-Claw* because it has a shape designed specifically for that," Junak added. "I like having a lot of space. Look at the size of our rooms. Maybe the Ursoids are on to something with their oversized gear."

"Have you seen the handheld comm units?" Sankar asked.

Junak hung his head before getting back to work finalizing the course. "Where are we going to drop you off, Akoni?"

The Ursoid moved to the astrogator's position and pointed over his shoulder at a map of Medved Central. He expanded the image until he had a picture of a small spaceport outside the city limits.

"I will need some bajingos. You can transfer them into my account, which I'll be able to access once in the city. Did you find where Maglor transferred the quarter advance?"

Sankar grumbled to himself as he brought up the external link. "I did. It was in my truth-hunting account, which is a bit disconcerting. That is, it was a secret account."

"Big money people don't move in the same circles as the little people. That's us if you haven't figured it out."

"Maglor made us painfully aware of that, as did your brother."

"And we're making others realize we're not to be trifled with, as evidenced by Koni's change of heart."

"You shoved your pistol down his throat."

"I was making a point."

"Would you have killed him?"

Akoni considered the question at length, then said, "He believed that I would. That's what matters."

Deathblade yowled at the noise, getting up and turning around to reposition himself.

"It's a hard thing to carry through on a threat," Sankar mused. "If we find the complete package of details for the screens, how far will we go to relieve Breon of them? Maglor wants the tech for exclusive sales. If we give it to everyone on the way out, we impact his competitive advantage. He may not like that."

"He may have no choice. It all depends on Breon. We're angling to take something he has. Maglor's probably not going to be too keen about it. I expect a fight, and I'm not sure I'm willing to kill him for the information."

"Then subterfuge is our weapon."

Junak transferred the final course to the pilot's station. Sankar adjusted the ship's flight path and rolled in front of the first gravity wave. He set the ship on autopilot and checked the time: three hours before the next course change.

"I'll be back," Sankar told those on the command deck.

"I have to get ready," Akoni replied.

"You have the chair, Junak. It's all you." Akoni went for his quarters while Sankar went to the cargo bay. They acquired more equipment and parts at each stop. He wasn't sure if he was supposed to be bothered by that or accept it as part of driving a freighter.

Or flying a ship where space wasn't at a premium, like living in an ancestral home for one's whole adult life. The accumulation of stuff was a threat to mobility. Sankar stopped by the lab on his way down the corridor.

Gwarzo was finally upright and starting to connect equipment. Bayane was elbow-deep, holding a metal bracket and wincing at the effort while Gene attempted to align bolts. Sankar would have reversed their roles, but this was Gene's show.

Bayane's eyes pleaded with Sankar. He helped stabilize the load until the bolts were started and ready to be tightened. Bayane rubbed his arms while glaring at the Goroid.

"The joy of setting up one's lab. What if we find at the very end that we are missing a tiny but critical adaptor?"

Bayane's jaw dropped open, and Gwarzo started to laugh.

Sankar tried to reassure his new friend. "You were elbows-deep in dust and old stuff. In the lab, we took everything. The only way we wouldn't have taken something was if it wasn't there."

"We shall see," Gene replied. The wolf trotted through the open door. "Look who's here." Crassius walked past Gene first before sniffing Bayane's hands.

Deathblade strolled in. Crassius ignored him.

"It appears we have a truce. Keep plugging away, Gene, and be ready to receive new samples. We'll be hitting the site on Medvegrad after we drop off Akoni."

"We're not going with him?"

"This team looks like a flashing beacon that says 'come arrest us.' So, no. We're not going with him."

"Fair enough. I don't want to spend any more time in prison. Please make sure that doesn't happen since I might go on a killing spree. It won't be pretty."

"I don't know if you're joking or not, but I don't want to go to prison either. Definitely not a Medvegradian one. Or any one, if I'm to be perfectly clear."

Sankar continued to the cargo bay, where he looked for equipment to help them penetrate deeper into the ruins. Metal to use as pry bars. Flat pieces to use as shovelheads. He pulled the welder out of the damage control locker and set up an area to fabricate the gear they would need.

Upstairs, Akoni rummaged through his quarters as if looking for something he knew was there.

Akoni used the callsign Veracity One to get clearance for a planetary landing.

"Now everyone knows our secret group name."

"Nothing can stop the truth!" Akoni shouted, making Junak jump.

Sankar chuckled and shook his head. "Nothing at all, my big friend."

Akoni hoisted a small pack onto his shoulder and headed for the airlock. "I'll check in every six hours but keep my comm off in between to conserve the battery. You keep yours on in case I need to contact you early, in which case, speed will be of the essence."

Sankar guided the ship in, taxied closest to the exit gates, and settled to the landing pad.

"Good luck," Sankar told him.

"Don't forget to come get me."

"You have money. You have purpose. And you're home. It would be hard not to have second thoughts, but I want you to come back to us. I don't want you to forget you're part of this crew."

"Where else can a bear have cats and dogs as pets?" He roared at his joke.

He continued to laugh as the outer hatch popped and waved over his shoulder while descending the extended ramp. It retracted when Sankar closed the hatch. Once back in the pilot's seat, he yelled, "Taking off."

The *Bilkinmore* lifted into the air and headed north on a loop away from the city before flying in a massive circle to come at the archaeological site from the far side.

Akoni strolled toward a security shack. He waved at the disinterested guards inside and continued through the gate into the outskirts of Medved Central. A small shop stood on a corner nearby. He walked in, purchased a Georgy snack bar of meat and berries, and asked the clerk to call a taxi cab for him.

"Use your own phone."

"I'm a weary traveler recently dropped off at the spaceport. I have no such device, only the desire to get a place near the research institute and visit some old friends before I'm back on the freighter for another year of indentured servitude. Throw me a bone, man."

"You're a slave?"

"In everything but name. But this next year relieves my family's debt, and then I'll be free. Maybe I'll be able to get on at the institute. I've learned a great deal on the ship because there is a lot of time to study. Our engineer is the kindest soul." Akoni smiled peacefully.

"I love a good story. You aren't much bigger than a cub. I bet your life has been hard. Expand your mind; that's what the missus tells me. With all of this?" He took in the expanse of the small shop. "I've my hands full. But the youth. Education never stops, does it?"

The shopkeeper tapped his phone, then tapped it some more, apologizing for not knowing a number he'd never called before. He finally realized success and connected with the rides for hire.

"They'll be ten minutes."

Akoni shook hands with the other in gratitude for the man's kindness. He interfaced manually with the pay system, inputting the numbers from memory. He paid the zeno double and took a second Georgy bar.

"You're helping me make this a great day." Akoni bowed his head to the rotund Ursoid behind the counter. He strolled outside and waited, thinking ahead. The rest of his day depended on what he found at the institute.

CHAPTER SIXTEEN

Sankar clenched his jaw and made minor adjustments to their flight path. To the casual observer, the ship would disappear off screens as it went from one remote colony to the next. They took their time on the way to the dig. He flexed and stretched as they cleared the last waypoint.

He took the ship to the treetops and maneuvered through the lowest areas to hide their approach. He split his attention between the holographic display and the front viewscreen. They weren't in a hurry, so he pushed it closer, enjoying the piloting, even if the *Bilkinmore* was a flying crate.

An angry, high-pitched snarl came from the passage. "What's going on out there?" Sankar called over his shoulder.

Junak stepped onto the command deck carrying the small domestic cat. "Since you knotheads brought your pets out, I brought mine. She's a little afraid, though. Bayane's uncouth beast appears to be less than taken with Supernova."

"You call your cat 'Supernova?'"

"And?" Junak pressed.

Sankar didn't look up. He kept the ship on course as he leaned into the controls to keep the ship out of the treetops. "And nothing. Introduce them properly, and they'll get along like family. We're going to need to leave the ship, and we can all go if we have these three guarding it for us. Otherwise, one of us has to stay behind. That almost did us in back on Cornelior."

"At this point in time, I find myself forced to add that there's something that has almost done us in everywhere we've gone. When is our luck going to run out, Sankar?"

Sankar guided the ship toward the archaeological site, picking a spot clear of the main area. A tent was set up on the far side of the extensive ruins. Sankar landed far enough away that whoever was at the site couldn't be sure the ship had been anything more than a tourist fly-by.

"Seems like our luck is going to be pushed once more," Sankar replied while powering down the ship's systems. "I don't know, Junak. I don't know if we should go faster or slower to be safer. I think we're going to live on the razor's edge from here on out. Every step is a chance for a misstep."

Junak bowed his head but nodded.

Bayane appeared, Crassius at his side. The wolf snarled, and Bayane gripped its ear until it stopped. "Here," he told Junak and took the cat out of his arms to hold in front of the other creature's face. The cat slapped the wolf's snout seven times in rapid succession. The call to play was on, and Crassius dipped his chest to the floor. Bayane put the cat down.

"They're fine now."

The cat vaulted over the wolf, dug its claws into the bigger beast's back, and launched into the corridor. The wolf trotted after it.

"We ready to check things out?" Bayane asked, blocking Junak from running after his pet.

"I think we wait until nightfall," Sankar kept the scanners active, adjusting them to get a view of anything higher than a blade of grass. "I'm surprised at how well these work on the ground."

"Ursoid technology," Bayane stated. "It's the best stuff from all the races. There's no doubt that's why Maglor partnered with someone from Medvegrad."

"Looks like we're alone. I don't see anyone out there. Maybe a reconnaissance is in order?"

"Let me," Junak offered. "I feel like a third wheel around here. You know I can move through the woods silently, not like an Ursoid." He stabbed a thumb over his shoulder as if Akoni were behind him, but it was only Bayane.

Sankar nodded. "Take a Goroid stunner and an Ursoid comm device."

"Will those work on these great furry beasts?" Bayane wondered.

"Let us know if you find out. Better yet, don't get into a place where you have to use one. Move like the wind."

"Like a whisper over a whitewater stream," Junak suggested.

"Being invisible will be your best defense. Take a look at the screen." They returned to the cockpit, and the two Tigroids studied the three-dimensional images showing the layout of the site and that it was clear of targets.

"Got it."

Bayane handed over a stunner and patted him on the shoulder. "I'll do it if you don't want to," he offered.

Junak shook his head. He shouldered the backpack with the comm device that kept his hands free and snapped the stunner onto his belt. They popped the hatch and Junak ran outside, quickly disappearing into the undergrowth. They closed the hatch and waited. Deathblade sniffed the air that had crept in during the short time the door was open. He looked from Sankar to the door and back.

"If I let you out, will you come back?" Sankar asked the tiger.

"You sold us on delivering these creatures to their freedom. Is the ship just a bigger cage for them? A gold-plated cage, mind you, but not freedom?" Bayane asked.

Sankar opened the hatch again, and the tiger ran outside. He closed the hatch behind him.

"If you love them, set them free. If they come back, they love you, too. Or they're hungry." Bayane winked and headed upstairs. Sankar returned to the command deck and watched as the scanners tracked Junak's progress away from the ship. Deathblade didn't appear on the screen. Sankar felt emptiness clawing at his insides.

Akoni cast his gaze on the blocky architecture common in Medved Central. A sign on the fence said the buildings beyond were the Traklan Research Institute. Despite the fence, the gates stood open, with no one on guard. Akoni strolled through like a casual visitor.

Being short gave him the advantage that others might consider him a juvenile without taking a second look.

He used that, lightening his step and walking like a starry-eyed teen ready to take on the fast-paced world of higher education. Inside the first building, an information desk stood front and center. Akoni approached with his shtick well-rehearsed.

"Good morning!" he called happily. "I'm looking for a lecture on a cycling power source and translational module. That is some fantastic research!"

The guard looked up at him from his seat. "A what? No. Don't say it again. That stuff makes my ears bleed."

"It is a research institute. I thought everyone here would be equally excited by the theoretical physics turned into real-world applications. Fascinating stuff!"

"If you say so." He picked up his magazine and held it in front of his face.

"The cycling power source and translational module are the work of a Professor Nober. Maybe you can just point me in his direction. I think one of his calculations is off and would like to discuss it."

"Nober..." The guard put his magazine down. He tapped a screen in front of him.

"There's no one at the institute by that name."

"I am destroyed!" Akoni declared, throwing a hand over his heart and falling to the high counter, leaning across it and giving his best puppy-dog eyes to the guard.

"Get off my counter."

"Translational module. Maybe you can look it up. I must have gotten the name wrong."

"If I find it, will you go away?"

"Most assuredly. We cannot abide incorrect calculations on such groundbreaking discoveries."

"Of course not." He pointed at the building opposite where he sat. "Third floor, Office Seven. Professor Magilon."

"Magilon! Superb. I shall bother you no more, good sir." Akoni bounded out the door to reward the guard for his help.

On the walk across the compound, Akoni scanned for other security, cameras, and an escape route. When he continued into the building, no one questioned him. Up the stairs to the third floor and to Office Seven.

A handwritten sign was taped to the door. "Back after lunch."

Akoni checked the time. He had a few hours to kill. He needed to look for a place to stay, but then again, lunch sounded like a better idea.

Junak hadn't been an outdoor Tigroid. His pursuits had always been more cerebral, more technical. He never filled out like his cubmates. When he went into the military, they had taught him the essential skills, even though he was destined for space.

But he remained a Tigroid. The nature of his being was most at home in the rough wood. He had taught himself otherwise, but he wanted to make a point to the crew. He walked without a sound, as Tigroids did, staying low to slink sinuously through the undergrowth and keep the leaves and branches from shaking and giving away his position.

He made it to the cleared section of the ruins. To stay hidden, he had to adopt a circuitous route to the other side. Junak remained in the woods and heavy brush, keeping the ruins to his left as he moved toward his goal, the tent. Movement caught his eye—a small tiger he knew was Deathblade. He wondered if he had escaped through the open hatch when Junak had gone through.

I didn't look behind me, he thought, cursing himself for not making sure. He was convinced Sankar would be angry. The cat strutted through the center of the ruins on a direct line toward the tent on the far side.

Junak hurried, accepting his brushes with the leaves and branches to keep pace with Deathblade.

He stopped when the cat stopped. Junak sniffed the air, looking for anything that smelled like it didn't belong, but nature was overwhelming: green, pollen, the air, and a hint of decay. Junak matched the tiger's pace when it resumed its journey.

As Junak closed on the tent, he dropped to all fours and crawled forward, remaining under the brush until he could see. The small tiger stopped outside the tent, sat, and licked its paw to groom its face.

A head appeared within the darkened rectangle of the tent's entrance. The Ursoid youth said something over his shoulder and stepped outside.

"Here, kitty, kitty," he called. Others appeared, eight before an elderly adult lumbered out, supporting himself with a cane. Not big but grossly overweight, the elder called for the children to take care.

Deathblade danced back to remain out of reach until he drew them away from the tent. Then, like an orange and black flash, he darted around them and into the tent. One youth ran after him. Seconds later, the cat emerged carrying a haunch of meat a third his size. It slowed him down, but not enough for the children to catch up. He loped into the ruins on his way back to the *Bilkinmore*.

Junak lost sight of him quickly. Some children ran into the tent while others took a few steps after Deathblade. The elder chuckled and called for them to come back. They rallied around him.

He explained the joys of nature and that he had more food than they needed but that they had best secure their provisions if they wanted to eat again before they were picked up in the morning. He told them he'd pass the warning to the next group of campers.

They trooped back into the tent before securing the flap against more wild beasts. Junak retreated to where they couldn't see him before walking into the open. With the youth group secured in the tent, he had the opportunity to check out the main structure at the site. In the depths of it, according to Sankar, there was a chamber that had not been discovered.

He hurried through the open area to the rising jumble of the partially restored pyramid-shaped building. Junak thought it looked alarmingly like one on Oterosan. His whiskers lay flat against his face as he jumped over a small fence and a roped-off entrance. Inside, he found a crude door secured with a padlock that hung open. He took it off and put it in his pocket to keep anyone from locking it behind him. He opened the door, wincing at the squealing hinge. He let it stand open as he went through, then waited for his eyes to adjust to the darkness beyond.

His Tigroid eyes adjusted quickly, and he could make out shapes and the way ahead even in the near-total black. Junak followed the corridor down and took a left at the t-intersection. As an astrogator, he had a gift for remembering maps and directions. He continued on the path Sankar had shown him.

To the bottom of the ruins. Even his cat eyes couldn't penetrate into the darkness. He used the emergency light they all carried because *Bilkinmore* could break at any time. Light could mean the difference between life and death on board a spaceship.

The room that appeared under the rays of the broad beam was exactly as he'd expected, based on the documents found in the Temple of Spheenix. A short passage was supposed to lead to another chamber, but a wall blocked the way. Not a walled doorway, but a complete wall that revealed no cracks or hints that anything was hidden behind it. Junak tapped, but it all sounded like solid stone. He checked the chamber, memorized the dimensions after walking it off, and headed out, keeping his light on as he retraced his steps.

At the top, he flinched at the door's squeal even though he'd expected it. He kept the lock, just in case.

He checked the open area before running toward the clearing where the ship was hidden.

CHAPTER SEVENTEEN

Akoni knew he had eaten too much, but it was home cooking and far better than what he got on the ship, although the meat was nowhere near as good as the fresh bovine they'd been enjoying.

He browsed a newspaper someone had left on a nearby table and made himself at home in the large café that saw more than its fair share of refugees from the institute. Most hurried in, ate quickly, and ran off. He ate casually, read the inane news of the day, and watched his fellow Ursoids.

It gave him a certain amount of comfort to be on his home planet surrounded by his kind, but it also gave him pause. His family had never appreciated him, only tolerating him because he was good with academics. Excelled even, but it wasn't enough.

He would catch *Bilkinmore* and leave Medvegrad no matter what happened in his search for the mysterious Breon. Akoni checked the time, folded the newspaper, dropped it on the table, and strolled out on his way back to the third floor.

For a second time, no one bothered him when he walked through the gates and to the building with the professor's office.

Three flights of stairs later, he found the door still closed and the sign in place. Akoni walked down the hallway to a bench, took a seat, and waited.

"I'm on my way in," Junak said into his comm unit's microphone. When he reached the ship, he found Deathblade waiting by the hatch, a haunch in his mouth.

The hatch opened, and the tiger loped inside. Sankar beamed like a proud parent.

"Don't be so proud of your so-called hunter. He juked the youth camper group and stole their lunch. He's not a hunter, he's a thief."

Deathblade remained oblivious to Junak's characterization and dragged the haunch up the stairs, leaving a greasy trail in his wake. Sankar wondered if it would end up on his bed.

"You've confirmed there are people here. But a youth group?" Sankar stared at the wall and contemplated the implications. No threat except in their curiosity. "Adults?"

"An ancient Ursoid. Doesn't move too fast, but they are leaving in the morning, and a new group will be dropped off."

Sankar blew out a breath and shook his head.

"There's more. We can get into the pyramid and to the bottom, but there's a wall that we'll have to get through. It looks like a solid wall, which is probably the reason they haven't gone through it." Junak held up the lock and shook it.

"The lock to your chastity belt?" Sankar quipped. "Or is that the lock to the pyramid?"

"Very funny, but yes. The main door to the subterranean chamber. It squeals, too, so we'll need a lubricant for when we go back tonight. Let's get this thing done before the new group arrives."

Sankar nodded. "There's no way we'll be able to put it back like it was no matter how hard we work tonight." He led the way into the cockpit and brought up the map on the main screen.

"I wish this thing was to scale," Junak complained.

"It's two thousand years old. We're lucky to have it. They didn't have graph paper back then."

"They should have!" Junak used his finger and knuckle to measure the image. He went through the process twice while Sankar waited. "I think they built a false wall to hide the final chamber as opposed to blocking the short corridor. Makes me wonder why."

"Demons from the abyss? Or they knew about grave robbers even back then." Sankar stared at the map. "It looks like this?"

"Exactly like that. You have a map of this site, and the fact that it was discovered in the Temple of Spheenix archive is most illuminating."

Sankar one-arm-hugged his friend. "You sound like an academic *and* a Heretic. My father recognized the importance, but he couldn't voice his revelation aloud. It had to be condemned as heresy, but they didn't destroy it simply because of the age and the opportunity to disprove its importance. I think they couldn't, and that's why they buried it."

"Do you know what we're supposed to find in there?"

"No, but my father thought it would be the keystone in the arch connecting the Hinteran people. One people, springing from a single source."

"I know what a keystone is, but I don't know what it'll look like in that chamber. Maybe it's like pornography. We'll know it when we see it."

"That's my hope," Sankar agreed.

"That it's pornography?" Junak clapped him on the back and started to laugh. He strolled off the command deck on his way upstairs. When he reached the upper deck, he shouted back down the stairs. "Sankar, you'll want to see this."

Sankar bolted from the cockpit and flew up the stairs. Junak stood by the mess, arms crossed, leaning against the doorframe. Sankar peeked in to find the three animals sharing the haunch. The domestic cat worked on a small piece of meat while the wolf and the tiger split the other half. All three crouched over their food.

"A peace treaty has been signed, it seems. I'm just thankful that thing wasn't on my bed. It also suggests that the campers are eating well. I wonder what Akoni would have to say about it. Is this the rich kids? Or maybe it's commonplace. We won't know because all things being equal, we'll be out of here before their ride arrives." Sankar strolled in and bent down to pet the tiger. It growled, and he growled back before giving its ears a vigorous scratch. He stopped when he passed Junak. "Good job out there. You collected the intel and answered all the questions. Tonight, we go in as soon as it's dark and for as long as the kids are tucked in their beds. What kind of equipment will we need?"

"You have it ready. Lights, pry bars, and maybe bring a plasma torch to help break out some of the ancient mortar, but these guys were good with their rock-cutting. There is just enough in between the stone blocks to keep air from flowing through. Do we have a rock-boring tool?"

Sankar chuckled. "No."

"Pity." Junak smiled at his friend. "A hammer and chisels then, to open up enough space to get the pry bars in. And Gwarzo to add some muscle."

"We're all going. This is what we came here for. We're not going to half-ass it."

A middle-aged Ursoid strode down the hall, eyes fixed on Akoni. He stopped in front of the door to Office Number Seven and removed the sign.

Akoni waved like a little kid. "Professor Magilon! Great to see you. I have a question regarding the translational module."

The youthful exuberance disarmed the man, even though Akoni was probably the same age as the professor. He led the way into his office. Akoni closed the door behind him and flipped the lock.

"What was your question?" Magilon sat behind his desk and leaned back. Akoni held the Goroid stunner in his hand.

"Where's the screening tech, Breon?" Akoni had decided to take the direct approach. He didn't have time for subterfuge.

The other Ursoid looked startled—but only for an instant. Then recovered himself.

"How did you find me?"

Akoni snorted. "You can't help yourself. You invented something that no one else has been able to get beyond the theoretical stage. Theoretical physics to pragmatics. Better engineering through breakthroughs. You are to be complimented. And keep your hands where I can see them."

Breon laced his thick paw-fingers behind his head and leaned back. "I'll never tell you where it is."

"Then our instructions are to kill you. I can do it right here, right now, if you wish. That'll settle things, and I can go on about my business. Have a care about me, please. This isn't all about you." Akoni moved closer to the desk. He remained standing to keep as much of Breon in sight as possible.

"I don't understand." The professor looked confused.

"If you're not going to hand over the tech you devised, then Maglor determined that it was best if no one had it. He can start over with someone else. Tell me for my own edification. Me and the boys have a bet. I think you took Maglor's money for your research and then balked when the screens actually worked. It makes me think you're the scumbag and not Maglor. He's always been upfront about what he wants the tech for."

"He's an arms dealer." Breon raised his head after playing his trump card.

"Of *course* he's an arms dealer. You had to know that before you took his money. What does that make you?"

"Wait! I *didn't* know that. Not until just now."

Akoni shook his head slowly, judgingly. "You are smart enough to break through the energy screen limitations, which tells me that you knew who you were climbing in bed with. And you're a terrible liar. So, I have an alternative proposition."

Breon hung his head and looked into his lap. "How much do you want?"

"No amount of money can save either one of us. If I don't complete this mission, then I'll be in the same boat as you. Since I don't want people like me coming after me, I'll save your life. If you don't want to turn over the tech, then fine. We'll go to Maglor, and you can explain to him why you're not going to give him what he paid for."

"You can't take me to him."

"I can, and I will. Either in a box, or self-propelled. If I have to off you, there will be a mess and logistics issues. Like I said before, this isn't all about you. You should consider my challenges and how they affect me." Akoni knew he was taunting the Ursoid because he'd been on the receiving end of such his whole life.

Breon screwed up his face as he thought through his options, and his eyes widened when he came to the conclusion that his luck had run out. He jumped to his feet.

Akoni pulled the trigger, and the shock jolted Breon back into his seat. The professor shook and vibrated as if a seizure had taken him, but remained conscious. His breath caught, and he gasped, then struggled to breathe normally again.

"That was the lightest setting because I wanted to get your attention. I can do this all day since these Goroid stunners are marvelous pieces of technology. Maybe it's best if you collect your notes and your engineering and let's go. We have to catch our ride."

"Bring your tech. No sense in trying to hide it because that will be the only thing that saves your life. I see that you are a stranger to pain. How much are you willing to put up with, or rather, how much do you think you can tolerate? I'm not into torture personally, but Maglor has people who seem overly fond of it. I wouldn't mess with him any more than you already have. Life can be good, and judging by what I see here, you like the good life. I think it can be yours once again if you deliver the screens and then look to improve on them. Maglor wants his ship to be the most powerful in the known universe. He won't kill you as long as you are working toward that goal. On the way, you're going to hook us up with the tech, too. Just because we need it to stay alive. Working for Maglor has significant risks."

Breon chuckled softly. "You got that right." He stood up, a little shaky. "Follow me."

Akoni stepped back, suspecting more duplicity. He held the stunner with his finger on the trigger.

In the office's private latrine, Breon removed a medicine cabinet above the sink and set it on the floor. He reached inside. Akoni held the stunner steady.

Breon held out a folder, a memory stick, and a squarish module with three wires.

"Here. Take it all, but let me go."

"I can't let you go until I've verified this. I hope you understand." Akoni gestured with the stunner toward the door.

"I knew I shouldn't have partnered with Maglor, but he was the only one with sufficient funds to make it happen."

"Now is not the time to second-guess yourself. The deed is done, and the technology, if it works as it's supposed to, is stunning. You are to be complimented on your genius."

The Ursoid smiled, but his eyes were sad as he met Akoni's gaze. "I don't feel like a genius."

"We all have our moments of triumph, punctuated by moments of despair."

Breon packed what he'd pulled from behind the cabinet into a briefcase and threw it over his shoulder. "You have to be the strangest hitman ever. You sound like a philosopher."

"I'll take that as a compliment. But no. I'm an engineer who is in the same position as you—working for the man. Trying to get by, day to day. I'd like to talk with you about your work, but engineer to engineer, and not two minions doing Maglor's bidding."

"I'd like that, too. I've only been able to talk about the elements that make up the end product, and not what the end product is. The screens are a magnificent piece of work. The translational module is the key element. This little piece of equipment, when married with the energy projectors, will wrap a nearly impenetrable shield around an object. I'm proud of the work."

"You have every right to be. But for now, let's go catch a ship."

They proceeded out of the room.

Breon said over his shoulder, "How did you find me?"

"Searched academics pushing a new mode of energy transmission. We expected Maglor to hire a research scientist and knew that's what it would take for a screening system to work. We also knew an academic would publish his work."

"Ah. My profession is my downfall."

"Or your rise. We'll see this thing through until you come out the other side. You'll like our ship and our crew. Down to earth. No judgment. No hair off our ears if you want to be yourself."

"Hair off our ears? Isn't that a Tigroid expression?"

"Now you're onto me. We are a multi-racial crew, which helps us no matter which planet we happen to be on."

"To include a Goroid?"

"Yes. You'll find out about him when you get on board. Until then, it's best not to know too much." Akoni nudged the professor. "I hope you understand."

Akoni was sincere but remained wary. Breon wasn't much taller than Akoni and had probably been in the same boat growing up: too small to be of any use, so he turned to science, where he'd found a home. If he ran, Akoni wasn't sure he'd shoot him. He said a brief prayer to the Tigroids' Furd gods, asking that Breon comply and join them on the *Bilkinmore*.

CHAPTER EIGHTEEN

Sankar watched the scanner display. The children had been out and about but had returned to their tent as nightfall approached. "Time to light this candle."

He stretched on his way to the airlock and found the others lounging in the corridor. Before he could say another word, the Ursoid comm device crackled.

"Catamar One to Catamar Primary. Package is in hand. Requesting pickup."

"On our way. Be there in an hour. Over," Sankar replied.

"Roger. Out." Akoni was brief—to foil any direction-finding equipment.

Sankar twirled his paw-finger in the air. "Time to light a different candle. Let's get this tub into the sky."

Gwarzo and Bayane secured the tools while Junak raced to the cockpit to start running the calculations for their course to Medved Central.

Sankar helped lock down the tools. The lights and the torch went in the damage control cabinet, and they strapped the shovels and picks to the wall.

"I know you guys were ready to do some serious digging," Sankar offered.

Gwarzo twisted his mouth before answering. "I was excited about what we'd find behind that wall. I almost have the genetic sequencers up and running. I'll be ready to test samples within a day, and then after any necessary calibrations, I can run the real stuff. Who knows? We may already have your answer inside the four of us."

"What?" Bayane looked sideways at the Goroid. "You're not drilling a hole in me."

"I can get by with a hair follicle. Are you okay if I yank a hair, or will that hurt too much?"

"What do you mean by yank?" Bayane looked skeptical.

"Don't worry about it, dog. We'll take what we want while you're sleeping," Sankar suggested.

"Wolf, thank you very much. There's a difference." Bayane punched Sankar in the shoulder. "Chow time."

"Nope. Engineering station. Akoni isn't here. You're now first engineer on the Furd one's stellar chariot."

Bayane shrugged before running up the stairs.

"Hey!" Sankar called after him.

"Getting a snack. I'll be there in two wags of a pup's tail."

Sankar started the pre-flight. "I'll keep us low heading out to the north so the happy campers don't see us." One by one, he verified the systems were ready. He fired up the engines as Bayane arrived.

Once the engineer confirmed nominal technical operations, they lifted off. Sankar flew out low but quickly gained enough altitude to increase their speed. The *Bilkinmore* was as sluggish as ever.

Junak sent the updated course to Sankar. With two shortcuts through opportune valleys, the trip would only take forty minutes.

"Give Akoni a call and tell him we'll be early."

Bayane handled the comm. "Catamar One, this is the biggest of all Catamars. Arrival in three niner minutes. I say again, three niner minutes."

"Roger," Akoni replied.

"How about a thank you, Runt?" Bayane told the closed comm channel.

"Scanning." Sankar examined the screen. "It seems busier than the last time we were at that spaceport. A lot busier."

"Which means we're not coming in for an unobtrusive pickup?" Bayane wondered.

"Gimme that mic."

Bayane held the Ursoid comm to the side of Sankar's head and keyed the button.

"Catamar One. What's going on down there? It looks like an air show."

The speaker crackled before Akoni's voice came through. "It's rush hour down here. Just get into the landing queue, and we'll run out to wherever they park you, but the ship looks like half the other ships down here. You'll have to wave or something."

Sankar smiled. Bayane let off the button. "That is the best news I've heard all day, well, besides the fact that Akoni has snagged our comrade already. Which doesn't thrill me because it seems like it was too easy. For what we're getting paid, I would have thought it would have been harder."

Bayane replied, "But Maglor is a Goroid. Maybe he didn't have an Ursoid contact he could trust. Seeing us, he knew we were a pack of misfits who didn't fit anywhere but could get inside because we represent all the races."

"All that we know. There was that one guy at the prison, but that's beside the point. Maybe you're right. Key the mic, please."

Bayane complied.

"Catamar One Three coming in. We'll flash the lights so you can pick us out of the crowd."

"Roger." Akoni signed off.

"I wonder how Akoni convinced Breon to come with him. That seems odd, too. My hackles are up."

Sankar looked over his shoulder. "Relax. We'll be fine. You've got me on the stick. And while you're figuring out the meaning of life, check the engine output. This thing seems to be lagging more than usual."

Bayane took Akoni's position, standing like Sankar. "Down ten percent. There's a leak, and we're losing pressure. Isolated to the main engine compartment. I'll wrap the pipe or hose or whatever it is. I'm sure this symbol means something."

Sankar's mouth dropped open before he turned to face the engineer.

"Got you," Bayane declared and started singing a Wolfoid ditty as he left the command deck.

Sankar looked at Junak for hope. His fellow Tigroid shrugged. "You've assembled a cast of strangers; key part of that word is 'strange.'"

"But they're our strangers." Sankar focused on the holographic display, then activated the comm channel, voice only. "Catamar One Three requesting permission to land and instructions to avoid hitting anyone else."

"You needed to submit your request a week ago in triplicate to get a slot in this afternoon's landing pattern."

Sankar stared at the screen. "We weren't in this system a week ago. Is there anything we can do? We're running low on crew and fuel."

"Nah, I'm having some fun with you. Course three seven, true. Landing pad four-four. It's the farthest one out. You can't miss it. You are third in line."

Sankar blinked rapidly. "Bring up the map."

Junak complied, and the airfield appeared on the display. "I hope Akoni isn't dragging this guy because that looks like an hour-long walk from the gate."

Sankar activated the Ursoid comm unit. "Catamar one, we are at spot four-four. It's as far as possible from the gate. See if you can catch a ride or put on your walking shoes. It's going to be a hike."

"Thanks for that," Akoni replied and cut the line.

They took their place in line on the indicated approach vector and watched as those in front of them descended and settled into spots across the field. *Bilkinmore* rolled in, banked hard, and landed almost immediately. The good news was that they were a long way from prying eyes.

Bayane returned. "Did you notice the surge in power?"

Sankar shook his head. "No. This thing is a scow and will always be a scow."

"I got eight percent back. We'll need to weld a patch over it. It's a hard pipe, and the crack is at the bend."

"Is there any way we can replace it? A crack in the bend suggests structural failure. That thing could come apart when we need it most. I don't want to die in a scow crash."

"You big baby!" Bayane replied. "The patch will reinforce it. We'll weld the crack and then slap the patch over the top, stretching it well down from the compromised joint. It'll be the last thing to fail. Have you been in there? We got bigger problems than a cracked elbow."

"Which means?"

"The more we fly this thing, the more likely it is that you're going to die in a scow crash. It is well past its useful service life."

"When we hit the shipyard, have a list of parts ready. We'll pay for what we need and rebuild as we go."

"I'm not sure that's going to get it, but I'll get started. I need Akoni's help for most of it, though." Bayane strolled away.

Sankar kept the scanners active so he could watch the holographic display to maintain situational awareness. He searched the panel for the external lights, finally finding them after a few taps through the correct screen.

They settled in for a long wait. Junak went upstairs to get something to eat. Bayane was probably eating on his way to the engine room. The creature contingent had eaten their fill of the campers' lunch and would sleep for the rest of the day. Gene had retired to his lab.

After a half-hour, Sankar flashed the lights to highlight the ship to the inbound Ursoids. Sankar popped the hatch and lowered the ramp. When he leaned out, he could see the spaceport spread before him, lit up like a gambling hall. He hurried back inside, closing the inner airlock hatch to keep the pets from getting out, and cycled the lights a few more times to get Akoni's attention.

Sankar took the comm unit outside with him and activated it. "Catamar One, are you out there?"

"Pin your diaper tight. We're almost there. Next time, maybe you can park farther away. Over and out!"

Sankar chuckled until he caught sight of the two Ursoids shambling toward the ship. One was only slightly larger than the other—the intellectual class, unlike the warrior class to which Koni belonged. Command came from size and not intelligence. It was the Ursoid way.

He loped across the ground to them.

"A Tigroid? I thought you were kidding," the taller of the two exclaimed.

"Why would you think I was kidding about that?" Akoni wondered.

Sankar offered to help, but the Ursoids refused. "We have it, little tiger," Breon said.

"My name is Sankar and I'll be your pilot today, so don't give me any of your scat." Breon raised his eyebrow at the unarmed Tigroid before him.

"You don't want to mess with him," Akoni advised. "He beat the hell out of my big brother. Fast as lightning. I'd watch my tongue if I were you."

Breon jerked his head to the side to stare at Akoni, who nodded with raised eyebrows. When Breon looked away. Akoni winked at Sankar.

"You must be Breon. Any way you can get those shields of yours working on this tub?"

"What will Maglor say if your ship arrives carrying the shields he's expecting for *his* ship?"

"We'll cross that bridge when we come to it. In the meantime, we need to survive. We seem to attract the wrong attention."

"Attention from types that try to kill us," Akoni clarified.

"Why am I coming with you? So I can risk dying on the way to *death?*" Breon asked. "You zenos have very odd senses of humor."

"We're the Veracity Corporation," Sankar said, "oddity is our stock in trade!" He led the way into the ship. When he stepped inside, he shouted, "Prepare to lift off! We're going back to the archaeological site. We have some digging to do."

"Do I look like a ditch-digger?" Breon asked.

Sankar looked at him from the entrance to the cockpit. "Do I? Secure the hatch, Akoni. Get our guest settled. We'll be in the air in five minutes."

Akoni led Breon to the upper deck.

Bayane bounded past them on his way to the command deck. He stopped at the bottom of the stairs. "Are you going to handle the engineering console?"

Akoni shook his head and pointed at the Wolfoid.

"I figured but had to ask."

Deathblade chased Crassius out of the mess and toward the rear of the ship, where they headed down the stairs into the cargo bay.

Breon tipped his head back and stared at the ceiling. "What have I done? I'm being punished before being punished. It's like a protracted series of painful events, culminating in an excruciating death."

"This is the good life," Akoni declared. "You're in charge of your own happiness. Accept it, and you'll have a lot better day. Here's your quarters. Give me the shield information, then join us on the flight deck when you're settled."

After Akoni relieved him of his briefcase, he stood there, empty-handed. "What is there to settle?"

"Go to the mess and get yourself something to eat, then. We have fresh bovine, but you have to cook it yourself. And then clean up, too."

"Fresh bovine? I take back my harsh and ill-conceived condemnations of this menagerie."

He hurried down the passage and into the mess. Akoni leaned into the doorway on his way to the cockpit. "And make me one, too."

He made it to the command deck before they took off.

"How long before you can get those shields online?" Sankar asked.

"I have the information right here, but I don't know if we have all the equipment we need or the power."

"About that," Bayane interrupted. "We had a leak on a secondary manifold. I threw a temporary patch on it, but it's going to need a sleeve. Maybe even a new elbow joint. But we're only down two percent on the power. We were down ten."

"What are you knuckleheads doing to my ship?" Akoni chased Bayane away from the engineering station.

Bayane held his hands up and walked away.

"Where are you going? We've got a broke ship to fix."

"And we have a guest on board who would benefit from this ship not being able to fly. What do you say we keep an eye on him?" Sankar looked at the two engineers.

Akoni tapped a few screens before coming to a conclusion. "I'll fix it, and I'll take Breon with me." He ran off. Bayane continued to hold his hands up.

"What are you doing?" Sankar turned his attention back to his flight screens.

"I don't know which way I'm being pulled. What do you want me to do?"

"Watch the screen, and if anything goes ugly, dial up the intercom and yell at Akoni."

"I like that order." Bayane resumed his place standing before the engineering station. He conducted his own pre-flight. "Systems are nominal. Ready for flight."

Sankar activated the external comm system and contacted the tower. "Catamar

One Three requesting immediate departure."

"Course three two six true, climbing to an altitude of one five, bank ninety degrees to the north at the outer marker. Have a pleasant day."

Sankar pulled the controls back and lifted off. He swung the ship to assume the designated heading and climbed slowly. He kept his eye on the screen to maintain his distance from other ships in the air. The seemingly frenetic pace of activity lessened with the loss of daylight. The screens showed mostly clear. When *Bilkinmore* reached the outer marker, Sankar turned the nose to the north and continued to climb until he cleared the city's air control zone.

That was when they dove to treetop level while maintaining acceleration. The ship bumped forward with a surge in power.

"We are at one hundred and five percent power."

"By the Furd gods, don't blow us up! What's Akoni doing back there?"

Bayane ran off before Sankar could clarify that his question was rhetorical. Junak worked furiously to deliver a course to the dig site.

Sankar leaned back in the pilot's chair and watched the screen. The ship continued racing north until Junak delivered the new course. Sankar banked easily on a slow turn that would eventually deliver them to their destination.

Two blips high in the sky turned with *Bilkinmore*, maintaining their distance and mirroring the freighter's speed.

"We have company," Sankar announced. Junak's head snapped around to look at the screen.

"What are we going to do about them?"

"I'm going to hit the ground in a number of spots between here and the site to throw them off."

"And then?"

"We'll dump you and Gene at the pyramid. You are going to break into the underground chamber and find what there is to find. We'll dust off and take them on a wild skeeter chase, and if they get aggressive, we're going to blow them out of the sky."

Gwarzo scowled at the others while he and Junak geared up to take on the underground chamber. They carried two pry bars, two shovels, a vial of lubricant, a drill, a plasma torch, and two bags. They also carried Goroid stunners in case of visitors.

Sankar yelled from the cockpit, "Setting down in five, four, three, two, one. Pop the hatch and go!"

Gwarzo hit the button, and they jumped through the opening to hit the ground running. They took a hard turn to avoid slamming into the pyramid that was between the ship and the tent on the far side of the site. *Bilkinmore* climbed above the trees and headed out.

"Just me and you, Gene, in the middle of nowhere on the bear planet."

"Shush," Gwarzo whispered, holding a long finger to his lips. He slowed and stalked ahead, stopping when he reached the entrance. He squeezed the lubricant onto the two hinges, then slowly worked the door back and forth. The slight squeals faded, and he was able to open the door the whole way.

They turned on their flashlights and shined them down the tunnel. Gene hesitated. "It's not as big a space as you implied."

"Looks big to me. I'll go first." Junak jogged down the slope. Gene grumbled as he followed. His head was near the ceiling, but he didn't have to duck. Junak couldn't understand Gene's discomfort. He slowed. "What's the problem?"

"Goroids live aboveground. A spaceship is pushing it, but *Bilkinmore* is huge, and my lab is the biggest room on the ship."

"This isn't a small space."

"But it's underground." His nostrils flared. "It smells funny."

"It's dry and dusty, which is better for the artifacts. I hope we find a book or a map." Junak looked to see if his attempts to distract the bigger creature were having any effect. "It's not much farther, and then we have to break down a wall. It'll be easy."

"If it were easy, it would have already been done," Gene countered.

Junak shrugged and hurried. He wasn't sure how many breaks Gene would need to take or if he would leave and not come back. "I can't do this alone, big man. I need your help."

"Let's get it done, then, and get out of here." Gene hurried to catch Junak before he rounded the corner. Down and down to the bottom chamber.

They braced their flashlights on the floor to cast the best light. Gene leaned close and studied the wall where Junak indicated the tunnel should be, then moved to the corners and peered at the stonework.

"This wall was put into place after the chamber was built. There is a slight variation in the mortar color, but I doubt you half-blind species would have ever seen it."

"You mean like Bayane, who doesn't see colors at all?"

"Bayane." Gwarzo chuckled. "You know he's playing you, right?"

"What do you mean?" Junak shoved at a gap, trying to get his pry bar in.

"He's probably the smartest one on the ship, but as long as you guys think he's dim, he gets out of the hard jobs. He's smart, but smart zenos are often lazy."

Junak gave up with the pry bar and grabbed the torch. He started to laugh. "That is something. He had me fooled."

"He's very good. Probably has done it his whole life. If you want Breon's shields to work, put him on it." Gene stepped back as Junak lined up on the crack in the middle of what he hoped was the entry to the tunnel. "And as an added incentive, tell him he doesn't get to eat until it's up and running."

"You should have told Sankar before we left. They're probably working on it right now, but if death is the result of it not working, he might surprise them."

Junak hit the torch and carved the mortar away bit by bit, tracing lines around the carved blocks from ceiling to floor. At the bottom, when the mortar was cleared out, the weight of the freestanding rock shifting, Junak jumped backward, shutting off the torch in mid-flight. He hit the ground in a crouch, ready to bolt. His whiskers stood on end.

Gwarzo stepped up and tried to find purchase with his pry bar. At the top, he could get it into the gap but couldn't get enough leverage to pull it out.

"Screw this." Gene braced his legs wide and pushed at the second block down from the top. He grunted, and a rumble grew deep inside his barrel chest. The rock started to slide, and then it was through. The next block up caught as it dropped, half-wedged into the gap. Gwarzo pushed it through as well.

Junak checked the time. They had only been there for an hour.

Gwarzo snapped his fingers as he tried to look through the opening. Junak slapped a flashlight into the Goroid's hand and stood on his tiptoes to see what lay beyond.

The tunnel the original Oteran map had shown. The entrance to the chamber was at a turn, so they couldn't see in.

"Grab your pry bar, and we'll pull these others out." With Gwarzo on one side and Junak on the other, they levered the stone blocks out. They fell with dull thuds onto the stone floor of the chamber, both zenos dancing out of the way to avoid getting a crushed foot.

When there was a two-block gap, Gwarzo hesitated.

"Not again?" Junak took one of the flashlights and headed through, staring at the roof as if it were ready to come down on his head.

"This wasn't a load-bearing wall," Gwarzo told him, remaining in the original chamber.

The tunnel narrowed until an Ursoid would have a hard time squeezing through. Junak shined his light around the chamber. Without taking his eyes off what was inside, he called down the corridor, "You're going to want to see this."

CHAPTER NINETEEN

Sankar shook his head and grumbled to himself. The others were attempting to install the shield technology and bring it to minimal operational capability. They couldn't get any greater functionality without the external mounts, but a functional forcefield could be created around the skin of the ship.

That was what Breon had said.

Bayane had shrugged, and Akoni had looked skeptical. The three had gone to the engine compartment to see what they needed to do.

Sankar needed a friendly face to tell him not to be concerned about the ships on the screen. The group of two had become four, and a new group of two stood off at a much lower altitude.

With a far quicker response time if they turned hostile.

Sankar keyed the intercom. "Akoni, can you join me in the cockpit, please? You need to fly the ship. I have to take the *Four-Claw* out. We have more company than we can ignore."

He landed the ship for a few seconds before lifting off and flying at a tangent to the last course. He hoped to confuse the ones following him. So far, it had worked. No ships had gone to the ruins.

All the attention was on the *Bilkinmore*.

"Isn't that what you wanted?" Sankar asked himself.

"Isn't what you wanted what?" Akoni attempted.

"To draw attention away from the chamber of horrors in the pit of the pyramid."

"When you say it that way, it sounds weird, but that's not why I'm here. What do you need, wildman?"

"You fly this bird. I'm taking the interceptor out."

"Hey! The *Four-Claw*'s power system operates at a hundred twenty percent faster cycle rate than this tug. We wouldn't need an adaptor for the translation module." Akoni moved behind the ship's controls. He tugged like an amateur, and the ship bucked until he settled in. He activated the intercom.

"Breon and Dogface, forget trying to shoehorn that thing into this power system. Install it on the *Four-Claw* instead. Sankar is taking it out to deal with the six ships following us."

He turned off the intercom. "Bayane will have to install it himself. Breon won't be able to get through the hatch."

"I'll help. I know my ship." Sankar stepped into the passage.

Akoni called over his shoulder, "You think you can take six ships?"

"How many do I need to take out before we can escape? No matter what happens, make sure you have a course back to the dig site charted and ready to execute. I don't want to leave without our people."

Sankar headed down the corridor to pre-flight his long-range interceptor. He could already feel the surge of energy that came with flying such a ship.

His face fell when he saw an Ursoid wedged into the open hatch.

"Right there, cross-connect that wire to the two, the red and the green."

"I can't tell them apart!" Bayane shouted.

"Just point to them, and I'll say yes or no," Breon replied with a new sense of calm. "Yes, no, yes." He waited a moment before continuing, "Insulate them against a short. More. Even more. A short would be bad."

"Fry the power system and I plunge to my death in a dead ship bad?" Sankar asked.

"The shield implodes and separates every molecule within the ship, sending a metallic spray to the planet below bad."

"Less pain that way. Tigroid, coming through." Sankar snaked his way over the top of Breon and into the ship. Bayane leaned over an open panel in the floor.

"Give me that." He pointed at a shirt hanging off Junak's bed.

Sankar pulled it out and tossed it to him. "This should hold it in place and shield it from percussive impacts due to someone's erratic flying."

"What are you saying?" Sankar asked, knowing he was being trolled. He took his seat and started cycling through the ship's systems. "You might want to take your hands out of there before something chars your fur."

Bayane closed the panel. He leaned over the pilot. "On your engineering systems screen, you'll see the system we tapped, water recycling. All you have to do is turn the recycler on, and the shields will envelop the ship."

"You may lose thrust momentarily until the antigrav compensates for the change in external force," Breon added.

"Lose thrust. Nice side effect. Anything else I should know?"

"These won't protect you against ion cannons of the type you have on this ship. Sorry. Their projectiles are far too small to be blocked by the screen. Electron gaps. Nothing you can do about it, so avoid anyone with those. But missiles and general concussive or brute-force weapons will bounce off. It's quite remarkable if I do say so myself."

"I'll have to trust you on that." Sankar activated the communications system. "Catamar One Three, this is Catamar Actual. Prepare for immediate departure. Somebody open the cargo ramp, and while you're at it, make sure my tiger doesn't get sucked out."

"It won't," Bayane replied. "It's in the bed behind you." The Wolfoid pushed Breon out of the hatch and secured it behind him. Bayane ran to the end of the cargo bay and lowered the ramp. Medvegrad swept beneath them faster than it had seemed from the cockpit.

Sankar lifted the interceptor off the deck and maneuvered toward the opening. Once he was lined up, he punched the acceleration and shot out of the *Bilkinmore* like a rocket.

He activated the scanners and painted a picture of his potential adversaries: four in a low orbit and two standing off.

"Let's take a closer look at you, shall we?" he told the two closer ships. He stood the ship on its tail and accelerated straight upward. The exhilaration made his arm hair stand on end. The two ships assumed a staggered front-and-back tactical formation on an intercept course.

Sankar nosed over to take them head-on and tapped his screens until he reached the water recycling system. His finger hovered over the button for a heartbeat, then two. *Might lose thrust...* The words grated on his fighter pilot soul. He gritted his teeth and tapped.

He was thrown forward as the interceptor seemingly stopped in mid-flight, then slammed back in his seat as acceleration renewed at a reduced level.

Systems showed forward acceleration at eighty-five percent of max. The engine was firewalled, set for maximum output.

"Fifteen percent loss of thrust to gain a shield? I'm now the same speed or even slower than my enemy. I already don't like it," Sankar mumbled. He maintained his course, juking randomly to foil a potshot should the other ships take one.

The scanner finally gave him a determination on the incoming. They were drones. He angled the *Four-Claw*, standing the ship on one wing to cut through the middle of the close formation. The drones never wavered as they continued their descent toward *Bilkinmore*.

"Catamar One Three, you have inbound. Bring them back toward me."

Bilkinmore slowly banked through a one-hundred-eighty-degree turn. Sankar pulled hard to bring the *Four-Claw* around and tapped the recycling button to turn off the shields. Without any resistance, the nose whipped around and faced the ground by the time thrust was restored. He was thrown back in his seat when the ship returned to maximum acceleration.

He started to close on the ships. He dropped below their trajectory and fired his ion cannons, walking the nose of his interceptor across the tight formation.

The drones disintegrated under the ion stream.

Sankar banked skyward in an effort to intimidate the ships in orbit. He counted on them having seen the destruction of the drones.

They split into two formations of two and raced away at ninety-degree angles to Sankar's approach.

He pulled back on the throttle. The ship quickly slowed, and when it hit zero acceleration, he activated the screens. There was no indication besides the button color changing from red to green. He nosed over and powered up.

Eighty-five percent. The screens were active. He flew in a lazy circle above the *Bilkinmore*.

"Catamar One, time to pick up our boys."

"Couldn't agree more," came the terse reply.

The ship assumed a new course, heading directly to the ruins. Sankar relaxed in his seat and held the overwatch position, keeping his eyes on the two pairs of ships in orbit keeping their eyes on him.

Gwarzo groaned, but forced his way through the opening. Each step was a trial. Junak waited without words despite his growing impatience. He forced himself not to tap his foot, focusing on slowing his breathing instead.

When Gwarzo reached the corner, he was shining the light into the chamber.

"I see what you mean."

A mummy lay on a stone table, desiccated by the dry air of the underground chamber. Shelves with documents of rough paper lined the walls. Personal items filled a last shelf closest to the door.

"Jackpot," Gwarzo said. "Rip off his hand. That'll give me what I need."

Junak winced. "How about just a finger? This looks to be a religious thing, and the

Furd gods will punish me for defiling their high priest's chamber."

"I see what you mean," Gwarzo said, and shined his light more carefully on a figure that was neither Ursoid nor Tigroid nor Wolfoid nor Goroid. Gwarzo snapped a digital picture with a device Junak had never seen Gene use before. "Bone, muscle, skin, and anything within. That is what I'll need for the sequencing."

"I'm sorry, ancient grandpa," Junak told the long-dead individual. He uncovered the dry and shriveled hand, then pulled on the longest of the fingers, the middle one. It came off far more easily than he'd expected, and he almost fell. He sealed it in a plastic bag and put it in his pocket.

"What about the documents? Is there any labeling?"

Junak started at one end and skimmed the covers. "Nothing." He opened one of the books and tried to read. "This is written in a language I've never seen before."

Gene stared into the chamber, his discomfort with confined spaces forgotten in the thrill of their discovery. "If we assume these are in chronological order, and I have nothing to base that on, then let's take the first book and the last one, at the very least."

"There's a million ways to organize these. How about the first and last from each shelf?"

"That'll take all the room we have, but the more we can get, the better off we'll be. We may have to find someone to help us translate this stuff."

"May have to?" Junak started collecting the volumes, taking the greatest care not to disturb the others on the shelf as he placed one book after another into the bag. Eight books later, when he reached the last shelf, he pointed.

Gene leaned in as far as he could fit. "I don't know what to take."

"Looks like old technology, stuff that predates all of us. I can't take it all, but I want to." He picked up and held out three different handheld devices. Gene took them one by one and secured them in his vest. Junak put what he could into his pockets. He filled the remaining space in the bag.

"The find of a lifetime, and here we are, acting like grave robbers." Junak took a knee next to the table and bowed his head. "May the Furd gods forgive me for disturbing one so august as to deserve this interment. May your legacy be reborn with this find. May we add to it someday when the peoples of Hinteran are enlightened. May you protect Sankar and the rest of us as we seek the answer to our origin. Thank you for bringing us together and watching over us."

Junak stood.

"Time to go," Gwarzo said. He'd waited through Junak's prayer, then hurried down the short corridor, taking care not to crush his pockets as he squeezed through the narrow opening.

Gene looked at their gear. "I'll try to carry the plasma torch, but we'll have to leave the pry bars and shovels."

Junak shrugged while lugging the bag of goods through the outer chamber. Gene carried the Ursoid comm device in one hand and the plasma torch in the other and lumbered after the Tigroid. Junak dropped the flashlight he'd clamped under his arm, but he could see the way. He left it.

Gene held his in his mouth, refusing to be plunged into darkness. At the top, Junak stopped and listened before going outside and around the corner of the pyramid opposite the young campers.

He activated the comm unit. "Catamar One Three, this is Catamar Two, ready for pickup."

"On our way," Akoni replied almost instantly.

"It's like they were waiting for us. How sweet," Junak offered. "It would have been nicer if he told us how long it was going to be. I have to take a leak."

"It'll be longer than that," Gene said. Junak put his stuff down and loped toward the woods. "I meant that you should go right here."

Junak had already disappeared into the darkness. Gene was tempted to mess with him by shining his flashlight into the woods but decided against it. He thought it best to finish the mission without making waves and get back into space so they could fly far away from Medvegrad.

CHAPTER TWENTY

The split pairs became fireballs as they ripped through the upper atmosphere. The distance between the two groups widened as they bracketed the *Bilkinmore's* course.

Sankar had to decide. Engage one pair quickly, then race to intercept the other. With the screens in place, could he fire? He'd failed to collect that key piece of information before chasing Breon off his ship.

He activated his comm as he flew toward one pair of unidentified craft. "Catamar One Three, can I fire while the water recycling is engaged?"

"Stand by," Akoni replied.

Sankar used the delay to toggle two of his four missiles, targeting one on each ship in the pair. Head-on shots were less effective. He tipped the nose away from the ships to get a side shot when the time came.

"Roger," Akoni confirmed.

"Fire," Sankar ordered the ship. Two missiles shot out of the internal storage banks. He dragged the ship to a new intercept course toward the other two unidentified ships.

The missiles cruised toward their targets, accelerating before the final impact. The ships twisted mid-air to throw the missiles off. The first missile tore past the ship, while the second impacted amidships, blasting the oversized fighter in two. The first missile continued on a ballistic trajectory, unable to maneuver further. The first ship changed course to get behind the interceptor.

Sankar kept the screens active after determining that his survivability was no longer dependent upon speed alone. He had sacrificed thrust for security.

He toggled the last two missiles and tried to acquire the other targets. Akoni had started to zigzag the freighter, the slow movements almost irrelevant to its survival. Any missile would come in far faster than the big ship could react.

Sankar angled to get into position to fire the ion cannons and get their attention. He sprayed rounds in their direction before he realized the archaeological site was in the distance beyond the *Bilkinmore*.

A rearward-firing missile answered the question of whether he could turn off the screens to increase speed. He maintained his eight-five percent acceleration and didn't deviate from his course. A missile ejected by the second ship left a smoke bloom as its rocket motors engaged and drove it toward the *Four-Claw*.

He blew out a breath and clenched his jaw in anticipation of the imminent impact. The missile looked like it was aimed between his eyes. Sankar jerked back in his seat, flinching an instant before it hit. The ship bucked from the loss of momentum but picked up after the missile debris slid off the energy barrier like water rolling down a windshield. The second missile impact was the same.

Sankar had no idea if the shields had weakened since the button was neither green or red.

Acceleration was down to eighty percent.

There had been some damage, but how had it affected the other systems on the interceptor? Sankar didn't have answers, and the middle of a dogfight wasn't the time to go looking for them.

The heavy fighters below zeroed in on *Bilkinmore*.

Sankar lined up and fired his ion cannons. There was nothing else that could stop them from downing their ship and destroying everything they had worked for.

And leave him stranded in the *Four-Claw*.

The pyramid erupted from the impact of the blasts from the ion cannons. Gwarzo dove for Junak, who screamed in pain, holding his ears. Gwarzo dragged him to the ground and covered him. The ion blasts walked from the pyramid into the open area. The shock of the concussion continued to vibrate their bodies.

Gwarzo stood and dusted himself off, checking the artifacts in his pockets to see if they were still in one piece while Junak rolled around on the ground in agony. Gwarzo grabbed Junak with one hand and hoisted him to his feet. "Look at me." He peered into Junak's eyes, watching his pupils dilate. "You're fine. You're *fine*."

They looked at the sky where a fight raged. Lights flashed in the distance.

Above the treetops, the moon shone on the shadow that was *Bilkinmore* lumbering toward them.

"That isn't good," Junak said far too loudly.

"Looks like we have company," Gwarzo said, picking up his gear. He gestured for Junak to do the same. "We're not going to have a whole lot of time."

"Let's rush on board in time to get blown up." Junak shook his head but picked up the bag and prepared to run.

"Have some faith. You know that's Sankar up there in the *Four-Claw*. He's the best fighter pilot around, isn't he?"

Junak frowned. "He is, but hardly immortal."

Gwarzo laughed. "We stole a zillion bajingos' worth of gear from a university, then we kidnapped a scientist, and now we just robbed a historic site because we are trying to prove that everything our races know about their history is wrong. Those things tend to upset people. Show a little sympathy."

"Are you jerking me?" Junak asked. "How can you take this lightly?"

"What else are we supposed to do? I can change nothing that's going on right now. Might as well enjoy this crazy ride that you and your madman pal brought us on. But now I can say that I've been on Medvegrad. Not many of my people can make that claim." He nodded at the ship. "Time to go."

"Get down here!" Akoni yelled. Every time he turned, he banked the ship off-course and had to drag it back. Scanners showed the pyramid before him, diagrammed on the holographic display. He slowed the ship, but it didn't respond as quickly as he wanted, so he banked hard to keep from hitting the pyramid. He rotated the ship and drifted into the open area before it.

"Pop the hatch!" he yelled, but Bayane was already there and had the door open before they landed.

Junak handed in a bag filled with books. Bayane took it and pulled the Tigroid through. Gene followed, pushing everyone ahead of him so he could close the door.

"Nice landing. Now get us out of here," Gwarzo shouted at the cockpit.

"Easier said than done, *Slick*!" The ship lifted off and started drifting toward the pyramid. He pulled back and forth until the ship moved toward the trees. Once he had enough forward momentum, he pulled back to lift the ship above the forest. It continued to rise.

Junak ran to his station and started plotting a course into orbit with a follow-on leg to the Cornelior black hole.

"Faster, please."

Sweat ran down Akoni's face, and he compulsively clenched and unclenched his hands between bouts of trying to fly the ship.

Junak sent over the easiest flight route to take the ship into orbit. Akoni set the autopilot to follow the course. He pulled his hands off the controls slowly and stiffly and rolled his shoulders to force himself to relax.

A flash in front of the ship blinded him before the buffeting rolled through. The ship stopped shaking and continued upward.

"Are we going to die?" Breon asked from behind them while bracing himself inside the doorframe.

Junak fixed him with a hard look. "Not if Sankar can help it."

"Time to die!" Sankar shouted at the screen. He laced the air with shots from the ion cannons, dancing them across the flight paths of the last two ships.

The Medvegradian heavy fighters jerked erratically. At the far edge of his screen, four more craft appeared on an intercept course as *Bilkinmore* lumbered skyward.

He closed the distance to the freighter to put himself between it and the attackers. With the screens surrounding his ship, he thought he could shield them, but when he approached, he realized he was too small and a target in his own right. Anything that missed him might hit *Bilkinmore*. He veered away from the freighter to take the big ship out of the line of fire.

The only way to protect it was to eliminate the attackers. Sankar tapped the water recycling icon to turn off the screens. The ship jerked and arced toward the ground before the thrust returned with renewed vigor. He stood it on its tail and accelerated straight up, then started a slow spiral to foil the enemy's targeting systems.

Sankar banked away from the *Bilkinmore*, and the *Four-Claw* responded almost as if it were reading his mind. He jerked it through a series of high-speed maneuvers to further confuse the enemy. They split up to catch him between them in a classic hammer-and-anvil strategy.

He picked the ship that maneuvered a little more slowly and turned on a looser corner. Sankar drove his bird at an angle to close the distance without appearing to attack. He smiled as his whiskers laid flat against his face. With a near-instantaneous turn, he unleashed a barrage from his ion cannons. The enemy started to bank, but it was too late.

Sankar nosed over to the second target an instant before the first ship exploded.

Had he kept watching, he would have seen a single chute appear as it carried a figure toward the ground.

The second ship started after the *Four-Claw* but thought better of it. It turned toward *Bilkinmore* and fired.

Sankar launched a missile, then filled the sky with a long burst from one ion cannon before firing the second. They were long shots, with the atmosphere eating up much of the momentum.

The ship maneuvered away from the cloud of projectiles. Sankar adjusted his heading and fired again. He jinked and fired. He yanked back and fired, trying to drive the heavy fighter away from an attack profile on *Bilkinmore*. Sankar risked a glance at the display to see the freighter continuing to accelerate toward orbit.

He relaxed since the ship was safe for the moment and continued on his trajectory toward the remaining enemy fighter. He fired more short bursts, wondering what had happened to his missile. He'd lost it in the excitement. Since the ship was still flying, the missile must have missed and was on its way to an unknown point on a ballistic profile that would bring it back to Medvegrad in the far distance.

Sankar adjusted his heading and fired. The fighter twisted away, but it brushed the edge of the ion stream, which ripped metal from the hull. The ship cleared the incoming but left a cloud of metal twisting and catching flashes of the sun. The ship banked over and accelerated toward the ground, one hundred and eighty degrees away from the interceptor.

Sankar turned the ship toward *Bilkinmore*, maintaining one hundred percent acceleration until he caught the freighter in the upper atmosphere. Together, they bumped through and into space.

The *Bilkinmore* headed for the nearest gravity wave to disappear into it and ride it away from the planet.

A heavier ship chased them, but it was barely faster than the freighter. The *Four-Claw* spun backward and sent a double blast from his ion cannons in front of it as a message that this chase would not be worthwhile. The ship broke off its pursuit.

"Open the cargo bay doors and let me in," Sankar pleaded.

"We're trying to secure the zoo so no one dies when we decompress the ship," Akoni advised.

"We have to do something about that," Sankar replied. He was thinking of welding air-tight doors in place to isolate the cargo bay for in-space recoveries. He knew this wouldn't be the last time they'd need to do it. Akoni and Bayane could figure it out. Maybe even Breon.

Sankar brought the interceptor in behind *Bilkinmore* and waited. He stared at the scanners to make sure they were in clear space, but the freighter had the better view.

"What does the universe look like from up there? All clear?"

"Five by five. Opening up now."

The cargo deck descended slowly. Minor debris flew into space with the explosive decompression since they had no way to pull the air into the ship before opening up. It wasn't designed for that.

He maneuvered the *Four-Claw* into the cargo bay, rotating it and setting it down with the nose pointed out in case they needed a rapid launch. By the time he powered down the engines, the cargo bay door was closed.

"How long before the ship is repressurized?" he asked.

"Give it about ten minutes. Just in time, Sankar. We are slipping into the gravity wave in five, four..."

Sankar activated the magnetic clamps to secure the ship to the deck before it bucked and accelerated like a surfer riding a wave toward the beach.

He left the pilot's seat to grab something to eat. Deathblade jumped out of the bunk and stretched, smacking its lips and looking at the hatch.

"We have to wait, buddy, until we have air. Relax and take a load off. That was a tough fight."

The tiger looked at him with his big eyes, a look that said, "I could not care less about your affairs. Feed me."

Sankar play-slapped at the tiger. It pounced, but Sankar had tiger blood too and dodged it, pushing the tiger aside. It hissed and lowered its head for a second attack. It was no longer playing. Sankar wanted to relax after the fight, maybe drink a glass of testle. There was no testle, and he lost his humor. His claws extended, and he slashed as the tiger came in for a second attack, cutting through an ear and leaving two clean cuts across its head. He caught it in his off-hand and pinned it to the deck.

He stabbed his claws at its face, stopping a hair's breadth from its eyeball.

"I am in charge. You will do as I say. You will not attack me. Your job is to defend me, and if the opportunity arises again, it's okay to steal food from the Ursoids. They already grow too big. It wouldn't hurt any of them to miss a meal or three."

The tiger relaxed, and Sankar retracted his claws. He cradled the cat and rocked it like a baby. Blood filled the cuts but didn't drip. They scabbed over quickly. The ear would be forever clipped, a sign that the tiger had lost its fight for dominance.

Deathblade had been marked with the scars of his name.

Sankar sat on the floor and leaned against the wall. The cat melted against him, quickly falling asleep. The tiger's change from aggression to submissive helped Sankar relax.

The sound of the hatch opening startled him awake. Junak's worried face looked in. "We tried contacting you, but you didn't reply. You had us *concerned*." He climbed in to stand over his friend, offering a hand up. Sankar put the tiger aside. Once the animal saw the open hatch, he bolted out of the interceptor.

"He'll need something to eat. Me, too. It's been a long day."

"We're still picking up the pieces in here. This ship wasn't designed for a deep-space recovery. We need to change some things before we do that again, but the good news is, we have three engineers on board who are already planning for it. We may have to stop by the junkyard for a day or two."

"Koni is going to love that unless we bring the screen tech. Then we may have free run of the place, for a short while at least."

"I think fresh bovine is all it will take to get us free run of the place," Junak countered.

They went upstairs, where they found the rest of the crew and the pets eating and joking. They cheered when Sankar entered. Gene waved a celery stalk at the fighter pilot.

"You are never going to be allowed on Medvegrad ever again," Gene mumbled after taking a bite.

"That goes without saying. We splashed three of their ships."

"And you shot up the pyramid." Gene pointed at Junak. The Tigroid nodded.

"That's not optimal. Did you find anything?"

"It would take a lifetime to study and understand what we found. Jackpot, Sankar."

Gwarzo nodded and took another bite before speaking with his mouth full. "It had zeno-ish mummy inside who didn't look like any of us."

"Did you take him—I mean, *it?*"

"We took a picture, and a finger. Even though we're grave robbers, that didn't look like something we should disturb. But we have enough. I'll be able to spin up the genetic sequencer, and I think we'll have some data before Maglor seizes our ship and kills all of us."

CHAPTER TWENTY-ONE

"Aren't you our little ray of sunshine?" Sankar walked to the Goroid and slapped him on the back. "Thanks for going with Junak into the pyramid. I look forward to seeing what you guys have. After dinner, of course."

Junak whispered into Sankar's ear, "Gene's afraid of small spaces."

"I heard that," Gene said but didn't expound. He focused his attention on his plate and went back to eating a meal that Maglor had provided, one suited for a growing Goroid.

Breon leaned close to Akoni, who leaned away. "Is it always like this?"

"Yes. Maybe someday we'll tell you the story of how we got together, but not today. Let's celebrate our victory over history and the task of finding you, which turned out to be much easier than we thought it would be."

"It's been two years since I went into hiding. I thought Maglor had given up. I should have known better."

"At least it was us, the Veracity Corporation, who found you and not a bunch of hitmen. We will get paid well for turning you over, but we don't have any intention of leaving you in Maglor's hands."

"We don't?" Bayane asked.

"No, we don't," Sankar confirmed. "We're the *good zenos,* remember?"

"I remember that you're the Heretic, and everywhere we've gone, people shoot at us."

Sankar pursed his lips and pushed his whiskers forward as he threw a steak into the hot pan. He seared it quickly before turning the heat down.

"I'd like to say that you're wrong, but only in perspective. They shoot at us because they're bad."

"Every planetary government is bad?" Bayane pressed. "Wait until you get to Angelos. You'll find my people warm and welcoming."

Akoni snorted, and Gwarzo stopped mid-chew to study the Wolfoid to discern if he was joking.

"We're not going to Angelos anytime soon. Assuming Maglor appreciates the work and we don't overstep our bounds by trying to keep Breon on the team, then we'll need to lay low for a while to work on the ship and let Gwarzo work his magic on the bits and pieces we've collected, as well as each of us, to build a baseline from which to backtrack."

Gwarzo turned to Junak. "I'm going to love carving a piece off of you."

"What did I do?"

Bayane barked a laugh once the focus turned away from him. Gene pointed at the Wolfoid. "You, too."

"Hey!" Bayane looked at Sankar for support, but he waved a hand over his shoulder. He had other concerns, like hitting the perfect medium-rare on his steak.

Once he was satisfied, he dropped it onto the last clean plate and settled at the table. He carved off a slice and held it below the table for Deathblade, who took it gently from his hand before gulping it down.

"How long until we exit the gravity wave?" Sankar asked.

"Another couple hours. We have time."

"We draw straws to see who does the dishes," Sankar stated. His look told everyone he wasn't kidding. The zenos looked away, embarrassed at the slovenly mess they'd become since boarding the ship.

"Hear, hear!" Breon shouted. "A clean ship is a happy ship."

"Suck up. Stay off the boss' nipple, would you?" Akoni nudged him. "No need to draw straws. We'll do it, but only because I want to pick Breon's brain on a couple things when we aren't elbow-deep in an engine component. Once we're done in here, we'll need to disconnect the translation module from the *Four-Claw* if we're going to install it on *Bilkinmore*."

"I can take care of that now. Beats doing dishes," Bayane offered and hurried away without taking his plate to the sink. Sankar and Junak cleared the table while the two Ursoids filled the space in the kitchen area.

"How did they have a whole crew of your people in here?"

"Only one cook who did everything. He was like the ship's captain, but more important. You know what they say. 'Too many cooks spoil the bovine stew.'"

"You eat stew?" Sankar asked.

Akoni and Breon looked at each other like they couldn't believe their ears. "You have much to learn about our people."

"Sounds like stew is on the menu," Junak mumbled. "Can't we just have steak?"

"Bah! Stupid cats!" Akoni gestured at them with two fingers.

"If you weren't so big, I'd kick your ass to Medved Seven and beyond!" Junak gestured back.

"You said it was always like this. I can't believe that. In academia, you would have all been shown the door three times over."

"Welcome to the real world, Professor." Sankar bowed. Gene watched with mild amusement, slowly eating his second bowl of vegetables and tubers.

The Tigroids left the others to it and returned to the cockpit. Sankar crawled into the cart and curled up. "Wake me when we're getting close."

"I'm taking hits myself. Maybe a catnap is called for. I'll set an alarm because we need to be awake and alert for our impending execution."

Sankar chuckled. "I think he'll love us, probably a bit too much. Mark my words, Junak. By doing his bidding, we'll get the opportunity to do a lot more of his bidding. He's going to own us, and we're not going to have any say in the matter."

"Sankar, my friend. We are alone in the vastness of space. Is it that bad to have someone watching over us, even if we have to do him favors every now and again?"

"The favors will get more and more dangerous until we die, and then he'll find someone else to burn out." Sankar tried to close his eyes, but thoughts of their benefactor kept him awake.

"No one else has you in the pilot's seat. You have never been bested in ship-to-ship combat. Look at what we've accomplished in such a short time. There is no one else like us. Maglor is lucky to have the opportunity to work with us. I like having regular meals and a warm bed with more space than a bunk on the *Four-Claw*."

"You make good points, Junak. I fear sleep will be elusive as these thoughts will haunt me. I had a purpose and a mission that mattered."

"And you still do," Junak countered. "Don't let Maglor pull you away from what you have to do, what we all signed up for, and that's to find the truth. Maglor accepts us while we do side jobs for him. You can sell that because we have already shown we get the job done. Where you go, we'll follow."

"I don't know what to say, Junak, besides thank you. I'll do my best not to fail you."

"See that you don't. And tell your tiger to leave my cat alone. I think she's going into heat."

Sankar snorted. "That would be madness. Lock her up because the last thing I want on this ship is a mess of kittens. They'll get into everything. Remember when you were little with your litter?"

"We only had four. Come on, man! It wasn't that bad. You had just one. You were lucky."

"Not to hear my parents talk about it. They thought they were being punished by the Furd gods for a litter of one."

"Ha! They were because that one was you. Now, shut your blood pudding hole. I'm trying to get some sleep over here."

"And our benefactor is a vegetarian. If we want blood pudding or testle, we need to make a trip to Oterosan." Sankar waited, but Junak didn't answer. "That doesn't sound too bad. I don't think a trip back there would be all bad. I'd like to tell my father about our progress. We've already accomplished more than he imagined, all he hoped. I envy you that you were able to see an ancient one. Was he the first? So much we have yet to learn. No. It's not time to go home. We have more to do."

The black hole was nothing more than a point in space blocking the stars behind it that registered as a massive gravimetric distortion on the scanners.

Sankar activated the intercom. "Hang onto your butts. We'll be back in Cornelior space momentarily. Be ready for anything."

Akoni took his seat at the engineering station in the cockpit. On Sankar's other side, Junak laced his fingers behind his head and leaned back, almost falling off his box. His job was finished.

"Taking us through." Sankar eased the ship forward into the black hole, getting a momentary feeling of nausea before they were through. The holographic display showed a free-for-all of ships engaged in an intricate death dance around a single large ship—Maglor's heavy cruiser.

"I recommend activating the screens," Akoni said.

Sankar didn't question it. "Bring them online, please, Master Engineer."

The loss of thrust was indistinguishable on the freighter, but the flickering lights and flashing screens left no doubt that the system was fighting for primacy in the ship's power hierarchy."

"Compensating," Akoni said as he tapped keys. Breon leaned over his shoulder and offered advice. Akoni adjusted. The systems settled down, and the lights stopped flickering. The systems display showed available thrust at seventy percent. "I didn't know it was possible for this hog to go any slower."

Breon threw his hands up. "This is the greatest technological achievement in this century, and all you can do is complain about the loss of thrust? Some people..."

Akoni added, "But we're protected against their weapons. The space fighters are using plasma discharge weapons. The screens are one hundred percent effective at eliminating the threat from plasma. It'll be like it passes around us without ever touching us."

"That's worth the loss of thrust. Thanks, Breon. I'm glad you guys got it installed while I napped. I was out of it."

"And now we could use some sleep, but it doesn't look like that's in the cards anytime soon."

"Akoni, take the controls. Time to launch the *Four-Claw*. We need to help Maglor."

"Let's not be hasty," Breon said.

"He owes us money, and if we save him, we save you too," Sankar replied.

Junak activated the comm as Akoni slid into the pilot's chair and Breon took over at engineering. "Secure the ship for space deployment of the *Four-Claw*. Hide your pets and your food, people. We'll be opening the cargo bay as soon as I get confirmation that people and things are behind closed doors."

"Wait!" Bayane yelled, his feet hammering the deck as he ran toward the cargo bay.

Akoni headed straight for Maglor's ship.

"Catamar One Three, will I be crushed and destroyed when I try to exit?"

Breon answered the comm. "Only if the deck is still up. You can pass through this way, but you can't come back through unless we drop the screen."

"It's a one-way trip. I'm ready to go whenever you can open us up."

"Are you sure? You aren't shielded," Akoni noted. Goroid fighters splashed *Bilkinmore* with multiple plasma discharges. They passed around the ship as if it weren't there. "I like this."

Breon beamed like a proud father.

"All clear up here," Bayane called over the intercom. Junak jumped up and closed the cockpit hatch.

"Gene?" Akoni asked.

"Clear."

"Opening the cargo ramp." He tapped the button. "Sankar, wait until we have free space behind the ship. Wait. Wait. Go!"

Sankar punched it, shooting out the back like a projectile. He banked hard to avoid Maglor's ship. Akoni closed the ramp, adjusted his heading, and slowed to take a position near the rear of the cruiser, where the vulnerable engine areas were located.

Weapons fired from all quarters, attempting to hit the fast maneuvering Goroid long-range fighters, heavier and larger versions of the type Sankar had downed last time they were in Cornelior space.

The *Four-Claw* flew into the middle of the Goroid fighters.

"What is he doing?" Akoni watched in horror at the risks Sankar took, drawing the fighters away from the cruiser and *Bilkinmore*. He twisted faster than the enemy. He juked and fired. One down, three remained.

Maglor fired indiscriminately into the formation.

"Ceasefire, ceasefire, dumbass," Akoni shouted over the comm.

"Come on!" Breon replied. "You can do better than that."

The cruiser stopped firing.

In that brief span, Sankar killed another fighter, leaving only two ships. They split wide, forcing him to decide which one to go after. He picked one and sent streams from his ion cannon in circles around it, spiraling in toward the rapidly retreating fighter.

The other turned, but Maglor's cruiser had not been idle. They focused all their firepower on the lone ship and hit it with enough ordnance to destroy a small fleet.

When Sankar's spiral reached the center, the fighter found it had nowhere to go. It powered down to show that it surrendered, but it was too late. Sankar stopped firing, but the fatal ion streams were already well on their way. They ripped the ship in half, clearing the space around Maglor's cruiser.

"Deactivating the screens." Breon verified his command by tapping the screen and nodded. "We can open the cargo ramp and recover your pilot."

"Our commander," Junak stated.

"I stand corrected. That was amazing flying, but we'll have to build another translation module as quickly as possible to outfit the *Four-Claw*. With screens, he would be more invincible than he already is."

"Dock at the airlock. Maglor wants to see you."

"That sounded like Wargo. He could have said thank you," Junak said.

"Opening the cargo ramp." Akoni cut the engines. There was no way he was going to attempt to dock with Maglor's ship. That would take Sankar's steady hand and piloting skill.

The interceptor eased into the cargo bay, rotated, and locked down. The ramp closed, and the repressurization of the ship's common areas commenced.

Akoni activated the comm. "We'll dock as soon as our pilot is able to take the controls. Ten minutes."

"You have two."

"Ain't happening. Ten minutes because we need the pilot who just saved your ass.

Akoni out." He turned off the comm.

"At least he knows who to be angry with," Junak suggested.

"I can take him." Akoni puffed out his chest.

"You couldn't even take Sankar."

"He has secret weapons."

"I expect Wargo does too, in odd ways. He's the type who likes to fight. You might want to steer clear of him."

"And pray tell, how do I do that?"

"Stay on *Bilkinmore*. Better yet, only Sankar goes over there with Breon's information. Tell us we have copies of everything."

"We have copies of everything," Breon replied, tapping the side of his head. Junak scowled, and Breon pointed at the computer screen.

"That's better. We'll leave it all to Sankar. He can fight the battle with Maglor while we keep Gene company over here. Maglor only wanted the research. He said we could kill Breon."

"What? You didn't tell me that."

"He said that, but we didn't have to because you're a good guy."

"I used to like you, Akoni."

"That's it! Now you're getting into the spirit of the Veracity Corporation."

"You are both on my list."

"You need a list to remember our names? I thought you were smart."

Breon looked at Akoni for help. The other Ursoid shook his head. "This is what people do in that in-between stage of not knowing if they'll be alive to see the end of the day. We think so. We're pretty sure we will. But then we have to hear Wargo's voice, and it casts doubt on everything. He's the dark cloud on our sunny day."

"But we're in space. There is no day or night," Breon replied.

"That's the spirit!" Akoni declared. "Numbers are nominal. Open up the ship."

Junak popped the hatch, his breath catching at the lower oxygen level in the passage. He steadied himself and hurried to the *Four-Claw*, where he pounded on the outer hatch. Sankar opened it and jumped out.

"You gotta dock us. Akoni is holding them off, but Wargo is unhappy. We need to hurry."

Sankar slowed. "In what scenario would Wargo be happy? The zeno doesn't know his place in the big scheme of life."

"I think he'd be happy to blow us up. Don't get us killed. I'll never forgive you," Junak warned.

Sankar smiled and jogged to the cockpit, where Akoni was still standing.

"Pilot on deck," Akoni called. He and Breon stood aside to make way for Sankar to take the controls. He pushed, but the ship didn't move, so he leaned into it. "It's

CHAPTER TWENTY-ONE

too easy to get used to the *Four-Claw*. If you engineers could make *Bilkinmore* fly like my fighter, I'd appreciate it."

"If we could make this tub fly like a fighter, we'd be the richest engineers in Hinteran." He waited for a reply, but Sankar was busy guiding the freighter to Maglor's airlock. "But since we can't, you're going to have to suck it up."

The ship bumped gently as the airlocks lined up and locked in. "I get it, but I think you should work on that and become rich so we can buy a better ship."

"After all the work we put into our baby, you want us to abandon her? Tigroids and their big litters don't care about the rest of us. Such hurtful words! I'm appalled. Now, go see Maglor."

"Maybe we should send Gene," Sankar said as the Goroid appeared in the nearby corridor.

"I'll be in my lab." He strode away like a zeno on a mission.

Sankar stood and sighed. "What do you say we wrap this mission up and then get some rest and recreation? Where could we take this motley crew where we wouldn't get any grief?"

"There's a habitable moon in the Beos system. Nobody there. No governments and no hassles," Akoni offered.

"Never heard of it, but that's what I'm talking about. Maybe we can open up a bar. We do have a freighter." Sankar spread his arms wide to take in the *Bilkinmore*. They walked to the corridor, and Sankar punched the airlock button. Once the system determined the air was pressurized on both sides of the hatch, it opened.

On the other side, Wargo glowered. Akoni waggled his fingers at him.

"All of you, come with me," Wargo commanded.

Sankar leaned back into the cockpit. "Give me the tech stuff for Maglor."

Breon remained out of sight as he handed over the briefcase.

Sankar took it and walked into the airlock. "Nah. Just me with the tech that Maglor paid for. I'll deliver it, we'll confirm that it's complete, we'll get our final payment, and then we'll be on our merry way. You're welcome for us saving your life. Shall we?" Sankar said in a flurry of words as he brushed past Wargo.

Akoni punched the button and secured the hatch, waving a finger at Wargo, who clenched his jaw and trembled with anger.

"I'm glad it's him and not us," Junak said.

"Although I have no fear of Goroids, I'm happy not to have gone back to that ship. But staying here, I doubt we'll get a resupply on food like we got last time."

"Unless..." Junak punched the button and opened the hatch. On the other side was a group of technicians and workers with carts and a great deal of confusion on their faces.

"Gene! Get up here. You've got some talking to do," Akoni shouted and started walking toward the lab. Gene popped through his door as if he'd been expecting to be summoned. "We've got the resupply crew waiting. Maybe we can let them through and blow off the folks who are trying to install more bugs on the ship. I still have to scrub the outside of this thing. I almost forgot."

"I'll handle it." Gwarzo walked to the airlock, stopped in the middle of the doorway, crossed his arms, and glared at the Goroids on the other side. "You with the food, come on through and leave it here."

Maglor's crew looked at each other.

Gwarzo uncrossed his arms, smiled widely, and strolled forward. "You know that we know that you're going to install more bugs on the ship. We're not going to let you. It's a huge waste of your time and ours. You're hoping that we might miss one. And we may, but for a relationship based on trust, we can't have subterfuge, but we can have a party. Bring that food in here and enjoy it with us. Come on." He gestured from them to roll the carts over, lifting them over the seals and into the airlock.

Akoni and Breon moved the carts into the corridor, where there was enough space to line them up. Maglor's crew looked even more confused as they stood there, the technicians behind them shifting uncomfortably since they had been blocked from doing their work. Gene waded in among them.

"Come, my friends! Eat, drink, and enjoy without bugging our ship. You," he pointed at the ones carrying toolboxes, "leave those here and join us for some of the finest Cornelior has to offer." He led the parade into the *Bilkinmore* while Akoni, Junak, Bayane, and Breon took positions where they could stop any of the visitors from going farther into the ship.

"This looks like fun," Bayane whispered to Junak, helping himself to a handful of something blue from the closest cart.

CHAPTER TWENTY-TWO

Sankar glanced over his shoulder to see Akoni waving as the outer hatch closed. Wargo fumed. Sankar thought he remembered the way, taking a right at the first passage and powering ahead until Wargo's long fingers wrapped over his shoulder and pulled him back.

He turned the Tigroid and tried to slam him against the wall, but Sankar twisted out of his grasp, dropped the briefcase, extended his claws, and slashed the Goroid's exposed forearms.

Wargo roared as he crouched, arms wide as he sought to draw Sankar into his grasp.

"And here I thought you were the right-hand zeno of a corporate mogul, but you're just a thug."

"I don't like people trying to show the boss up."

"What sewage is coming out of your pipes?" Sankar asked. "We completed the mission, and we drove off the Goroid fighters giving you grief. Why were they out there, by the way? Never mind. Looks like you need all the friends you can get. Alienating us won't get you what you want. We've done Maglor's bidding, and this is how he thanks us?"

Wargo drew up short, eyes blazing with hatred for the Tigroid, but behind that, there was fear. *Ah,* Sankar thought. Maglor had not directed Wargo to attack Sankar.

"Lead the way. I'll follow," Sankar said, picking up the briefcase, never taking his eyes off Wargo. The claws of his right hand remained extended, muscles bunched and ready to strike.

Wargo's attention turned to the Tigroid's natural weapons and the damage they had done to his forearms. "If you ever cross Maglor, I will kill you."

"You saw what I can do with the ion cannons of my fighter. I'm just as good with a blaster, or my *kabbar,* for the record. And I have no intention of crossing Maglor, so put your misplaced anger away and lead on. I have a delivery to make."

Wargo shouted down the corridor, and when they reached the antechamber to

Maglor's workspace, an aide was waiting with salve and towels. Wargo let the aide doctor his arms before continuing down the short corridor, through the doors that stood open, and before the massive desk raised above the level of the visitors.

Maglor spun around from his monitors to face his visitors. Sankar put the briefcase on the desk. "There it is. Everything you paid for."

"Indeed," he said slowly. He snapped his fingers, and a door opened to the side. A Goroid in a lab coat rushed in and took the briefcase, bowed, and quickly departed. "It appears that you have installed the technology on your ship."

"Of course. I demanded that we be sure the technology worked and that you hadn't been scammed. It also saved us since I'm driving a flying pig."

"That you are, but not that fighter craft of yours. That was an impressive display. Do you know why those four ships were attacking me?"

Sankar shrugged one shoulder. He didn't care to hazard a guess.

"They were auditioning to be my security," Maglor said, dead-pan.

"Well, now, that changes things a bit," Sankar admitted.

"This was a life-or-death audition, and they failed, but you did not." Maglor soft-clapped his ape's palms together.

"We weren't auditioning," Sankar said firmly. "Veracity Corporation had a mission to complete, and that meant clearing the void of space trash so we could dock and hand over the screening technology."

"Once I hear from my scientists and engineers that they have what they need to produce the screening system, I'll deliver the final payment for your services, minus ten percent holdback for future contracts." Maglor leaned back and crossed his arms as if expected a fight from Sankar.

The Tigroid didn't take the bait. "Changing the terms after the fact. How ruthless of you."

"You retained the technology for yourself," Maglor said, smirking an ape's smirk. "Ten percent is a low cost for what you've gained."

"Fair enough, but you sent us on a dangerous job where we were shot at by more than one group." Sankar licked his whiskers and nose before continuing. "Besides Medvegradian security, a second group came at us from space. You wouldn't know anything about that, would you?"

"Interesting. What kinds of ships were they flying? Say, heavy fighters?"

"Exactly. All black."

"A competitor, I believe. I have several. No matter. You don't need to go to Medvegrad. Your next job is something I think you can start on right away."

"We need a Furd-gods-break after this," Sankar said truthfully. "What now?"

"Time is of the essence, Sankar. In addition to Breon's miracle shield device, I've become aware of a new formula for a theoretical alloy which—assuming it could be successfully mass-produced and employed for industrial purposes—might revolutionize spacecraft construction. Among other things."

"Naturally, you want us to find and bring you this thing?" Sankar said.

"Naturally," Maglor said, still smirking his ape's smirk.

"How much?" Sankar asked, conceding to the inevitability of having to take the job.

"Twenty thousand, but half upfront, and we'll reprovision your ship."

"We'll take the job," Sankar said. "You've seen that when we agree to a job, we do it. The only way we won't complete it is if we're dead, so there's no need to track our ship. Once we get the bugs cleaned off, we expect them to stay off."

"I have invested a great deal in my business. You're outsiders, and I never trust outsiders." Maglor steepled his fingers and studied the Tigroid before him. "I wish you luck on your quest for the truth of our existence. I have no interest in such matters. Your revelation will neither unite nor further separate the species of Hinteran. But that won't stop us from conducting a productive relationship, now, will it?"

Sankar looked down and shuffled his feet before replying. "We had an animated discussion on board *Bilkinmore* about working for you. We feel like we have the choice to say no, but we also understand the importance of having a benefactor. Each contract is separate, but if you can provide us safe haven between jobs, provision us with food and supplies, then we believe that this will be a mutually beneficial arrangement. After this gig, we will take a vacation."

"Of course. Wargo will see you out. And Wargo," Maglor glared at his assistant, "please avoid future misunderstandings with my guests before you get yourself killed."

Sankar waited for Wargo to lead the way. Despite Maglor's veiled threat to his right-hand man, Wargo was now Sankar's enemy, looking for any excuse to kill the Tigroid.

He bowed deeply to Maglor before leading the way out. Sankar followed at a safe distance, both hands free and claws partially extended. He walked lightly on the balls of his feet to best react should Wargo attempt to ambush him.

But the Goroid kept his head upright and walked without looking around. He took Sankar straight back to the airlock, where voices drowned each other out and music played. Wargo sped up until he reached the crowd. He pulled the first Goroid aside to find a drink in his hand and a dull smile on his face.

"Hey! It's the life of the party," Akoni shouted. "Drink, drink, drink..." The group chanted, and everyone raised their glasses.

Wargo turned to face Sankar. He thought he saw a wisp of steam trail from the Goroid's ear.

"Get your people back on your ship and get out of here."

"For this once, I agree with you, but it's nice to see our people having a little fun. See you on the flip side, Waggle Tooth." Sankar pounded Wargo's shoulder as hard as he could hit, but the well-muscled shoulder didn't give even a millimeter. "Damn. You've been working out."

Sankar danced his way through the crowd, grabbing someone's glass as he passed and taking a drink. He coughed and choked, leading to an uproar of laughter from the Goroids. He handed the glass back and twirled his fingers in the air. "We'd love to stay because this is the best party I've been to in years, but we have to get going. Sorry, guys."

Breon blocked the way into *Bilkinmore*. The majority of the bodies were stuffed into Maglor's side of the airlock and the corridors of his ship.

"Bayane!" Akoni yelled and gestured for him to come.

"Woohoo!" he yelled as he body-surfed above their heads, Goroid hands passing him along until he was dumped unceremoniously into the airlock. Sankar caught him before he smashed his drunk face on the deck.

He pushed his people back into the ship, waving at the happy crowd before closing the hatch and locking them out. "I was gone five minutes."

Gwarzo grabbed Sankar by his shoulders and lifted him up and down, bouncing him off the floor. "We made the most of our time. It turns out they weren't given orders to kill us but to resupply us for our next run and that we're now the cool kids." Gene put Sankar down and turned serious. "What did you agree to?"

"I got us re-stocked, and paid. But we're immediately on the clock again. Something about a mystery metal that Maglor thinks will be worth a kingly sum."

"A complete shock," Akoni said, half-mocking. "Did you mention that we have Breon on board?"

"It never came up. Who am I to volunteer information to a zeno who seems to know it all?"

Breon offered his hand. "Thank you. I'm happy to join your crew if you'll have me."

"Junak," Sankar ordered, "plot me a course to the Pangea system. And you don't have to pick the most expeditious course, either. We need some downtime, while we pick up leads. Akoni, check the input and see what we received to help us with this mission. Bayane, go get something to eat. We'll need you sharp. And Gene, where are my results from that genetic sequencing?"

"I haven't spun it up yet. We've been busy."

Sankar shook his head. Gwarzo grumbled and strolled away, grabbing something from the cart and unwrapping it to eat as he walked.

Akoni glanced at Sankar. "Is this our life now?"

"The road to the truth has many detours, but it goes through that lab, first and foremost." He pointed at Gene as he disappeared into his space. "I think we're a sideshow."

"A sideshow with guns."

"Damn! I forgot to ask Maglor if I could get some more missiles for the *Four-Claw*. We're out."

"But we have our health, and how about those screens!"

"We'll survive to fight another day, my friend."

"Maybe that should be our calling and not the Veracity Corporation."

"No." Sankar shook his head. "Our job is to look for anything that can help lead us to the truth of our existence. That has to be first. The screens keep *Bilkinmore* alive so Gene can do the work that others have avoided for too long."

"Roger." Akoni was along for the ride. "Wherever you go, and for whatever reason, I'll follow. We all will, Sankar."While you're waiting for the next story, would you be so kind as to leave a review for this book? That would be great. I appreciate the feedback and support.

The End of *Heretic*, but wait, there's more!

Reviews buoy my spirits and stoke the fires of creativity so if you could leave us a few kind words about this story, we would greatly appreciate it. https://geni.us/Zeno1

Book 2, in The Zenophobia Saga. ***Messenger*** can be ordered right now! Reserve your copy of *Messenger* today. https://geni.us/Zeno2

And while you're at it, why don't you pick up book 3, ***Extremist*** too? https://geni.us/Zeno3

CHAPTER TWENTY-TWO

Don't stop now! Keep turning the pages as I talk about my thoughts on this book and the overall project called Zenophobia.

DEDICATION

We can't write without those who support us

On the home front, we thank you for being there for us

We wouldn't be able to do this for a living if it weren't for our readers

We thank you for reading our books

The Zenophobia Saga team Includes

BETA / EDITOR BOOK

Beta Readers and Proofreaders - with my deepest gratitude!

Micky Cocker

James Caplan

Kelly O'Donnell

John Ashmore

Author Notes - Craig Martelle

Written November 1, 2021

I can't thank you enough for reading this story to the very end! I hope you liked it as much as I did.

It was great to bring Brad R. Torgersen on board to work with me on this series. I'm happy with the direction it's gone.

I'll let you in on a little secret. I originally wrote this book to satisfy my contract with Aethon Books as a military science fiction story, but it wasn't military enough and I didn't like it. I powered through, wrote the story, but couldn't find it in me to write the next two books. So I put this aside and wrote the Battleship: Leviathan series for my three-book contract.

And that series has launched huge and is sustaining its momentum. It was the series I needed. But I still had Heretic written and doing nothing for me. So I dropped it off with my insider team and asked what they thought. They all liked it a lot! So, it left me in a conundrum. I now needed two more books (I already had the outlines done) but didn't want to write them myself. I dropped a request on my Facebook page and was humbled by the top talent who offered to write the last two books in the series.

Enter Brad R. Torgersen. He's been friend for a while and had just won the Dragon for Best Science Fiction Novel of 2019 for his traditionally published title (Baen), The Star-Wheeled Sky. It is an excellent read if you don't have it. I have a signed paperback along with the rest of his books, signed. Coincidence? I think not. Brad tells a great story.

And he's done so with Messenger and Extremist, the last two books in this series. Once, again, I can't thank you enough for reading to this point. And I'm glad that my insider team convinced to publish the first book and finish the series. They are my sounding board and truthsayers. Jim Caplan, John Ashmore, Kelly O'Donnell, and Micky Cocker. They keep me on the straight and narrow and telling stories that you like. If there's a problem with it, then it's on me. If you like it, then they had a hand in it.

On November 1st, outside Fairbanks, Alaska where I live, I woke up to 42F temperatures. This is unheard of for November. A chinook wind blew threw over the past few days, but this week, temperatures will plummet. Next week, it looks like highs of around 10F with lows around zero. Much more like our common temperature for November. Although technically Fall, October is the start of Winter in the Sub-Arctic. We have six months of solid winter, except this year, where October was mostly mild. Every day it's nice is a bonus for us.

I'm not saying 0F isn't nice, but it's different. We spend a lot less time outside when it's that cold as I have a hard time breathing. At freezing (32F) or thereabouts, I breathe great, better than when it's warmer, but that tapers off fast as it gets below freezing.

In any case, Stanley is doing great, our new dog – a six-year-old pitbull rescue. He lived in California, so every new low is a new record for him. He likes the colder temperatures, I think. But we'll see how he handles next week when it gets cool. He has shirts, coats, and boots. He's good with getting geared up when necessary.

And watch for Zenophobia 2 – *Messenger* comes out on December 27, or you can pre-order it now https://geni.us/Zeno2

and it'll automatically upload to your Kindle come midnight, December 26.

Peace, fellow humans.

If you liked this story, you might like some of my other books. You can join my mailing list by dropping by my website craigmartelle.com or if you have any comments, shoot me a note at craig@craigmartelle.com. I am always happy to hear from people who've read my work. I try to answer every email I receive.

If you liked the story, please write a short review for me on Amazon. I greatly appreciate any kind words; even one or two sentences go a long way. The number of reviews an ebook receives greatly improves how well it does on Amazon.

Amazon—https://www.amazon.com/author/craigmartelle

Facebook—www.facebook.com/authorcraigmartelle

BookBub - https://www.bookbub.com/authors/craig-martelle

My web page—https://craigmartelle.com

Thank you for joining me on this incredible journey.

Other Series by Craig Martelle
 # - available in audio, too

Terry Henry Walton Chronicles (#) (co-written with Michael Anderle)—a post-apocalyptic paranormal adventure

Gateway to the Universe (#) (co-written with Justin Sloan & Michael Anderle)—this book transitions the characters from the Terry Henry Walton Chronicles to The Bad Company

The Bad Company (#) (co-written with Michael Anderle)—a military science fiction space opera

Judge, Jury, & Executioner (#)—a space opera adventure legal thriller

Shadow Vanguard—a Tom Dublin space adventure series

Superdreadnought (#)—an AI military space opera

Metal Legion (#)—a military space opera

The Free Trader (#)—a young adult science fiction action-adventure

Cygnus Space Opera (#)—a young adult space opera (set in the Free Trader universe)

Darklanding (#) (co-written with Scott Moon)—a space western

Mystically Engineered (co-written with Valerie Emerson)—mystics, dragons, & spaceships

Metamorphosis Alpha—stories from the world's first science fiction RPG

The Expanding Universe—science fiction anthologies

Krimson Empire (co-written with Julia Huni)—a galactic race for justice

Zenophobia (#) (co-written with Brad Torgersen)—a space archaeological adventure

Battleship Leviathan (#)– a military sci-fi spectacle published by Aethon Books

Glory (co-written with Ira Heinichen) – hard-hitting military sci-fi

Black Heart of the Dragon God (co-written with Jean Rabe) – a sword & sorcery novel

End Times Alaska (#)—a post-apocalyptic survivalist adventure published by Permuted Press

Nightwalker (a Frank Roderus series)—A post-apocalyptic western adventure

End Days (#) (co-written with E.E. Isherwood)—a post-apocalyptic adventure

Successful Indie Author (#)—a non-fiction series to help self-published authors

Monster Case Files (co-written with Kathryn Hearst)—A Warner twins mystery adventure

Rick Banik (#)—Spy & terrorism action adventure

Ian Bragg Thrillers (#)—a hitman with a conscience

Not Enough (co-written with Eden Wolfe) – A coming of age contemporary fantasy

<u>Published exclusively by Craig Martelle, Inc</u>

The Dragon's Call by Angelique Anderson & Craig A. Price, Jr.—an epic fantasy quest

A Couples Travels—a non-fiction travel series

Love-Haight Case Files by Jean Rabe & Donald J. Bingle – the dead/undead have rights, too, a supernatural legal thriller

Mischief Maker by Bruce Nesmith – the creator of Elder Scrolls V: Skyrim brings you Loki in the modern day, staying true to Norse Mythology (not a superhero version)

Mark of the Assassins by Landri Johnson -

For a complete list of Craig's books, stop by his website—https://craigmartelle.com

Made in the USA
Las Vegas, NV
01 July 2022